PARADISE UNDERCOVER

Fernando Fernandez, P.I.

CREDITS

Author: Fernando Fernandez, PI, BAI, CCDI, CII, CAS

Editors: Yasmin Rodriguez & Colin Grubb
for The Writing Ghost

Cover Design and Graphic Art: Colin Grubb

Photography: Yolima Rey from Dream Photography
Olga Cortes from Covert Intelligence, LLC

Book design and production for print: The Writing Ghost

Translation: The Writing Ghost

This book and all of its contents are the result of the author's imagination and thoughts, based on his real-life investigations. Names and places have been changed to protect the individuals and organizations involved.

Published by Covert Intelligence, LLC
www.covertintelligencegroup.com
www.paradiseundercover.com
facebook: ParadiseUndercover

ISBN-13: 978-0-9861059-0-6

First Edition, 2015

Beyond Content

DEDICATION

There is one person who loves me unconditionally, trusts me with her life, and makes me believe I can do whatever I set my mind to. Olga, you rock my world. Thank you for giving me the chance to be a father, a lover, a friend, and for showing me the path to become a man I can be proud of. I grow more in love with you every day. I am looking forward to the rest of our lives together.

I am blessed to be the father of four beautiful girls. Elisabet, Alondra, Adriana Lakshmi and Shanti, you are my reason for being. Every day I wake up looking to make a better future for you. Never doubt that everything I do, I do it for you. Dad loves you, forever.

TABLE OF CONTENTS

ACKNOWLEDGEMENTS

I had wanted to write a novel for a long time. My work as a Private Investigator for the last 10 years has been full of adventures, both on the field and in my private life. Whenever I would tell someone about my anecdotes, the reaction always was: "You should write a book!". I finally did it, and there is a group of people without whom I would not have this career, the reputation that goes with it, and the interesting life that inspired this book.

My father, Fernando Fernandez Sr., was able to raise me with values, honor, and a good sense of right and wrong, good and bad, before departing this existence way before his time. My mother, Isabel Correa, took on the task of taking care of us during difficult times. My sister Solymar Fernandez and I didn't get to spend time together throughout her childhood. However, we have grown into a wonderful sibling relationship, where she is my number one fan, always letting me know how proud she is of my accomplishments. I want to take this opportunity to tell the world how proud I am of her, for overcoming so much, and getting so far ahead in life.

I want to thank my mother in law, Aurea Rivera. In hindsight, she gave me my first case when, just after I obtained my degree as Private Investigator, she told me I would be the one to solve her husband's murder. She has become a second mother to me, and continues to trust me to this day. Thank you, Aurea, for allowing me to talk about this sad and hurtful event in this book.

I would like to acknowledge the people who help me every day, either from the office or from the field. My executive assistant, Jose Medina, who keeps me organized and keeps the office running when I'm not around, and my junior P.I., Edrick

Narvaez, who in the time he's been with us has proven himself to be a great asset, a valuable team player, and a friend.

There are some industry colleagues that I'm proud to also call my friends. The people in this amazing group are all examples to follow, the kind that set standards, and I want to take this opportunity to thank them: Mr. Jimmy Mesis, P.I., B.A.I., editor of PI Magazine, for his invaluable advice, and for believing in me enough to refer me and make me a collaborator to his magazine; Mr. Richard Marquez, C.F.E., for giving me the opportunity to work on a lot of these amazing insurance cases; Mr. Ian Withers, P.I., for opening my eyes to a different world of investigations; Mr. Jim Carino, C.P.P., V.S.M., from Intellenet, for honoring me with his trust and allowing me to belong to a most prestigious association; and Mr. Steve Rambam, P.I., C.F.E., C.P.P., for setting the highest standards for other investigators like me to follow.

Some of my colleagues played an intrinsic role in the development, and eventual closing, of some of the most important cases of my career. Mr. Ponno Kalestree, P.I., from Singapore, and Mr. Bob Rahn, P.I., from New York, both proved how a true network of P.I.'s can collaborate from different parts of the globe to bring closure to a family in grieve. I thank them for their camaraderie, professionalism, and trust. Guys like you keep our industry honest and loyal to our mission.

Mr. Brandon Perron, P.I., C.C.D.I., was the instructor who gave me the insight and methodology to pursue criminal investigations more passionately, and effectively. Thank you for your kind words of encouragement. Also, there is a certain news reporter who has always believed in me, and followed my cases with hope and trust in my ability to solve them. Istra Pacheco, I'm forever in your debt.

Finally, I want to say "thank you" to my editors, Yasmin Rodriguez and Colin Grubb from The Writing Ghost, Inc. They went over and beyond my expectations in helping me bring my stories to the world of fiction without losing the investigative criteria and techniques that helped me solve the actual cases. Even when I decided to change the tone and angle of the book mid way, they stood by me and brought these stories to life. We definitely became a team, and I'm grateful.

Fernando Fernandez, PI, BAI, CCDI, CII, CAS

WHAT OTHERS HAVE TO SAY

"Paradise Undercover reads like a cross between Ellery Queen and Magnum, P.I. To any unsuspecting reader, this unlikely hero –Fernando Fernandez– and his sordid cast of characters and situations might seem just like a figment of the author's imagination. But is it? You might be surprised. Very entertaining and even hilarious at times!"

Paco Correa

Award-winning writer and producer for American television networks such as Telemundo, Nickelodeon, Spike TV, Discovery, Fox and HBO.

"Private Investigator Fernando Fernandez is an internationally recognized private investigator well known for his insider knowledge of Puerto Rico and the region. He is also the only Board Certified Criminal Defense Investigator operating in the entire Caribbean! My own experience with Fernando reveals that his professional standards and ethics are beyond reproach. He is tenacious in his pursuit of the truth and leaves no stone unturned during the course of his investigations. Fernando has enjoyed a truly exciting career as a private investigator and his stories of adventure and intrigue are as educational as they are entertaining!"

Brandon A. Perron, PI, CCDI

National Director of the Criminal Defense Investigation Training Council Nationally Recognized Award Winning Private Investigator and National Top Criminal Defense Investigator.

"While there are many private investigators throughout the world, there are those who clearly stand out amongst their peers. Fernando Fernandez is such an investigator, recognized internationally as the "go to" private investigator for Puerto Rico and the Caribbean. I've had the opportunity to meet and work with Fernando on several projects and have always been amazed at the amount of information he has been able to acquire and the professionalism he puts into every assignment he works on. Conducting investigations in the Caribbean offers many unique challenges and Fernando shares his many stories and in a truly enjoyable and entertaining way."

Jimmie Mesis, LPI, BAI
Editor-in-Chief - PI Magazine, Inc.
Nationally Recognized Award Winning Private Investigator

"This is a book that is long overdue. Fernando Fernandez has been a friend and colleague for many years, and so I have had the pleasure of watching Fernando bring his unique skills and dedication to bear on a wide variety of difficult cases. Private Investigators are a critical part of the justice system; they handle the cases that traditional law enforcement can't, or won't, pursue. A P.I. finds missing persons and witnesses, gathers evidence that frees the innocent and finds the guilty, reunites families, fights fraud, recovers stolen property and monies and makes victims whole again. Fernando has handled these types of cases successfully throughout the Caribbean region, and more. This book, detailing selections from Fernando's extensive case files, will no doubt amaze the reader."

Steve Rambam, PI, CFE, CPP
Director, Pallorium, Inc.
Renowned International Private Investigator
Host of Investigations Discovery Channel's Nowhere To Hide

Prologue
The Furniture Man
2013

Fernando Fernandez, Private Investigator, looked up from the sink and immediately realized it was almost impossible to look at his mirror image in the eye. His pupil could never quite lock with his brother's on the other side. Looking at himself straight on, his focus seemed to automatically shift slightly to the left or right. If he did, for a split second, manage to meet the eyes of his reflection, the person on the other side was frighteningly wide-eyed, unfamiliar, and not him.

Was he lost in thought and didn't know it? Was it astigmatism? Was it nerves? He decided it was nerves.

The two ladies from Singapore would be arriving tomorrow and it was shaping up to be a media circus.

"Yeah, that's it," he said aloud, nodding to his reflection in confirmation.

A forgiving island breeze came through the window bars and worked its way into every corner of the bathroom, eventually curling around and cooling his wet face. He turned on the faucet and splashed himself another coat. The afternoon was dying. The palms gently sang. The frogs would be coming out soon. He could hear the children finishing their lesson in the next room and Nicole answering the phone in the adjacent office.

Nicole.

Nicole was the problem. He didn't have to even tell her he'd been scratching at the Furniture Man case, she would be able to tell. The last two months of domestic bliss had been purchased by virtue of the fact he'd let it go.

Then five minutes ago he'd listened to the voicemail. The lady in red in Forensics had a lead on the evidence. After ten years, simple as that.

It wasn't the Asian ladies arrival giving him an anxiety attack.

It was his wife. She would be able to tell.

Beijing Joaquin was in the can, done and dusted. After months of work he'd found the old man's family. And when he should have been sitting at the Hostería beach bar opening his third beer, practicing the humble and charming manner with which he'd accept the coming accolades, he was instead standing in his bathroom looking at himself in the mirror, terrified to face his own wife.

"Fernandez you're a fucking mess," he said quickly drawing his voice down to a whisper so the kids next door couldn't hear. Not quick enough. He noticed that Sra. Mendoza stuttered briefly in the middle of a sentence about the legislative assembly, and Angelic, his youngest, was giggling uncontrollably. Great. They always told their mother about his swearing. Throw this on the pile of crap to deal with.

Nicole had been fighting a marriage-long war against his profanity. It was a losing battle mainly because Fernandez didn't understand why he shouldn't curse. Which, of course, made things even worse. It was impossible to control. Once, at an A-list dinner at the El Convento Hotel, he'd used the word "dickhead" in front of the Governor. Nicole didn't talk to him for a week after that. Yeah, the cursing was a sore spot, but his children found it hilarious.

"Ok settle down, the upper house normally consists of 27 senators, the lower house has 51. All senators are granted parliamentary immunity," Sra. Mendoza resumed as the giggles died.

Fernandez dried off his face and started back through the classroom toward his office. He briefly locked eyes with Angelic and attempted to convey a silent message. It was useless, Nicole had heard, she was at the file cabinet waiting for him. He tried to make the short walk as long as possible by thinking.

Maybe looking himself in the eye was hard, but looking other people in the eye was not a problem. In fact, it was absolutely essential in his situation. At 40 years old, 5'10", 260 pounds, he looked, dressed and sounded more like a corporate IT guy than a private investigator. And that had been his angle his whole career. He flattered, he disarmed, he flirted, he came in under the radar. He was your friend; the jolly but overworked tech coming to reestablish your Internet connection and not pump you for information regarding the savage beatdown of an unfaithful husband.

This approach had paid off. Fernandez had been extremely successful and work was plentiful.

And now with Beijing Joaquin came his greatest achievement yet. He had beaten Interpol. His tiny, four-employee firm working out of his house in Carolina had got the drop on Interpol!

He paused at the water cooler and poured a glass he didn't want, all the while cursing his nature for not being able to relish this achievement, at least for a day or two.

The trouble was Beijing Joaquin had not existed in its own universe. Because of what he dug up during the investigation it was now inextricably tied with the Furniture Man, and hence the cause of his current and conflicted misery. Why did he ask Garcia? All he had to do was not open his mouth. Why did he bribe that woman in Forensics when he should have been concentrating on the dead Chinese man? All these years Nicole had been happy enough to leave it alone, and she had a much bigger stake in all of this than anyone.

He couldn't leave it alone. The Furniture Man was the ultimate loose end. And if there was one thing Fernandez hated, even more than coffee, it was a loose end. Now he was apparently going to talk about real evidence, and all it took was a crate of Tequila and some innocent flirting.

"Where's Simon?" Fernandez said sitting down at his desk.

"He's meditating," Nicole responded.

"Meditating?"

"Yeah, out on the patio."

Fernandez took a look outside and saw his secretary in a lotus position next to the girls' trampoline, surely getting eaten alive by mosquitoes at this time of day.

"He's supposed to be working, Nicole."

"It's ok. I already emailed all the invoices. There's nothing left to do today."

"That's not the point. I'm not paying him to…" Fernandez trailed off as he noticed Fiona, one of the two family dogs, begin licking the meditating man's face. Simon attempted to shoo the big husky off, which the dog promptly took as an invitation to play and jumped on him. The two went down in a pile.

"Good," Fernandez was satisfied.

"It's not good honey. It's very dangerous to break concentration like that, he could have been entering a Jhana."

"Excuse me?"

"You should try it," Nicole tried to sound innocent. "It would be great for you, focus the mind, be able to see clearly some of your…habits."

So she had heard the swearing.

"No thanks."

Simon entered the office through the side door wiping dirt and dog drool from his face with his sleeve.

"Do you think I could meditate in the garage from now on, Nicole?"

"Of course Simon. I'm sorry about Fiona."

Fernandez took this opportunity.

"Hey, I got an idea. How about instead of meditating, or Jhana-ing, or yoga-ing, you send out some of these invoices?"

"I told you it was already finished," Nicole said in a low voice. "I told him it would be good for him. Simon, why don't you teach him?"

"Mr. Fernandez?" Simon laughed. "No way, he's not the type. He couldn't sit still for two minutes."

"I sit still for hours at a time surveilling people."

Everyone let the subject drop. It was Friday, and almost time to call it a day. Next door he could hear Sra. Mendoza finishing the days' lesson. He suddenly realized the message indicator on all the office phones was still blinking. He'd hung up and bolted for the bathroom before the end of Estrella Leon's voicemail and the system was still counting it as new.

As he went to delete it his girls ran out of their classroom and jumped him.

"Daddy, daddy! Are we still going to Moisty Water Park?" Lakshmi, his older daughter was now big enough to clasp her arms around his neck. Angelic attached herself to his leg. The force of impact rolled the three of them to the back wall, away from the telephone.

"You said we would. You said that we could bring Lisa and Juan too. They have a new slide that's like 100 stories tall!"

"Of course we're still going, I remember."

In fact Fernandez hadn't remembered that this was the

weekend he'd agreed to take the tribe to the unfortunately named water park up in the mountains. He winced as he thought of the drive, narrow twisting, barely kept roads with locals accustomed to the conditions barreling through at 50 miles an hour. Why didn't these kids like the beach? The beach had a bar.

"There's no such thing as a water slide 100 stories tall, you dumbass!" Lakshmi was older, but apparently not old enough to humor her younger sister.

"Yes there is, craphead! I saw it on the news."

This was enough for Nicole.

"See Fernando! Look at what these girls have learned from you. I never talked like this in front of my parents and look what we have, a couple of sweet little girls that swear like pirates! For the love of God! The two of you get cleaned up right now. We're going to dinner and believe me, if I hear any more language like that, you're going to be sorry!" Nicole hustled the two girls out the office door toward the bathroom, but managed to look at her husband just before leaving the room.

"You're going to be sorry too, Fernando. I'll be right back."

Still sitting, he began to push himself back toward his desk. Simon picked up his line and hit the voicemail button.

"Simon! Simon! Hang that up right now!" he shouted.

Simon threw the phone onto his desk as if someone had just told him he was holding a live grenade.

"What!" he yelped in terror.

"I wanted to ask you something," Fernandez searched for something to say.

"Yes?" Clearly suspicious, Simon quietly hung the phone

back up. The red message light was still blinking.

"I think Nicole's right. I want you to teach me to meditate," he lied.

A look of peaceful joy came over Simon's face.

"I should say you need it," he said. "You are incredibly wound up right now, more than usual. You have a loud aura."

"Yeah, I've been told that before. Come over here and show me," Fernandez instructed, trying to get Simon away from the telephone.

"There's really not enough space on the floor here. It would be better outside," said Simon getting up from his desk.

"I'd prefer to do it here. It's hot out there."

"Ok, sit like this."

Fernandez sat down next to Simon on the hard office floor, feeling like an idiot.

"What we want to do," Simon began. "Is to concentrate on our breathing without controlling it. Don't try to force out thoughts, but don't follow them either."

Fernandez was sure he would regret this later. He closed his eyes and humored Simon all the while wondering how he was going to get to the phone to delete Estrella Leon's message. If anyone heard it he'd be fucked in two or three different and distinct ways. Nicole reentered the room and he opened one eye.

"The sound of your wife coming in, just notice it," Simon continued completely unaware of the possible looming disaster.

Nicole went for the message button and put the phone on speaker.

"Oh shit," Fernandez said getting up.

"I know," Simon sympathized, his eyes still closed. "It can initially be very nerve wracking. We want to get up and move but we must just notice this as well."

"Hello Fernando! This is Estrella, your little Charo," cooed a woman's voice from the speaker.

Too late.

"Thank you so much for the gifts. How did you know Tequila was my favorite? I'm such a lucky girl."

Nicole shot him a look of amused confusion.

"Fernando?" she squeaked quietly as the message continued.

"I'm so sorry I wasn't here to receive you. You come and see me. I think I know where to get what you want. Bye," she said breathlessly and punctuated it in the end with a loud kiss.

Rooted to the spot he turned to look at Simon. He was no longer meditating and his eyes were bulging out of his head in disbelief.

"Simon, go home," Fernandez instructed.

Without a word his secretary gathered his things and left. When the door slammed he turned his attention to his wife, who had now collapsed into Simon's chair with a disoriented look on her face. This was a rock and a hard place. Fernandez had to tell the truth. He couldn't let her think he was sleeping with Estrella Leon and he didn't have enough time to make something else up.

"Nicole, this isn't what it seems," he explained. "Come on, think about it, would I be stupid enough to give her the office number? Think."

He knelt down behind her and gathered her in his arms.

What he said made sense. She sat in consideration and didn't pull away.

"You know this is something else," he continued.

"What then?" she asked.

"You're going to like the truth less."

Nicole searched for a scenario she'd find less appealing than infidelity. As she scanned the possibilities her suddenly froze into a mask of anger. She'd found it.

"No."

"The woman on the message works in Forensics."

"It's been two months. You'd said you'd leave it alone. What's wrong with you?" she fumed.

"Her name is Estrella Leon, and she has a lead on the evidence on your father. I just have to go talk to her about it. That's what she was talking about."

Nicole swallowed slowly, and spoke as though she was gently telling a five-year-old that his imaginary friend wasn't real.

"There was no evidence on my father's case, Fernando. You've always said so."

"I was wrong, Nicole."

Fernandez could hear his own heart. It started to rain outside and the frogs tuned up for their nightly symphony. "Co-qui! Co-qui! Co-qui!" Despite the noise the air between him and his wife was dead with tension. This subject was closed to her and she didn't want it opened again. That being said she certainly wasn't ignorant enough to persist in denial. If new information came to light, she'd have to consider it. But she'd want to know why he'd brought it to light.

She'd made peace with her father's death ten years ago. If she was ok, if her family was ok, what right did he have to bring it all back again? He knew that she knew he had an obsessive streak bordering on a disorder, about not leaving loose ends. He knew that she knew this was a selfish act.

She swallowed again.

"Do I want to know what's there?"

"He was killed Nicole, you know it. That evidence is going to help me find who did it."

He let the words hang and waited for his wife's response.

"Fernando…you've got to be fucking kidding me."

The Big Leagues
2008

Two loud Americans were arguing with each other over the phone in two very loud American voices. One was in Houston, the other in London.

"There's no way this shitbag didn't pull the same shit with the bank as the shit he pulled in the past," the world-famous detective bellowed into his cellphone. "C'mon Dirk, you can't tell me you don't see this shit. Shit!"

Jay Lauderdale was not known for his diplomacy, or his creative use of expletives for that matter, but Dirk Saban was used to his bluntness. After all, he had dealt with Jay for years. The guy was one of the top investigators in the world, a radio personality, a celebrity media resource to tap when they needed the voice of a P.I.. He even had his own true crime TV Show on the ID Network called "Fraudbusters." But under all the fame and media trappings, Jay was still an in demand investigator functioning at the absolute top of his game. Shrewd, knowledgeable, experienced and seasoned, when you wanted a top-notch private eye, you called Lauderdale.

Though his credentials were beyond questioning, Dirk Saban was not so sure about Jay's detachment or objectiveness when it came to this particular case. The shitbag in question was Lionel Carter, one of Jay's nemeses. He had been trying to nail Carter for years, following his trail of scams all throughout Central and South America, and then the Caribbean. Carter had slipped through the eminent investigator's fingers every time. The fact that Lauderdale had never been able to bust Carter's particular frauds was a thorn stuck mightily in his side, and his ego.

"Jay," Saban closed his eyes and paused to consider his words carefully. Dealing with Lauderdale could be remarkably similar to dealing with his teenage daughter. No, scratch that, his daughter was less of a diva.

"Jay the case is closed. The guy is dead. The bank is happy, and because of that, Alliance Insurance is happy. Let it go. So how's the weather? I hear London is beautiful this time of the year."

"Oh, it's great if you don't have any particular attachment to the sun, and you like the feeling of being soggy right up into your asscrack 24/7. Who the fuck cares about the weather? Stop trying to change the subject Dirk! Carter is alive! His pussy-ass is sipping margaritas on a beach somewhere with a fresh 20 mil of Alliance Insurance's money in Freeport earning 20%. I know you don't work for them anymore but you still gotta be...concerned," Lauderdale purred slyly.

What was this fucker getting at? Saban thought.

"Jay..."

"I'm telling you, Carter got away with murder. Again! Twenty million in life insurance? You're telling me the sneaky bastard gets diagnosed with cancer, dies, and the family files the claim within, what was it? A week?"

"A month. It is Puerto Rico Jay. It takes a lot for the red flag to go up," it was half a joke, and Saban let out a long painful breath. He was quickly realizing Lauderdale wasn't going to go away anytime soon.

"Puerto Rico, Schmuerto Rico. That's a lame excuse Dirk and you know it. I know the bastard, and you know that I know the bastard! You let this drop too easily last time and now I'm back to bite you in the ass. Ruff! Ruff!"

Jesus, was he actually barking? What the hell time was it in London? He must have hit the Queens Arms Pub early. Saban could hear a soccer match on the television and glasses clinking in the background. He tried to imagine the looks on the regulars' faces confronted with this hulking Yank half-pissed and barking into his phone like a Rottweiler. Surely Lauderdale was about one whiskey away from being cut off.

He took another deep breath.

"Jay, there are witnesses to his illness and a death certificate. What's more, Sweetwater Bank says he was a model employee, they have no gripe with him. This is the same bank, may I remind you, that bought the policy that Alliance Insurance paid off. You're the only one who keeps flogging this. Again, let it go."

"Yeah, the same Alliance Insurance where you were Claims Investigations Director at the time, Dirk. The same Alliance Insurance that's now contracting your brand ass spanking new firm to carry out the job you used to do for them internally. At a premium, I must add."

"So?" Saban didn't like where this was going.

"So if I am right, and Alliance dished out a whole bunch of money incorrectly, it's on you."

The motherfucker. He would actually go over his head to Alliance. Saban knew he would. He didn't even need any evidence. His profile was sufficient. He'd say there were flaws in the initial investigation. It had nothing to do with money. It was vendetta, it was ego, it was reputation. And the one who would undoubtedly come out of it smelling like shit was Dirk Saban.

"The only person rocking this boat is you my friend," Saban proceeded cautiously. "No one is still thinking about this."

"What about the money?"

"Twenty million to Alliance is what your lunch is costing you right now," Saban laughed. "Even without half a bottle of scotch." He couldn't resist the dig.

"I wish. The pours here are tiny. I couldn't drown a mouse in this drink."

There was half a giggle in Lauderdale's voice. The mood was lightening. Perhaps this wasn't the threat Saban was perceiving.

"What about doing a good job Dirk? Justice?"

Saban chuckled.

"I'm serious. Just because Alliance can write it off doesn't mean we still don't want the job done right. It doesn't niggle at you? I didn't get where I am by cutting corners, and neither did you, buddy."

Saban looked around his nice, polished, well appointed office. His shiny, brand new Interference International office. An office that Alliance Insurance had helped build, with their generous retainer. He looked outside his window, with a beautiful view of Houston's downtown business center. There was a hint of rain in the clouds. Yeah it was hotter than the sun, but Saban loved everything about the city. Raised in the Fifth Ward, his mother worked two jobs to send him to school on the white side of town. She could barely afford the rent after Dirk's tuition. He'd busted his ass, and now he surveyed the gleaming metropolis from his own personal eagle's nest. Jay was right. No corners had been cut.

"Dirk I'm not the asshole you think I am. I'm not going to Alliance Insurance. I called you because ultimately this is your baby." Lauderdale put down the phone and Saban could hear him talking to the barman.

"Just one more, thanks. Hey, can you get the Cowboys on that thing?"

Saban couldn't make out the irritated cockney response.

"Jesus, testy."

"Did you actually just ask an English person to preempt a soccer game for the Cowboys?"

"Whatever. Look, alright I hate him. I hate Carter and I'm dying to get him. Satisfied?"

"So I'm supposed to open this whole thing up again because of your particular hard-on?"

"Partly. But let me ask you this? What happens when the shitbag shows up again?"

"He's got 20 million, I think it's a safe bet our Lionel will be laying low on a straight shot to the grave. What the fuck am I even talking about? You've got me thinking like you. He's dead!"

"No. Fucking. Way," Lauderdale spat. "Trust me Dirk, he rolls high. Remember the five mil he got in Barranquilla? That was more than enough to set himself up for life in Colombia and what happened there?"

"The Ponzi thing in Antigua with the cricket team," Saban sighed heavily. Unfortunately, Jay Lauderdale was beginning to make sense.

"And this is what, wife number three? It might take a little longer, but this one will blow through that 20 million too. That's when we're both screwed."

He had a point. Up until now Saban had filed that annoying little possibility deep in the back of his brain. He couldn't lie to himself now, he must have been harboring doubts as well this whole time. Subconscious, inconvenient doubts kept buried because no one was rocking the boat. Had his standards slipped so much? Two years into the CEO-ship of his own firm and his life was already beginning to reek of politics; the speed at which he'd dismissed Lauderdale's talk about doing a good job now alarmed him. He'd done a good job for Alliance and now they were his main client. The Alliance retainer was the financial bedrock upon which he'd built his private investigation firm, Interference International, where he'd continued his policy of doing a good job for all his new clients. Doing a good job, it turns out, was good business.

Dirk spun in his chair and once again looked over his city. Back in the 90's a lot of money went into brand new skyscrapers and other impressive buildings. He had an excellent view of them all. One Park Place, the Green Street complex, the Houston Ballet Center. His building, the shiny new Calpine Center, was finished in 2003. He saw the place go up while he was making a name for himself at Alliance Insurance and admired the 32-story tower, with its curves in a city known for its straight lines. Its grid over blue glass made it look sort of like 1500 Louisiana Street. When he started his own firm, he knew that's where his headquarters would be.

He mentally chastised himself. Lionel Carter showing up and making a fool of him shouldn't be the motivator. Neither should pissing off his main client and benefactor. Lauderdale was right, if he had doubts they must be addressed. Saban didn't make a name for himself by taking the easy way.

Alright. He was prepared to entertain the notion, for now, that Carter had faked his death. But he was not going to drag Alliance Insurance into reopening the case unless he had absolute evidence to support the expense.

"Hey are you still there?"

"Yeah. Ok, what have you got, Lauderdale? Make me a believer. I'm listening."

"I knew I could count on you!" Lauderdale exploded with glee. "You da man dog!"

Saban winced.

"You're going to the WatchNET conference in St. Croix next week, right?"

"Of course."

"Change your ticket and come to Puerto Rico a day early. I want you to meet someone in San Juan."

"Who?"

"When we worked the Carter case the first time, I found an extraordinary resource there. This guy is gold. He's a relatively new P.I. but man he's got the contacts and the chops. I've never seen anything like it. I got him working on gathering the necessary evidence as we speak."

"You what?"

"Relax, it's on my dime. That's how sure I am, brother."

"What information does he have? I'll go with you on this Jay, but just know I'm not going to Alliance with anything less than irrefutable."

"Yes. He's getting shit you can take to the bank. The guy is dynamite! He's got the goods on Carter and his whole crooked family. He's ready to blow the lid off the entire thing!" Lauderdale yelled loud enough for the Queen to hear.

"Ok, ok. Who is he?"

As the plastic water bottle he was filling with his own piss drew close to overflowing, Fernando Fernandez couldn't help but ponder the undignified turn his career had taken.

"Son of a bitch," he whispered. Putting his camera down on the passenger seat he began to blindly fish around the back of the van for another empty bottle.

This was a delicate operation. In order to maintain aim he had to keep his eyes on the bottle while pawing around the cab of his converted minivan for one of the four or five empties he knew were rolling around the floor. His fingertips finally touched plastic.

"Nice." He brought the bottle forward and carefully began the transfer process.

Just then a panel of storm shutters on the house he was supposed to be surveilling creaked open. The docking with the new bottle successful, Fernandez looked up to see a shadowy outline of a man inside the house.

"Dammit."

This was it. He needed to get the shot but now held two bottles of pee. Hands full he desperately scanned the car for a cap but found none. A smaller figure appeared beside the man inside the house.

Fernandez gingerly placed the first bottle on the floor of the passenger side and grabbed his camera. In taking his eyes off the second bottle there was some spillage, but not much as he was basically finished. He snapped a couple of shots and the two figures disappeared back into the house. He flipped the camera to view mode. Just as he thought, even with the night vision it was entirely too dark to make out anything. His only hope was getting these two out of the house somehow.

He was here because he'd been hired by a woman named Miriam Alonzo. Miriam suspected her husband of cheating. After two-weeks of watching Sammy Alonzo at work as a municipal policeman and at play in his free time, Fernandez had finally tailed him to this dark backstreet in the sleepy seaside town of

Loiza, a street nobody went to in a town nobody visited.

It was risky. Residents of a street like this surely were familiar with the cars that came and went. What's more the guy was a cop; he probably knew every square inch of the neighborhood. Fernandez was worried he'd stick out like a sore thumb. He'd parked half in a ditch at a dead end and turned the engine off. The windows were sufficiently tinted. If he stayed quiet, people would most likely think the car belonged to someone visiting a friend or relative.

He'd already managed to get a clear, zoomed in shot of cheating Sammy's license plate. This was damning in itself, given that it was 11:30 on a Sunday night in a town 20 miles away from the man's house. Fernandez just needed that one shot of the two together in order to put the nail in the coffin.

The house shutters rolled back down. Fernandez put down his camera and began the tricky process of zipping up with one hand. He managed to get the zipper to the top but found it next to impossible to get the clasp on his slacks to fasten under his gut. After fiddling for a few seconds he let out a long sigh, and his eyes retreated into his forehead.

Undignified turn.

It wasn't so much being caught with his pants down, that could happen on any surveillance. It was the job. Following cheating husbands around was a money maker. And let's face it, he could make a comfortable living doing little else.

It just was too easy. There was no challenge and it seemed so inconsequential in light of what he could be doing. The cash was all well and good but he wanted to be involved in something more substantial. Times like these Fernandez saw his future as an endless series of infidelity cases, and despaired. The unchecked libidos and shaky ethics of his fellow islanders would give his wife a new kitchen, put his girls through college, and ultimately buy his retirement house on the beach. What happened to all the cool shit he used to be doing? Was he destined to settle for this?

"Fernandez, get it together," he said to himself as the anxiety began to mount, knowing he had the tendency to blow things out of proportion. Suddenly and unwelcomely, his secretary Simon's voice came into his head.

"Bring your thoughts back to the now. Now is all you can cope with. Now is all you will ever will be able to cope with. The future is unwritten and..."

"Shut up Simon," he said aloud, now firmly convinced that sitting alone in a car for hours on end in the dark was really driving him batshit. He could have brought his new assistant Ruben, but Ruben was still having trouble learning the finer points of how the office coffee machine functioned.

Someday, someday he'd manage to find a good assistant. Ruben was his third try. All three had been spectacularly inept in a variety of ways. On a night like tonight it would have been fruitless to drag Ruben along. He needed someone he could teach. Ruben wasn't ready, and what's more, Fernandez doubted he would ever be.

As domestic cases went, this one wasn't that bad. Usually the jilted woman was in a state of hysterical panic, calling him up every five minutes and making it next to impossible to do his job. "Did you find him? Where is he? Are her tits bigger than mine?" It was intolerable.

In the last few years Fernandez had come to understand that there was a certain kind of woman that was prepared to make keeping tabs on their husband a full-time job. He found this to be an exercise in futility. If the man's inclination was to roam, shouldn't that be addressed? No matter how short a leash he's on, something is eventually going to happen. Can't leave town. Can't sleep till he's home. Sounds like fun sweetheart, knock yourself out.

Miriam Alonzo was not one of these. Or if she was, she'd gone firmly beyond the point of panicking.

Miriam ran her own small ad agency in Hato Rey and was far too busy and important a person to be following her dumbass husband around all night. In her dealings with Fernandez she was calm, and she'd never called him once during surveillance. Being a confident businesswoman, Fernandez never at any point had to play Doctor Phil with Miriam.

Alonzo struck him as a woman who was probably not that much interested in marriage in the first place but did it for tradition's sake, only to find out the man she'd casually picked turned out to be a liar and an asshole. She'd hired Fernandez to correct the situation.

Everything all neat and convenient, right? The only problem was that Miriam and Sammy Alonzo were insensitive enough to have a child along the way. And by no fault of his own he was about to have his little life changed forever. More than anything else, this was the part about these jobs that made Fernandez queasy. But at the end of the day money was money.

He had another go at his pants to no avail.

"For the love of...what the fuck?"

A stray dog had propped himself up onto Fernandez's minivan and was quietly staring at him through the window, his wet nose creating circles in the condensation.

"Go away dammit!"

The dog barked.

"Shut up, you fucking dog!"

A pack of other strays appeared over the dirt pile at the dead end and casually began to congregate around Fernandez's car, nosing at the bumper and pissing on the tires.

"Oh no, not now. Not now!"

When you saw packs of animals on the Discovery channel they all looked basically the same. To Fernandez, the motley crew of canines that now congregated around his car looked like something out of a Tom and Jerry cartoon. He tried to pick out the head dog. Like in the cartoons, it wasn't always the biggest. Maybe he could throw the bottle at it.

A few others began to bark as well.

"Leave, you dicks!"

The dogs were calling attention to his car and there was nothing he could do that wouldn't call more attention. Fernandez fell once again into a state of heavy brooding.

Undignified turn. One year ago things had been completely different. His career was ready to blast off.

He'd been subcontracted to do some due diligence work by none other than Ken Grimes. Based in the UK, Grimes was arguably the best private investigator in Western Europe and was taking a huge gamble on the relative newcomer.

Grimes had gotten in touch with Fernandez on behalf of a venture capitalist firm to check out a new company that was opening on the island. Some P.I.'s might find researching the viability of an international corporate branch office and the criminal records of its Board of Directors boring, but it was right up Fernandez's alley. Certainly a lot better than chasing around grown men who couldn't keep their dicks in their pants.

The fact that Grimes had trusted him enough to do this kind of work was huge. He'd completed the research to Grimes satisfaction and within a week his profile increased substantially.

Grimes was so pleased with Fernandez's performance that he used his considerable influence to sponsor Fernandez's membership to WatchNET, the international affiliation of P.I.'s. Usually WatchNET only considered an application after ten years of operation. Fernandez had only been in business for three. Needless to say, it was an incredible honor.

Now a year later, his career seemed stuck in neutral. All the fanfare had petered out. The criminal or international investigations hadn't materialized and he was stuck on the domestic side playing psychologist to women in the middle of nervous breakdowns.

Work would pick up, Fernandez told himself. At the very least, his name was out there attached to prominent investigators like Grimes, and for that matter, Jay Lauderdale, another high profile international investigator.

Suddenly Fernandez was shook out of his pity party. The porch light of the house went on, undoubtedly due to the canine disturbance.

Then three unfortunate things happened almost simultaneously. One, in grabbing for his camera Fernandez knocked the first bottle over spilling piss all over the car. Two, a state police car appeared behind him and flashed its lights. Three, he received a call on his cellphone from Jay Lauderdale. The ring pierced the silence and lit the entire car from the inside. In an instant a policeman was knocking at his window with a flashlight while Fernandez furiously grappled with his pants.

"Fucking great!" Between the dogs and the cops, the ruckus that was being created would surely send two weeks of work right down the tubes. Fernandez rolled down his window.

"Can I help you officer?" Fernandez smiled.

It took a second for the policeman to process the scene before him. Fernandez sat in his minivan smiling with a bottle of pee in one hand and the other hand on his crotch. On a deserted street. In the middle of nowhere. In the middle of the night.

"Sir," he began wearily, kicking a dog away from his boots. "Just what..." he paused as the smell from the passenger side hit his nostrils.

"Ah sorry about that officer, little accident. I've been sitting here for quite awhile. I'm on a case, I'm a P.I." Fernandez pulled his license from a lanyard around his neck and handed it to the policeman.

"I see." The cops demeanor began to change as he inspected Fernandez's credentials.
"You know sir, those flashing lights on your car aren't doing me any favors," Fernandez offered.

"Right." The officer motioned back to his partner and the turret went dark.

"Thanks."

He took a look around the car, smiling and interested. Fernandez realized in horror he'd encountered a talker.

"So how did you get into this kind of thing?"

"Sir?"

"Investigations, I've often thought about it. See, I am going to be retiring soon and God knows I'm not ready to be sitting around the house all day. I can hardly stand my wife as it Is, huh? Ha!" his final exclamation might as well have been a pistol going off.

This happened once a month at least. The police never hassled him but always were curious about breaking into the business.

"Officer, with all due respect, I don't mean to offend you, but..." Fernandez cocked his head in the direction of the house he was in front of, not the one he was surveilling.

"What? Oh yeah, sorry about that."

"Here's my card, give me a ring tomorrow morning and I can tell anything you need."

"Thanks," he whispered. "Hey, just out of curiosity." He looked toward the house Fernandez indicated.

"Cheating wife," he explained.

"Oh," his eyes narrowed as he looked knowingly at the house.

When doing jobs like this, especially in areas where he wasn't known to the cops, Fernandez always fed them the wrong information. These communities were tight. It was totally within the realm of possibility the officer was friends with Sammy or his lover and would tip them off about the portly gentleman snooping around their front yard. More so in this case, where the cheater was a municipal policeman and this officer was a state cop.

"Ok, we're out of here. We'll be in the area if you need anything."

The cop returned to his car and sped silently off the street. Fernandez quickly scanned the area, it didn't appear that the incident drew any onlookers. Everyone was undoubtedly sleeping and flashing lights were hardly a curiosity in Puerto

Rico. Marked cars, unmarked cars, party buses, school buses, tow trucks, even funeral body transport all had some sort of light thing going on. Flashing lights were all over the roads and you didn't immediately panic when they appeared behind you like in the States. It could be anyone.

The front door to the house opened and out stepped none other than Sammy Alonzo, wide-eyed, mouth open, looking down the street for the cop car like a moron.

"Hello gorgeous," Fernandez whispered as he snapped away. Ironically the dogs and cops Fernandez was sure had blown his cover ended up luring Sammy out of his mistress's house.

Sammy was joined by his lover on the street corner.

"Alright, here we go, don't be shy, you two are making this easy."

They were deep in conversation, but Fernandez was too far away to make out the words. Sammy was yammering sleepily and pointing down the street in the direction the cops left, then back up to the dead end where Fernandez was parked. The slack jaw woman then seemed to be offering her expert appraisal of the situation. They got closer and he put his arm around her waist, practically looking right into the camera lens.

"These two geniuses really have their shit together."

Fernandez wondered why the soon to be former Mrs. Alonzo even needed to hire him. Her husband was clearly a special kind of idiot.

Sammy and his lover got into a tongue-happy kissing match. Bingo.

"That's all she wrote, folks." Fernandez quickly cycled through the shots to make sure they were clear. There were two that were absolute gold. Sammy and the woman returned to the house arm in arm, giggling.

It was heavy. This kind of thing always was. The Alonzo's little boy was his younger daughter's age. Fernandez was now the sole possessor of information that would inalterably change, or maybe even ruin, at least three lives. Not even reviewed yet, just sitting in a tiny camcorder on his passenger seat. Basically minuscule slices of information, that together created a picture Sammy Alonzo would probably kill in order to erase.

Was Miriam really better off knowing? What if he went back to her and told him her husband was spending his nights away volunteering at an animal hospital fixing little birdie wings and helping find homes for pussy cats?

Pointless. From tonight's events it was clear Sammy was the kind of chowderhead that would fuck up somewhere along the line. Being the catalyst was just business, and ultimately it was Miriam Alonzo that had come to him. She would keep the boy. She'd be stressed out but sane. He'd be confused, but in the new apartment there would be no yelling. She'd do her best. Maybe she'd find someone else, or maybe she wouldn't.

He pulled off the street onto the broad and breezy causeway that cut through Loiza. Pitch black, he decided the first order of business was to get out of town and find a gas station on Route 3. He remembered Lauderdale's missed call, and things looked a little bit brighter. Considering his negative reminiscence on his career state of late, he was very eager to talk with Lauderdale indeed, but the smell from the front seat was grossing him out and making it impossible to concentrate.

Coasting through the dark and desolate back road, flanked by the shallow ocean on the left, Fernandez let himself get a little bit excited. He hadn't heard from the famous detective in almost a year, when he was helping him out on the ground for the Lionel Carter fraud case. Ken Grimes had referred him after his due diligence work. The two world-class detectives couldn't possibly have been more different. Grimes was quiet and dominating, reminding Fernandez of a university dean. Lauderdale was like an enthusiastic football coach. Fernandez admired his swagger, but found being in his company a bit overwhelming.

He wondered what Lauderdale had for him. It could be a ticket back to the big time. Feeling like he was on the verge of being rescued from exile, he gunned his minivan into the night.

Twenty minutes later he was at a gas station in the town of Canovanas, vacuuming out the passenger side when the voice-mail chime popped up on his Blackberry. Lauderdale must have left a message when he called but because of spotty coverage the voicemail didn't show up until now.

"Fernandez, buddy boy, this is Jay!"

He could barely hear Lauderdale over the background noise. Sounded like he was at a party.

"Big news, I'm going to be down there on Wednesday with Dirk Saban. I need you to pull everything together from the Lionel Carter thing from a year ago. I know there wasn't much but I've got some incredible shit to add to it. I have a plan, call me back ASAFP brother. We'll get that fucker good!"

The time ran out and the vacuum switched off leaving Fernandez leaning against his car in a deflated silence disturbed only by the tweeting of frogs and sparse, late-night traffic. He plunked in another couple of quarters and set about finishing the job.

"We'll get that fucker good," he repeated as he worked the floorboard. "There's no fucker to get."

He looked anxiously at his phone lying on the seat, not sure if he even wanted to respond to Lauderdale. In any other line of work this behavior would be borderline insane, refusing to believe someone was dead, chasing ghosts. But Carter was slippery, to be sure. He'd made an ass of Jay more than once. Had he been stewing on this all year?

How could he possibly have something new? Barring obtaining a photo of the corpse the entire thing had seemed pretty cut and dried. What's more, although Carter had a string of wives who had undoubtedly been involved with his scams in the past, the current widow's grief was unquestionably real. As was his coworkers'. Everything at the hospital checked out.

The massive payout to his family was tough to swallow considering his impressive career of ripping people off, but to all accounts Carter had happily settled into a middle management lifestyle. Toyota Highlander, Costco Chardonnay, photo of the family riding Space Mountain on the mantelpiece next to the kid's baseball trophy. It didn't happen often that people reformed, but it did happen. And unless he'd managed to execute some elaborate five-year setup, then fake having cancer? Fool his friends and family not to mention the doctors? It was simply inconceivable. They don't give you chemotherapy just because you ask for it. Everything checked out.

Fernandez returned the vacuum and sighed heavily. This was going to be difficult. Jay Lauderdale was an important man who could do a lot to shape Fernandez's future. The Dirk Saban he referred to was also a huge deal. His new firm Interference International had burst upon the scene in the last two years and quickly established itself as a hub of investigatory activity. Their profile couldn't possibly be higher and they subcontracted work all over the world. From suspicious wives to major corporations, if you were looking to hire an investigator, Interference International was going to be the number one Google hit.

Conflicted, Fernandez returned to his car. This could be the golden ticket. He called up Lauderdale, silently praying that he was just going after some sort of technicality on the insurance payout. Ruthless as it would be toward Carter's family, it would certainly be preferable to the paranoid shit he was preparing himself to hear.

"Fernandez, what took you so long? I've called you three goddamned times," came a groggy voice from the other side. Fernandez tried to stay upbeat and light.

"Jay, buddy, how are you doing? Listen I just got your message now and..."

"Now? I left it last night."

"Huh?"

"I'm in London, Christ, it's six in the morning, man."

His cell service had been almost nonexistent in Loiza. Lauderdale must have left it at the beginning of the stakeout, late night in London.

"I was on surveillance, in the middle of nowhere. I can call back..."

"No, we need to talk now. Jesus, we're going to have to buy you a satellite phone with the fucking reception down there. Just give me a second."

Fernandez could hear Lauderdale coughing violently. The investigator had a penchant for cigars and no doubt Cubans were easily obtainable in the UK. It sounded to Fernandez like

Jay had a hell of a night. Hopefully, the booze had been fueling his enthusiasm and he'd get the more sensible Lauderdale now.

Unlikely, Jay was one of those lucky people who seemed immune to guilt and self reproach, even during a scorching hangover.

Lauderdale concluded his coughing fit with a mighty expectoration that Fernandez could actually hear hit the back of the sink. He almost gagged.

"Ok, here it is, Fernandez. You know Dirk Saban, right?"

"Of course, Interference International."

"Exactly. What you might not know is that Saban was the point guy at Alliance Insurance when we were working on the Lionel Carter thing last year."

"I didn't know that." Fernandez couldn't help but notice Lauderdale pronounced the con man's name like someone had just farted directly into his mouth. There was no way Jay could still be harboring such unabashed dislike for a dead man. He was despondent and didn't like where this was going.

"Saban is still working for Alliance Insurance in an independent capacity. He's got the clout to get Alliance on board and we can open this thing back up! How's that sound, man?"

Shitty, he wanted to say.

"Oh...wow."

"Wow is right, motherfucker! We are going to be there on Wednesday, we're going to make a little stop on the way to WatchNET. Let's meet for lunch around one-ish. What's that restaurant near the beach where those two girls liked me?"

A year ago Fernandez had spent a weird night in a place in Ocean Park where Lauderdale had spent the entire evening slobbering over two girls in bikinis who were being paid to pay attention to him because of a Medalla Beer promotion. That's what he must be talking about

"Papayas, in Ocean Park."

"Papayas. Do you think they'll be there again?" Lauderdale laughed, a little more than half serious.

"Probably not at lunch."

"Well anyway, all I need is for you to back me up. I'm going to send you a bunch of attachments via email today: photos, pdfs, that kind of thing. I need you to print everything out and bring it to the restaurant in a binder or something. Do you have an official looking one with a CO logo on it?"

"CO?"

"Covert Operations? What the fuck is the name of your outfit, Fernando? Sorry, I can never remember it."

"Covert Intelligence."

"Right, Covert Intelligence. You might want to think of changing that man, it's extremely forgettable."

"Well...," Fernandez couldn't help but be a little offended even if he agreed. "What about IBM?"

"That's already taken."

"No I mean, it's a pretty forgettable name too, and they've done pretty well."

"You're no IBM Fernandez. You run a tin-pot investigation firm with two full-time employees other than yourself, one of whom is your wife," Lauderdale chuckled. "Anyway, wasn't IBM started by the Nazis?"

"No, I think you're a little confused there Jay. I believe they had some business dealings during the war with Germany. You know come to think of it, I recently read an excellent book on the subject..."

"Fernandez?"

"Yeah?"

"I drank enough scotch last night to kill or stun the average mule. I am on the cusp of a world class hangover and I feel a cluster headache coming on that will have me praying for death by noon. I want to end this conversation as soon as possible, pop a vicodin, and attempt to sleep through as much of it as I can, which shouldn't be difficult as the sun doesn't appear to visit this country."

"Gotcha."

"I will then board a plane tomorrow afternoon, spend seven hours in the Admiral's Club or whatever the fuck it's called in JFK, and arrive in San Juan mid morning. By that time my hangover should have passed and I'll be sipping a Medanga Light at Papayas with Dirk Saban, eating food that actually tastes like something other than boiled bread."

"Medalla Light."

"Whatever. None of that is going to happen until you understand where I'm coming from and I hang up this fucking phone, capisce?"

"Yes."

"Get everything together and make it look like a pile of evidence you amassed."

Fernandez groaned then quickly checked himself. After all, this was still Jay Lauderdale he was talking to.

"Look, it's all above board, Fernandez, don't worry. This isn't an affront to your ethics, I just don't have the time to fill you in on the contents right now but trust me, it's all above board."

"So you want me to pass your stuff off as mine?"

"In a nutshell, yes."

"I'm sorry Jay," Fernandez tiptoed, "but I have to ask why can't you just..."

"Because he thinks I have a dog in this race!"

You don't? Fernandez wanted to ask.

"Plus Saban has kind of turned into a pussy since he opened up his own firm. Don't tell him I said that."

"I won't, Jay."

"Having you there will make my position much stronger, you know that. I just need that little extra push, your confirmation to get him to reopen the case with Alliance Insurance. I've already talked you up as the point person in all of the Caribbean. Saban's got a ton of work, this could be an extremely lucrative connection for you."

Lauderdale paused for effect. Fernandez looked across the desolate highway and saw an open air, late night bar. The entire edifice was plastered with beer and liquor sponsorships. Inside, a group of old men were playing pool and drinking Johnny Walker with coconut water. The tinkling patter of Bachata, at a mercifully low volume, radiated into the balmy night.

"Listen, I know things haven't been that great in the last year," Lauderdale continued. "You told me you were just on a surveillance, right? Where were you?"

"Work is work, Jay. We do what we gotta do."

"Where were you? No cell reception? You were getting pictures of some jerk off cheating on his wife, right?"

Fernandez was silent.

"I'm not talking down to you. I've been there too, believe me. But look at me now! Fraudbusters is the #1 rated show on the ID network. People write books about me and my cases. I'm in a position where I can pick and choose the work that I want. I probably turn down more work in a month than you take in a year."

"Thanks a lot Jay, you really know how to twist the knife."

"That's not my intention, Fernando. I'm saying you could be there too. Easily. You're excellent at what you do. I've never seen someone with such potential. You'll get there by getting on board with me right now. Everything will be in the email, when we find Lionel..."

"When?"

"What do you mean?" Lauderdale asked.

"No, Jay, it's just that, you know, with the stuff I found before..."

"Christ, not you too! You can't tell me the fuck has fooled you too? What the fuck has happened to this business? You've all become pussies!"

Fernandez heard the disappointment and disbelief in Lauderdale's voice. There was obviously no gray area here. He was as sure Carter was alive as he was sure the sky was blue. Fernandez could see the future slipping away. The only thing that could save him and not compromise his principles at this point would be good old fashioned ambiguity.

"C'mon Jay! I know Carter's resourceful! Of course I'm open to the possibility, I mean anything can happen. Let me take a look at the evidence. I'm sure I'll be able to help you in some way."

"Good, that's a relief. I knew I could count on you, Fernandez." Fernandez once again listened to Lauderdale hack into the London sink from 4,200 miles away. Having just stepped away from the ledge, he took a deep breath and let it out slowly.

"Don't take too close a look though. I'll admit some of it is a little flimsy but it doesn't matter. Like I said I just need you to back me up. The photos are the absolute clincher. Just nod and confirm what I say. You can improvise a little but stay in tight circles around me, get it?"

"Ok."

"Don't worry, Fernando. I've never been wrong before."

"I know, Jay."

"If you have any questions just hit me up on the email. I'm sure I'll have wifi the whole time. Let's shoot for around 1:00 Wednesday at Papayas. I'll call you when I land, though."

"Sounds good."

"This is big time, Fernando. We'll put you back on the map. Now, if you'll excuse me I'm going to throw up."

"Good luck!" Fernandez was so flustered and distracted he couldn't think of what else to say. Lauderdale hung up the phone before he'd finished anyway.

Fernandez pulled out of the gas station. This was all too much, and he was exhausted. He decided to compartmentalize and put everything that had to do with Lauderdale and Lionel Carter on the back burner until he's presented his findings to poor Miriam Alonzo tomorrow. Then he'd open the email and see what was to be seen. But right now it was home and bed. He pointed the minivan in the direction of Carolina and rolled down the windows. The noise and wind would keep him from falling asleep.

The next day Fernandez arrived at his office at ten. Everyone was already there and working. Simon filing while humming a happy tune, Nicole was typing away, and Ruben was struggling with the coffee machine again.

"Mrs. Fernandez, it's on, but nothing is coming out," he huffed.

"Did you put the water in, Ruben?"

"Oh no, what an idiot," he laughed. "Good morning Mr. Fernandez."

Fernandez shook his head, not laughing. He sat down at his desk. His computer was already on and he could see the email from jlauderdale@fraud_busters.com in his queue marked at the highest possible priority.

Later.

He was scheduled to meet Miriam Alonzo at lunchtime. He'd have to prepare his report which included the photos, a detailed account of everything he'd observed, and his hours and expenses etc. It would take him an hour or so to organize all his scribbled notes from the car and transfer them into the report template.

Then the meeting. Over the years, Fernandez had learned more or less how to predict the wife's reaction. He usually met the woman in a wide open, public place like a government building or university campus. If there was a scene, it made less of a disturbance in these places.

There usually was a scene.

A woman who went through all the trouble to hire an investigator to chase her husband was a certain kind of animal. Ballsy and hot blooded, righteous and determined not to be made a fool of. There was no tip toeing around. There was no "thank you Mr. Fernandez I shall take these documents and discuss them with my husband forthwith."

Half the time they didn't even read the report, or wait for the first sentence to be out of his mouth. Upon seeing a photo they were on their cellphones in seconds, in possession of the hard evidence of shit they'd expected for weeks, months or even years.

Fernandez had one such meeting in a crowded restaurant in Isla Verde. The woman was up out of her chair so violently she upended the table and spilled Fernandez's lunch all over his shirt. He then jumped up as well, yelping in pain as the scalding hot soup seeped through his Polo.

The combination of the woman screaming into her cellphone and gesticulating wildly with her free hand, and Fernandez frantically blowing on his shirt in an attempt to cool the spill silenced the whole place. The customers stopped eating and the workers stopped working to watch this real life novella taking place before their eyes.

When Fernandez realized the ruckus they were making, he gently tried to nudge the woman outside.

"Hands off, tubalard!" she screamed and delivered a punch to the gut that sent Fernandez ass-first onto the dessert tray. A sympathetic busboy brought him to the bathroom and helped him clean off both sides.

After this, Fernandez made it a policy never to conduct meetings in restaurants again. Even though Miriam Alonzo was certainly more even-tempered than most, he wasn't prepared to take the chance. He was scheduled to meet her outside the Energy Authority building at 12:30. If she freaked, there would be more than enough traffic and conversation to drown her out.

"Mr. Fernandez?" It was Ruben.

"Yes?"

"I completed the task Simon assigned Friday afternoon."

"The affidavits?"

"Yes," Ruben said slowly, with a hint of uncertainty. "I dropped them off at Mr. Gonzalez's office on my way home after work. His secretary said he was in an important meeting with an official from the Treasury Department, so I left them with her."

Julio Gonzalez was the guy Fernandez used to notarize his affidavits of process serving. He operated out of a one room office in Ocean Park and had a penchant for hiring fleshy Dominican women that were half his age, which usually put them at around 35. His "employees" usually had a shelf life of about six months due to his in-decorum. Although on the whole these women were pretty dismissive of political correctness, there were only so many times any woman could be goosed by a lascivious 72-year-old Jewish lawyer in a seersucker jacket before calling it quits.

"Wonderful, thank you Ruben."

He wasn't going back to his desk.

"Mr. Fernandez?"

"Yes Ruben," Fernandez replied exasperated.

"Do you know what is today's date?"

"It's Monday."

"I've been here three months today, and I completed the task you assigned last Friday."

Fernandez despaired. The three month review was huge in

Puerto Rico. Everyone had it. Whether you were working on the Governor's staff or Wendy's, the three month review was mandatory, and all jobs were strictly probational until it was completed. Employees never felt safe until it's completion; it was no wonder Ruben was asking.

Fernandez had no idea what he was going to do. After three months Ruben had basically proven himself an idiot. Giving him the simple task of dropping off some stamps had even been a stretch that made Fernandez nervous. The fact he felt this was the firm ground he stood upon to ask for his three-month-review just reinforced his obliviousness in Fernandez's eyes.

"I understand Ruben, it's just that I'm pretty busy the next couple of days."

"It's been three months..."

"I am aware of that Ruben. I have a meeting this afternoon and some things to attend to that will stretch into tomorrow. We'll have your review tomorrow afternoon, ok?"

"Ok."

"Can you get me some doughnuts in the meantime?"

"Of course. Oh look, I didn't put the filter in the coffee machine again. I have to clean all this out. Sorry."

Ruben then unplugged it and took the entire machine into the kitchen.

"What are you..." Fernandez let it drop as his assistant left the room.

Simon was smirking at his desk.

"You think this is funny?" Fernandez asked.

"Yes I do. You can't catch a break. This is the third one in a year. It's bad karma. You must have been an inept assistant in another life," Simon laughed.

"Simon, it's funny to hear you laugh, you don't do it that much."

"I know."

"I suggest you continue your policy of not laughing in the future."

"C'mon sir, you got to admit it's a little funny." Simon continued unfazed by the admonition. "First you had Gloria, she was a real piece of work."

"She was a little nervous."

"A little? She was a wreck. She was popping Klonopins like they were tic tacs."

"Not exactly the ideal temperament for dealing with the criminal element."

"You think? Remember that day I asked her if she wanted a mofongo for lunch and she started to cry?"

"Could have been a childhood thing? Some kind of freak mofongo accident?" Fernandez suggested.

"Well, whatever it was I have no idea what she thought she was doing. Taking an assistant P.I. position, and that edgy."

"Times are tough Simon. If they're breathing down your neck for rent you do whatever you can. I mean, what's unemployment here? $120 a week. C'mon, have you been the ideal candidate for all of your jobs?"

If Simon picked up on the gibe he'd decided to let it go.

"And then there was Vicente."

"The thrill seeker."

"The 350-pound thrill seeker."

Fernandez had to laugh. Although thoroughly unqualified, he'd hired Vicente because he liked his enthusiasm. Plus his fearless and outgoing personality was refreshing after Gloria's timidness. He'd thought he could shape him into a first-class assistant but he was too brash and thought he already knew everything about people. It was impossible to go under the radar with Vicente in tow, it was like walking around with a gorilla in a leather jacket.

"He didn't even show up half the time," Fernandez remembered. "That Harley Davidson was constantly breaking."

"Of course it was! It wasn't meant to handle the tonnage," Simon laughed but then checked himself.

"He was a lot bigger than you sir."

"Yes, he was." Fernandez's eyes narrowed.

"How did he hurt himself again? Was it surfing?" Simon asked.

"Kite-boarding."

Fernandez's second assistant was sidelined by a freak water sport accident.

"Amazing. I mean, you have to admire the courage, a man of that size."

"I don't know if it was balls or sheer stupidity. Have you seen those kite-boarders? I'm pretty sure you have to be in relatively good shape to hold onto that thing. I'm surprised they let him do it."

The kiteboarding school put Vicente in a dingy, which he almost capsized, and took him way offshore so he'd be miles clear of all the swimmers. His 16-year-old "instructor" had apparently fit Vicente's fleshy feet into the one-size-fits-all bindings incorrectly. Once the kite went up poor Vicente was ripped from the board and unceremoniously dragged through the water face first, too shocked or afraid to let go of the ropes. To make matters worse, the unsupervised young man in charge had chosen an unfamiliar stretch of water.

Vicente smacked painfully into a coral reef, dislocated his shoulder, and stepped on a sea urchin. Then he let go of the ropes.

"Yeah, he wasn't the same after that," said Simon. "He just kind of sat here with his foot in a bucket of peroxide watching extreme sports on youtube."

"It was sad, he really did think he was in a Red Bull commercial. I was gonna let him go sooner, but under those circumstances I felt badly for him. You're right though, Simon, now that I think of it. Stupid is too harsh."

"Determined?"

"Determined and immune to criticism."

Simon laughed as Ruben came running back into the room with the coffee machine brewing and smoking.

"It's working now. Ouch! It's hot, though."

"Ruben, why did you..." His assistant glared innocently up from the machine and handed him a cup of coffee.

"Ruben, I don't drink coffee."

The phone rang and Simon answered.

"It's Mr. Gonzalez for you sir."

"Thanks Simon, I'll take it here. Julio! How are you doing you dirty old bastard?"

"I know how badly you want this gentile trinket but it's gonna take a lot more that $8.40 to get it, Fernandez," droned a bored, Long Island accent from across the line.

"What the hell are you talking about?"

"The little statue of the fairy stepping on the guy's head, the one Esmerelda threw at me that time."

"Saint Michael?" Fernandez had an affinity for the Archangel Michael. It was in fact one of the symbols he used for Covert Intelligence. Improbably, Gonzalez had a figurine of the archangel on the coffee table in his office. He refused to let Fernandez have it even though a former secretary had gotten fed up with the lawyer's advances and used it to clobber him in the head. The incident had apparently created some kind of weird attachment.

"Yeah, that's the one. I'm not letting it go for $8.40, it has to be at least 40 bucks and a bottle of Brugal," Gonzalez laughed.

"I'm lost here, Julio."

"I hold in my hand a book of US postage stamps," Gonzalez explained. "With a note from my secretary which reads as follows."

The old lawyer cleared his throat and Fernandez could hear him fetch the paper from his desk.

"Mr. Julio, De men fron Fernandez leaf dis wit me today when you were engda track. We olready haf dis kyna estamps."

"Wait a minute Julio, you're not telling me this..."

"You've actually managed to depress me, Fernandez. I initially thought it would be nice, in this day and age, to send some handwritten letters to my family, friends, or some old army buddies. But then I realized that they all were either long dead or refusing to ever speak to me again."

"He brought you postage stamps. God, Julio, I'm really..."

Fernandez used Gonzalez frequently to notarize affidavits. Ruben was supposed to pick up the affidavit stamps from the Department of Treasury and deliver them to the lawyer. If this was true, if Ruben had delivered postage stamps instead, he was even more staggeringly incompetent then Fernandez ever dreamed.

"This in turn got me anxiously brooding over faults in my character," Gonzalez continued, bringing Fernando back to the conversation.

"With all due respect, you should be doing that anyway."

"You're still a young man, Fernando. You don't yet realize the futility of such endeavors. I believe it was another one of your people who said: 'He who is fretted by his own failings will not correct them. All profitable correction comes from a calm and peaceful mind.' I can't remember exactly who, but I read that in 1988 and not by coincidence that's precisely when I stopped giving a fuck."

"Thirty years of not giving a fuck," Fernandez let out a low whistle. "I'm not sure that's what that quote means, Julio."

"I take it to mean you're not going to get anywhere by beating yourself up," Gonzalez explained. "It's a first step Fernandez. I still have plenty of time to change, I'm just waiting for my mind to be peaceful."

"It's not going to get peaceful at the horse track," Fernandez shot back. "Official from the Tax Collectors, huh? Were you gonna pay your back taxes after you hit the trifecta? You know, Julio, you're going to give Jews a bad name. Saint Michael statue, quoting Saint Francis de Sales, and what's with that huge painting of the mosque behind your desk?"

"It was here when I moved in. It's the Dome of the Rock. I keep it as a reminder. I yearn to once again step foot in the motherland."

"Right. The only thing you yearn for is..."

"I don't know who you're yapping at Fernandez. It was your assistant who did this. It's none of my business but I'd say he's gotta go."

Fernandez was absolutely certain of that now.

"You're approaching my track record," Gonzalez said with glee.

"No, I'm just unlucky. You, on the other hand, are a dirty old bastard."

"I can accept that Fernando. Listen, I'm not going to spend all day playing patty cake with you on the phone. I got things to do."

"Races to watch? Asses to pinch? Husbands to dodge?" Fernandez suggested.

"I've installed a trap door under my desk exactly for that eventuality. Anyway, when can I get the real stamps?"

"I'll run them by today Julio, and sorry again for that, buddy."

"De nada. See you soon. I'll be waiting with a calm and peaceful mind."

Fernandez slowly hung up the receiver in an amazed fog, contemplating Ruben's stupidity. Three months, well, at least he had an answer now.

It seemed to defy the imagination. Gloria the basket case, Vicente the plus-sized daredevil, and now Ruben the mailman, all in less than a year. Fernandez was coming to the realization that there must be something inherently flawed in his own character when it came to identifying potential employees. For all Simon's eccentricities, he'd been the only employee of Covert Intelligence ever to prove himself reliable and competent, and he was hired by Nicole. Maybe it was a sign.

Ruben was at his desk with headphones, Fernandez motioned for Simon to come over.

"What did you tell him to do on Friday? I mean exactly," Fernandez asked.

"I told him to take the stamps to Gonzalez's office in Ocean Park."

"Did you say affidavit stamps?"

"I don't remember. Why? What other ones do we use? What did he do?"

"Never mind."

"Strike three?" Simon asked.

"Strike three."

Fernandez collected Miriam Alonzo's report from the printer. On the third page were the two grainy, but unmistakable shots of Sammy and his lover on that isolated street in Loiza the night before. The rest of the report was a more or less a formality.

"I'm leaving hiring up to my wife from now on. I'm out of here."

"Oh, one minute," Simon called after him. "There's a State Police Officer Fuentes on the phone. He said he met you last night..."

Simon looked up only to see the door close.

Halfway across the Atlantic, at 35,000 feet, Jay Lauderdale finally started feeling like a human being again. The previous day had been spent not exactly awake, not exactly asleep, in a breathless and oppressive bed-ridden limbo waiting for the will to live.

In the evening, he'd at least found the will to do and walked across the street to Sainsbury's where he purchased a triangular sandwich in plastic and four liters of Evian. At that point he could just about make out shapes and colors, which was handy at the crosswalk. He then unceremoniously collided with another night and was required, by tradition, to once again sleep.

"Sleep" consisted of basically waiting for the piercing headache in his right eye to subside and trying not to smash his own head against the bedpost. By morning the headache was gone but had left in his brain a raw afterimage of sizzling disorientation that was strange to call relief.

On the train to Heathrow that afternoon he was once again forced to admit to himself that hangovers were a young man's game.

"Would you like something to drink, sir?" The pretty flight attendant smiled down at him.

"Just some more water thank you."

The cool, dim business class cabin felt like an oasis in the sky. While all the other passengers slept through, Lauderdale busied himself on his laptop, reveling in the return of purpose and energy.

He could see through his email plugin that Fernandez hadn't

opened the files on Lionel Carter yet. He began to wonder what he was waiting for. Had he made a mistake bringing Fernandez in?

A year ago he'd been certain, regretfully so as well. Lauderdale could gauge the kind of man Fernandez was by his regret. It was clearly hard for an up-and-comer to disappoint someone like himself. And even though he was pissed off at the time, Lauderdale admired Fernandez's honesty. There and then he'd filed Fernandez under "reliable".

That's why he needed him to open the damn email. Lauderdale considered harassing Fernandez over chat but he was offline.

"Jay, sometimes things are actually what they seem."

That's what Fernandez had told him at the conclusion of the case and it had been ringing in his ears since.

True. Actually most of the time things were what they seemed. But every once in a great while, in a business like his, life really did mirror the movies and books. Ironically, it took someone with a lot of experience to detect the obvious.

Lionel Carter was an invention. He actually was Moriarty or Keyser Söze. The fiction has to come from somewhere, and men like Carter had provided the template for hundreds of years. Those new to this line of work run the constant risk of considering themselves too smart. He now wondered if he was running this risk with Fernandez.

Fernandez hadn't run across someone like Carter yet. Maybe he even found what Lauderdale was suggesting absurd, even cartoonish.

He fired off a quick follow up email.

Fernando,

It's true sometimes things are what they seem. But every so often the movie comes to life. The best of our profession never lose their imagination.

Jay

That ought to do it. This would be a good lesson in reality for Fernandez. He'd realize some things now in working to get Carter that would kick him up a notch or two.

Just then he received an email from Dirk Saban. It was short.

Jay,

I changed my flight regardless. It wasn't cheap, this better be worth it.

D

Lauderdale was momentarily puzzled over the wording. What did he mean "regardless"? For a split second a dreamy and sodden half formed memory floated across his cerebral cortex and was gone.

He reestablished consciousness in the now by pulling up the two photos of Lionel Carter in Martinique, sitting by the pool, smiling. The rage welled up immediately.

"What a fucking smart ass."

Keep smiling asshole, because here I come.

He wrote back to Saban.

Dirk,

It's worth it. You're gonna come out of this looking like

a hero.

Jay

And Carter, I'm gonna wipe that shit-eating grin off your dumb fucking face.

Miriam Alonzo was waiting outside the Energy Authority. It was closed and the broad courtyard where Fernandez had planned to conduct their meeting was behind a locked gate. Fiddling with her phone, she didn't seem to notice.

"I'm sorry Mrs. Alonzo. I had no idea they were closed today."

"You mean you didn't know this was one of the 174 paid holidays these turkeys get?" She was shaking.

"I'm sure it's not 174."

"It's close though, isn't it? We have to bust our ass twice as hard in the private sector to make up for this shit. Do you have any idea the kind of free ride these people have?"

"No, not really ma'am. I've always worked in the private sector and I'm tired," Fernandez laughed.

"I'm sorry Fernando. I'm still trying to run my business, take care of my son, all the while this shit is going on with my husband. I have to just keep going. I've worked myself into a position of authority and I can't break down. Sometimes I think people don't look at me as human."

"They don't. That's why you get paid the big bucks Miriam. Let's go to that cafe across the street."

Fernandez kept it cool but could tell she was cracking. Hard.

The place was empty aside from an old man at the counter drinking an espresso. It didn't matter. Despite her agitation she'd keep her composure. There'd be no Jerry Springer action today, she simply wasn't the type.

Miriam took her glasses off, ordered a cappuccino and smiled weakly at him. Fernandez was then surprised by an overwhelming wave of grief and sadness. It surged slowly over his head and shoulders and came to an agitated rest in his stomach. An irresistible urge to take this woman in his arms and whisper in her ear like she was one of his daughters confronted him. The high-powered bitch was gone, they were both children again. So were we all ultimately, just putting on a show. What if they'd known each other in 2nd grade? Had they? On the swings? Only to meet 30 years later like this. What happened in your life? They always asked us what we wanted to be and now we're it. Do you feel any different? Cause I certainly don't. I'm still a little boy Miriam. What if they find out!

For this split second, he glimpsed that control was a fool's illusion and life was something that happened to us. She was still a little girl, she'd stayed a good person, there was no objective reason he had the good marriage and she had not. There was no objective reason he looked forward everyday to being comfortable and settled in front of the TV with his wife and daughters, and she was likely contemplating suicide. She didn't deserve it.

The sadness was deep and seemed to come from another universe. Embracing and rocking her would not alleviate it because there was nothing he could ultimately do. Life was set four dimensionally, and beautiful, longing sorrow seemed to be the cosmic background radiation. Geez, he had been listening to Simon for too long.

"I'll have a cheeseburger and fries please," Fernandez said to the waiter. "Miriam?"

"I'm sorry, I can't eat right now. I seem to have lost my appetite."

"How long has it been gone?"

She didn't answer.

"Miriam, be honest with me."

"About a week."

"How about a fruit salad and some juice or something?"

"I'd have to force it down."

"Of course you would. You're in a state of extremely high anxiety, but you have to eat. It will just make it worse if you don't," Fernandez explained.

"Ok."

She was different, singular among all the other women who had hired him for this job. She wasn't volatile, she was fair and nice. That's what made this hurt. He usually saw the husband and wife as a couple of low class jerk offs he'd have nothing to do with in the usual run of things. Miriam could have been his friend.

"So here we are," he said nervously.

"I can already tell by your demeanor Mr. Fernandez. This is going to be what I was afraid of."

"Funny, I've spent a lot of time perfecting my demeanor for this very eventuality," he half laughed.

"I've spent a lot of time learning to read people."

"Touché."

He reached into his satchel and pulled out the report.

"It's all there, I'm afraid."

Miriam shuffled through the papers and predictably came to a stop at the photos. She shook her head back and forth and smiled. Then somewhat unpredictably, she started to laugh. It began as brief stuttered nasal exhalations that after five seconds became full on snorts. After ten seconds she was belly laughing and slapping the table, tears streaming down her cheeks.

"Did I give you the right report, Miriam?"

It took a while for Miriam to catch her breath.

"What an asshole I married! I'm such an idiot!"

She resumed laughing, but even harder this time. Fernandez studied her and could quickly deduce this wasn't maniacal laughing of a woman who had gone over the edge. She was clear eyed and matter of fact, like she was finally getting a joke someone had told her years ago.

"Are you ok?" Fernandez asked.

Miriam calmed down and began smoothing the front of her shirt.

"Yes. Yes Mr. Fernandez. I'm fine."

She motioned to the waiter.

"What's your name son?"

"Felipe," the kid smiled.

"Felipe, what's the least healthy thing you have on the menu?"

"Probably what this gentleman is having ma'am."

"Ok, give me a burger as well but with extra bacon and a chocolate milkshake. Wait, do you have beer?"

"Of course."

"Do you like beer, Fernandez?"

"Usually not this early in the day."

"Don't be a pussy."

"Ok."

"Two Heinekens, and I still want the shake too," she yelled after him.

"Mine is a Medalla, not a Heineken!" yelled Fernandez immediately.

"I'm glad to see your appetite is back, Miriam."

"It was that laugh," she explained. "Somewhere during that laugh it came raging back. I'm starving!"

"You sound good."

"I'm relieved Fernandez. I mean, look at this idiot."

She held up the photo of her husband and pointed at the short, dumpy girl next to him, both staring mouths agape after the cop car from the night before. She started laughing again.

"They do look kind of stupid," Fernandez admitted.

"Where the hell was this anyway? The hood?"

"Pretty much. Relieved?"

"Relieved."

She downed half the beer in one gulp.

"I'll try and explain. You see, I thought this nightmare was my life and I'd just have to get used to it. Not just his bullshit but the whole relationship, the whole mockery of a family. I didn't think it could end, do you know what I mean?"

"I guess we're afraid to lose whatever we're used to, even if it's a nightmare?" Fernandez suggested.

"Exactly. You trudge along, you wake up, it's the same again, miserable. You keep moving forward even though you know with every fiber of your being the situation you are in is inherently fucked. It's a slow growing cancer that won't actually shorten your lifespan. You just live with it because..."

"You're used to him." he completed.

"It really is that pathetic. You're used to your unhappy and miserable life, you've settled into that layer. All the brooding, all the worry that looks indefinite and unchanging, it was all just paper thin and in one second you cut me a window. I feel like me again."

"I'm happy to be of service, Mrs. Alonzo."

"It's a funny feeling to have someone thoroughly by the balls. I'm kind of excited."

"I'm married."

"I'm not ready to start yet," she laughed. "Besides there's only one man on my mind right now and he is eight. Ok, is everything in order between us? Do I owe you any more money?"

"Nope. You are up to date in your account."

"Jesus, Fernandez, let's eat then."

After a passable and unhealthy lunch, he left Miriam Alonzo at the cafe, smiling. She'd ordered more beers and was letting the new situation wash over her. No doubt she was planning her next move.

As he rode home to his town of Carolina, Fernandez was glad he'd helped her. He was surprised to feel that level of satisfaction for this type of case. If all the women that hired him were like Miriam Alonzo maybe exposing cheating spouses wasn't the worst thing in the world.

"You just don't want to open up Lauderdale's email, Fernandez," he said aloud.

He realized he was in danger of settling into a comfortable usual, just as Miriam had.

"Alright, lets get this over with."

Maybe Lauderdale really had managed to raise the dead.

Fernandez stared at his monitor dumbstruck.

"No fucking way!"

There he was. Lionel Carter poolside in a lime green Speedo and yellow tank top. The file was named Martinique_1. He was sitting on a deck chair holding a piña colada with an "oh, hi there" smile, which was undoubtedly driving Lauderdale crazy.

"A walking corpse!"

The first thought that popped into his mind was photoshop. But there was no way Jay Lauderdale would tamper with evidence like that. For all his bluster, Jay's ethics were beyond reproach. Anyway, it didn't make any sense for him to invent evidence in this case even if he wanted to.

No, Jay was convinced. This was all the evidence he needed. And Fernandez had to admit he was beginning to see the light himself.

"No, there's no way. I don't believe it!"

"Are you alright sir?"

"Yeah Simon, fine."

Could someone have doctored the picture and given it to Lauderdale? Again, this made no sense. Jay was as good as

Fernandez with computers, maybe even better. He would have caught the tampering almost immediately.

No. This man was either Lionel Carter reanimated, or someone who looked exactly like him.

Martinique_2 was an intimate shot. It was from behind. Carter was at the edge of the pool, poised to dive into the inviting crystal blue water. Fernandez realized that the Speedo wasn't a Speedo at all but in fact a g-string. He then made a stunning realization.

"Cheeky," Simon had silently sidled up behind him and was whispering uncomfortably close over his shoulder.

"You can say that again," Fernandez concurred. "Extremely cheeky and apparently loud and proud. You would look good in something like that, Simon."

"I don't know if I could pull that off. I could give it a shot if you want sir. Not my color though."

"Jesus, who the fuck wears something like this?"

"It's either a hyper-masculine joke, or he could always be gay."

"Not necessarily Simon. He could be from the Netherlands, or France or somewhere like that."

"A distinct possibility. Who is this anyway?"

"It's supposed to be Lionel Carter," Fernandez explained. "Remember the fraud case from last year?"

"Supposed to be?"

Fernandez selected a zoom box and dragged it over the man's backside. The entire ass filled his screen. At high resolution the pool water glistened off the cheeks in the sunlight. The two straight men were impressed, it really was a pert and gloriously toned specimen.

"See? Check it out." Fernandez pointed to the man's left cheek. Simon adjusted his glasses and moved close to the screen leaning forward and putting his hand on Fernandez's shoulder for support.

"Where?"

"Right there, the ass. Don't you remember Simon?"

"Oh yeah. The assssss..." Simon whispered in a way that sounded uncomfortably seductive. They both were smiling lasciviously.

"What in the name of God are you two doing?"

Fernandez whirled in his chair to find Nicole and his two daughters staring at him, puzzled. They'd clearly been standing there for the whole exchange.

"Daddy, why are you looking at a hiney?" Angelic, the younger one asked.

"I'd like to know the same thing, Fernando," Nicole clucked sarcastically.

"No, you don't understand," Simon pointed to the screen. "You have to look close right here."

The two girls ran forward eagerly. Fernandez corralled them in his arms before they could reach the screen.

"Nicole, this is an extremely important ass," he tried to explain as they struggled against him, trying to catch a glimpse of the screen.

"Ass! Ass!" Angelic started to yell.

Nicole grabbed the two and angrily escorted them out of the room. Fernandez could hear from the kitchen the two had created an impromptu song consisting of "ass, ass, hiney, hiney" sung to the tune of the Micky Mouse Club march. Usually he would have been preparing himself to get reamed but he was completely absorbed in the current epiphany.

"Wait a minute," Simon interjected. "I don't understand. Is this an old photo?"

"It doesn't matter. It's not Carter. I have to tell Lauderdale it's not him."

"You mean the Fraudbusters guy?" Simon asked.

"Yup."

"I'm sure it'll be ok. He seems like an even tempered and reasonable fellow. Did you see the episode where he put the dude in a pitch black room with the agitated Rottweiler?"

"I missed that one," Fernandez sighed.

"Yeah, it was awesome. The dog was in a cage but the guy didn't know, of course."

Fernandez put his head down on his desk.

"You'll be fine! It's time for my breathing exercises." Simon went back to his desk and sat cross legged in his swivel chair.

"Maybe I should try that too."

She found him sitting outside in the dark. A squall kicked up and was peppering the backyard. He sat looking over the side wall, eyes fixed on the porch light of their neighbor, getting pelted by intermittent windy drops.

"What are you doing out here?"

"Look, I'm sorry about that ass thing, honey," he began.

"Don't worry, I'm used to it. What's the problem?"

"I've called Lauderdale three times and no answer. I don't want to spring this on him. I'm going to have to disappoint a very important man," he explained. "For the second time."

"The truth is the truth. Simon filled me in on the particulars before he left."

He looked down at his phone accusingly, the culpable source of all his current misery.

"Did I tell you on Sunday night I spilled a bottle of piss all over the car and was mauled by a pack of wild dogs?"

"I don't see the connection."

"I feel what I'm doing is undignified, Nicole. I'm sick of spending all my time chasing Felix Fuck-a-Lots."

"And if you disappoint Jay Lauderdale you're worried that's all you'll ever do."

She sat down next to him and put her hands on his knees. She was getting wet too, her hair would be ruined, but she didn't care. She smiled. She wanted to help him work it out. He loved his wife because of moments like these.

"Well, let's break it down. What choice do you have?"

"I could lie. He'd be pleased. I could help him on a cause that I knew was lost. His vendetta would drag on and on, but ultimately come to nothing. No one would ever be any the wiser that I lied, it would just be an oversight. Carter's widow would be harassed, dragged through the mud again. Carter's children would go through the hell of thinking their father was alive, when those wounds were just beginning to heal. Then they'd have to let him go twice. In the meantime tens of thousands, possibly hundreds of thousands of dollars would be spent chasing a ghost. Alliance Insurance would be pissed. Saban, Lauderdale and myself would all come out looking like shit initially, but it would pass. All this so I could float Jay Lauderdale's nuts and play with the big boys again."

"You won't do that."

"Of course I won't fucking do that."

It began to thunder. He stood up and took her by the hand back inside.

"It just sucks, that's all."

"Fernando, you didn't get where you are by lying, or playing politics. I'm a firm believer if you do the right thing, things will eventually go your way. And you know what? Even if they don't, at least you'll be able to sleep at night. There really isn't a dilemma here, you've made up you're mind. You're just having a pity party."

"I am," he admitted.

"Maybe he'll admire your honesty like last time? Maybe he'll be impressed you cracked this. No pun intended."

"You didn't hear him on the phone. This is some Lex Luthor versus Superman shit."

"Well, even if you're chasing Johnny-Pants-Around-The-Ankles the food's always been on the table and your family loves you. Remember that. I'm going to bed."

She kissed him and he followed her inside.

Dirk Saban emerged from the baggage claim at Luis Muñoz Marin International Airport and was promptly assaulted by three overzealous taxi drivers. Although he was black, his clothes and mannerisms clearly made him stand out as a gringo mark. A veteran of international corporate investigations and world travel, Saban was immune to intimidation. All it took was one sharp look to send the three men scurrying off to find the bachelorettes from Garden City, or the sun-struck and disoriented couple from Steven's Point. No, he wasn't interested in El Yunque National Rain Forest. No, he didn't want to see the bioluminescent bay. No, he didn't want to go to a wild party in Old San Juan. Thanks.

He hadn't been to the islands in some time and was struck by just how pleasant the weather was this time of year. He briefly started thinking about vacation homes, or time shares, when a loud bark jolted him out of his reverie.

"Dirk!"

Jay Lauderdale had arrived 30 minutes earlier and decided to wait for Saban outside.

"I figured we'd rent a car together instead of taking a cab. I know this place like the back of my hand. Then we can just take the puddle jumper tomorrow morning. You fixed up for a place to stay tonight?"

"No, not yet. This all happened so fast," he tried to mitigate his growl. If Lauderdale noticed, he didn't show it.

"Ok, I got a place. Let me take care of it, Dirk, it's the least I can do."

Forty-five minutes later, after a confused exchange at the car rental where Lauderdale wanted to speak Spanish and the guy at the desk wanted to speak English, both very badly, the two investigators were coasting down the expressway headed for the beachfront community of Ocean Park and the restaurant Papayas, where they were to meet Fernandez.

"I'm pretty impressed with your Spanish, Jay. You seemed to have that situation well in hand."

"Oh yeah? Thanks. It's kind of difficult here, being a territory and all. People always want to practice their English. You have to be forceful if you want to fit in and be treated like a native. Stick with me and you won't get the gringo treatment," he explained.

"I see," said Saban, stifling such a powerful giggle it emerged as a loud cough.

"You ok?"

"It's the fresh air. I'm not used to it."

As they made their way through the back streets of Santurce, Saban's keen eye spotted a shady transaction going down right on the street in broad daylight.

"So this is the area where we're meeting your boy?"

"A little ways from here. It changes pretty quickly."

In the space of one block, garbage and broken pints of rum gave way to the relatively well kept and affluent streets of Ocean Park. The dealers morphed into surfers, the obese woman in spandex angrily dragging three kids behind her became the sandaled and Ray Ban-ed dad, orbited by eager little children in soccer jerseys.

"It reminds me of Brooklyn," Saban offered. "No middle ground, no warning, just BANG, you cross the street and you're in a different world."

"It's a small island. Things are kind of packed in."

As they turned left onto McCleary Street, Ocean Park proper came into view, a gated and patrolled community. Unlike a modern guarded development, Ocean Park looked as if the walls had been constructed around a community that was already there, and indeed had been there for a hundred years. A modern bulwark that continued the ancient tradition started by the Spanish in the Old City.

Here there weren't 350 slightly different versions of the same house, impossibly green, surgically weeded lawns and weekend car wash regulations you come to expect from the suburbs in the US. Here there was a collision of independently constructed edifices that jaggedly cut through the horizon looking like a Tetris game. It was as if a kindergarten teacher had gathered all of her students' drawings of houses and given them to the contractors as blueprints. Fourth floor, rooftop party balconies hung menacingly over squat rectangular one story Florida houses. Hulking, square proletarian monoliths cast their shadows over ornate, colonial grottos. All dotted with satellites, antennae and crooked telephone poles. The five access gates were sealed at 6:30 sharp every night and the only way in was then through the guard post.

It was an oasis of peacefulness and normality. The kind of place where every night felt like Halloween.

"Here it is, Dirk."

They pulled off McCleary and parked at Papayas. Known more as a nighttime party spot, it was liberally attended by the midweek lunch crowd. Lauderdale payed the valet and the two looked for a second lost in the huge outside bar.

"There he is."

Lauderdale spotted Fernandez in the air conditioned area waving at him. He'd chosen a high bar table in a secluded corner. When Fernandez proffered his hand Lauderdale embraced him in a huge bear hug, giving an extra "I know I can count on you" squeeze. Fernandez could barely breathe.

"Fernando Fernandez, meet Dirk Saban of Interference International."

The two shook hands. Saban did the thing where he simultaneously grabbed the other man's forearm while shaking. Before even speaking, he took a long second to size up Fernandez. He seemed bemused by his short, stocky stature and honest face. Saban was a good judge of people and he made a mental note to remember in the future that he immediately liked Fernandez. This didn't happen often. It was something about his face. Maybe he looked like an old school chum from way back.

Fernandez picked up on the warmth in his eyes. He concluded that he automatically liked Saban too. There would be no awkward conversation between the two of them, they'd go right to friends.

"You were working for me last year, Fernandez, but you didn't know it."

"That's what I understand, Mr. Saban."

"And we're here to right the wrongs of the past, gentlemen! Fernandez, why are you drinking water? I told you I wanted to be exactly right here drinking Middleyas, it's been a long trek from the Old World."

"Medallas," Fernandez corrected.

"Yeah that's it. We'll have three Medallas," he yelled at a waiter that was attending to another table entirely.

"Of course sir, just one moment."

"A little rude, Jay?" Saban offered with a raised eyebrow and smiling at Fernandez.

"No one cares here, right Fernandez?"

"It's a little early in the day for me," Fernandez breathed

apologetically.

"Don't be a pussy."

"Ok." Fernandez wondered how many times he was going to be called a pussy for not wanting to drink at lunch.

"Anyway, it's nice to meet you, Fernando. Jay says you're doing a hell of a job. I heard WatchNET let you in last year, that's pretty unheard of. I'm impressed."

"Thank you sir."

"Call me Dirk. Are you going to St. Croix tomorrow?

"No Dirk, I'd love to but I can't really swing the trip... monetarily right now," Fernandez tried hard not to sound like a charity case, especially in light of the praise from someone like Saban.

"It's hard times to be sure, man," he said not without sympathy. "Maybe next year."

"We'll get you on the map," Lauderdale spoke out the side of his mouth, his lips locked to the icy beer bottle. He seemed to be waiting for Fernando to make a move.

"So how was London, Jay? I've got a standing invitation to visit from Grimes but..."

"C'mon Fernandez," Lauderdale interrupted grabbing the beer. "Out with it, show Dirk what you found. That's why he's here."

Fernandez squirmed in his chair. Through no fault of his own he was now in a situation where there was no good way out. He didn't want to reveal Lauderdale had sent him the evidence, he'd be making a lifetime enemy, and he'd look unscrupulous by association to Saban. He sucked it up and took the least bad option, fully knowing it would probably relegate him to the minor leagues forever.

"Jay I'm really sorry but I've made a mistake."

"What the fuck are you talking about, Fernandez?" out of respect for the establishment he lowered his voice to a boom.

"You see, I tried to call you about a million times since yesterday," he apologized.

"Fernandez, do you think we could go offline for a second?" He grabbed him by the arm and began to pull him out of his chair. Fernandez's girth shifted the barstool dangerously off balance and the two almost went down.

"Hold up Jay, you're out of order. This is Alliance's money we're talking about. I'm in charge here. Sit down, Fernando, and explain. Jay, have another beer for Christ's sake."

"Well, the photos I got," he measured out the words painfully, the half-lie leaving a bad taste in his mouth. "I thought initially it had to be Lionel Carter, God knows it's his spitting image, but last night I made a realization."

Fernandez produced the blow up shot of the man's backside.

"What the fuck is this, Fernando?" Lauderdale growled.

"This is the alleged derrière of Lionel Carter."

"Alleged?" Saban scrutinized the photo.

"Yes. I was privy to the report from his autopsy last year, and the photos as well. Lionel Carter has a huge birthmark on his left buttock. You can see clearly that this man, whoever he is, does not."

"Are you kidding me, Fernandez?" Lauderdale shot back.

"I made a mistake. I'm sorry."

The last sentence hung in the afternoon air. Several of the

patrons had obviously picked up on the escalating tension and
the place had become quiet, the silence broken only by the slap
of Lauderdale's beer bottle against the glass tabletop.

"Did you ever think he had it removed, Fernandez?"

"Yes Jay, of course I took that into consideration, but
according to the report Lionel's birthmark was a vascular
malformation. Removal of these always leaves some kind of
trace. I didn't get a chance to print this out on photo paper but
trust me, it's mega hi res. The file was huge, the camera was set
to something in the neighborhood of 600 dpi. When you pull it
up in photoshop it's not pixelated at all, even at this magnifica-
tion. The man's posterior is unmolested, there's no sign of any...
ah...interference."

"Smooth as a baby's," Saban whistled as he examined the
printout. "Fernandez, you seem to know a thing or two about
computers."

"Before I was an investigator I worked in IT for ten years."

"How useful."

"We could go back to my office and pull it up on the screen
if you want to be sure," Fernandez offered. "I'm just sorry you
came all this way."

Fernandez watched Lauderdale smolder as Saban examined
the menu with a smirk on his face. What would Jay do? Now he
was in the bad position and Fernandez could tell he still wasn't
letting it go. The only sensible course was for him to play along
and berate Fernandez, or accept his apology for the mistake.
The tables had turned. If he further pushed the issue of the
photo at this point he'd be on his own again, stroking his own
particular hard-on.

"Not a problem Fernando. I'm finding the neighborhood

enchanting," Saban smiled. "Hey, isn't that what they call it? The island of enchantment? Anyway, I'm determined to make the best of it. This place smells amazing. What's good?"

"The conch mofongo. They use the real thing here. A lot of places use fake conch these days. It's a scandal," Fernandez said tightly and distracted.

Saban eyed Lauderdale clenching his fists and fidgeting, looking at the Lionel Carter photos like a lottery ticket that was one number off.

"Out with it Jay, you're a terrible actor. Show your hand. He told me he gave you these photos, Fernandez, when he was in London. Do you remember Jay?"

"Kinda," Lauderdale replied dejectedly.

"It must have been killing you, even if it was basically a little fib. His standards are too high, Fernandez, but there's something about this one guy Carter, isn't there Jay?"

Lauderdale sat considering the new information, looking slightly ashamed he was just become acquainted with his actions that one drunken night. The unfamiliar self reproach made him angry and he jumped out of his chair.

"It doesn't matter Dirk. Look, this second shot here, you see? It's not him! It's just his back. The first one is. I mean look at him! It's Lionel Carter in the flesh!"

"Jesus, Lauderdale, let it go, this is getting sad," Saban issued this as more of a command at this point. "You think there were two guys at the pool that day in the same ridiculous swimsuit, same hair? Look at these time stamps, about 45 seconds apart. This is clearly the man who was sitting in the chair, he put his drink down and went for a swim with his smooth ass. Can we please just enjoy lunch?"

Lauderdale desperately turned his attention to Fernandez. His slicked back, expensive haircut, his Versace suit that had clearly been pressed in the Admiral's Club at JFK, his cologne, just a faint whiff of something that to Fernandez would be an absolute indiscretion.

"You failed me, Fernandez. You totally failed me and I won't forget it. Here I am trying to do you a favor and this is how you repay me?"

"C'mon Jay," Saban moaned.

"And you're a pushover, Dirk. You've lost your courage. So has this entire business! It's all politics because the whole thing has been steadily corporatized and you're fucking leading the way with that firm of yours."

"Don't be afraid to say what you really think Jay," Saban teased.

"Trust me I won't. I never am. Ten years ago when we were pounding the pavement we would have totally gone after this, we would have cracked some fucking heads. But now? I'm finished before I even start."

"And ten years ago you'd have wasted a lot of time and come up empty just the same," Saban calmly laughed. "What's wrong with efficiency? Times are changing Jay."

"Not for me they aren't. I didn't get where I am by sitting behind a fucking desk. I'm out of here. You, Interference International, WatchNET, you can all kiss my ass. Especially you, Fernandez. I'm going back to New York. Have fun at your pussy conference, Dirk."

The great detective stormed out of the restaurant like he was storming out of the 21st century. Fernandez stared after him but Saban was unfazed. Silenced by the outburst, the customers gradually regained interest in their own business.

"Fernandez?"

Fernando couldn't take his eyes off the swinging doors, thinking his future was in ruins.

"Fernandez!"

"Yeah."

"Well, that was interesting, don't you think? Jay Lauderdale, transatlantic restaurant silencer," he laughed to himself at the joke Fernandez would never get.

Fernandez sat dejectedly and didn't answer. The waiter brought the food and lay Lauderdale's lunch at the empty chair. He looked at the fish tacos like they had done something to him.

"You want them? I'm sure Lauderdale won't mind."

"I'm not hungry anymore."

Saban regarded Fernandez cooly, his lips pursed in a knowing smile, his cheeks bulging with salad. He was waiting for something.

"Dirk, I'm sorry..."

"Do you always apologize this much?"

"No, it's not that. I really didn't know what else to do in this situation."

"I fully understand that. This was borderline impossible for you, and I'm impressed with how you played your hand. In your situation, the fact you were willing to take the fall, piss him off at the same time and risk looking incompetent to me...doing the right thing and covering his ass and in the process hurting yourself royally. It's not lost on me Fernandez. Most men I know wouldn't have done it and I've been in this game a long, long time."

Fernandez wasn't sure where Saban was going. Was this an "it's nice to have ethics but this is the real world now go back to your mommy" speech?

"I'm saying you have balls, Fernandez," Saban explained. "And character. Lauderdale was right, things are changing, but that's one thing that's always gonna make you come out on top if you're patient and not stupid enough to get involved in interoffice bullshit. Keep doing it that way Fernando, and every single person that's got a personal gripe with you will dig their own grave. Every. Time. That's one thing that will never change, man."

Fernandez felt his appetite coming back. He began to probe his mofongo and Saban looked pleased.

"Jay left his message before I switched the flight. I switched it anyway because I wanted to meet you."

"Because of the work last year?"

"Partly, but I also had a talk with Ken Grimes. Lauderdale thought he was keeping you a secret but it was easy enough to figure out. Grimes couldn't say enough about you. Listen, I have a lot of work coming in from here, Dominican Republic , the Virgin Islands, all over the Caribbean, and I have zero staff acquainted with the area. Some of it is some pretty heavy stuff like fraud, huge dollar amounts, fugitives, that kind of thing. Are you up for it?"

"Yes."

"Perfect. I know it's short notice but can you accompany me to the pussy conference tomorrow? My treat? There are some people there that you are going to need to meet."

"Yes."

He slapped him on the back.

"Fernando, I think this could be..."

"Don't say it."

"Ok I won't."

Two days later Fernando Fernandez returned from St. Croix, tanned but agitated. His initial relief that his fortunes were changing had given way to mild panic. Interference International did have a lot of work for him, and it was coming in fast. After trying to take the weekend easy, he entered the office Monday morning intending to plan the next month and get a hold on all the cases Saban was sending him. Simon and Nicole had other plans, though. They'd brought in a young man to interview as Ruben's replacement.

"Fernando, this is Felix Rivera, he's my friend's stepson," Nicole explained.

"Nice to meet you sir!" the young man shouted.

"Take it easy Felix, this isn't Fort Bragg. It's nice to meet you too," Fernandez smiled but Felix stared straight ahead, taking far too firm and nervous a hold of Fernandez's hand.

"His resume sir!" Simon handed Fernandez a piece of paper and saluted. Fernandez ignored him.

"This is quite impressive Felix. Legal Investigation Certificate from Texas A&M, graduated with honors. You could have started a nice living on the mainland, why come here?"

"I was born here sir, in Caguas."

"That didn't answer my question, Felix."

"Well," the young man squirmed in his seat already showing chinks in his armor. "I feel too much slips through the cracks here, the police are...overstretched. Some of the things I saw growing up, things that happened to my family disgusted me. This society must be raised up to a certain standard. It's lazy and a disgrace now. I wanted to get the best education available so I could come back here and..." he hesitated.

"Clean up the island?"

"In a manner of speaking sir, yes."

"Bruce Wayne didn't go to Batman school, you know?"

"I'm not sure I understand."

Simon let out a long sigh from his desk.

"Felix, I like your enthusiasm, but the education is just the groundwork. It's important for sure, but most of this stuff you can't teach. You have to check your ego at the door and be willing to shut up and listen for a year, or maybe two or three depending on your aptitude."

"My aptitude is, uh, more apt than normal, above average I would say," the words tumbled out of his mouth a mess.

Fernandez wasn't sure if it was eagerness or arrogance. He couldn't help but think Felix was a Puerto Rican that had contracted an annoying case of mainland syndrome. If he'd been infected, his mind was already made up that he could learn nothing from Fernandez. Useless. In the normal run of things it might be fun just to knock him down a peg or two, but there simply wasn't time. There was too much work.

"How did you do on your certification?"

"Ninety-five percent. The highest score last year," he proclaimed.

"Hey, didn't you get a ninety-one in you test for P.I., Mr. Fernandez?" Simon offered with an innocence that was the furthest thing from genuine.

"Thank you Simon. So it looks like you're four percent better than me, Felix," Fernandez joked fishing for an inkling of humility. Felix continued to stare straight ahead in confirmation.

"I have the tools I need sir. I have been taught by some of the best. I will bring all the weapons in my arsenal to bear..."

"That's nice Felix. I know why you got into this business now. Who's your hero?"

"Pardon?"

"Who do you look up to? Who would you like to emulate?"

"Do you know Jay Lauderdale?" Felix responded.

"I've heard of him."

"He's the standard. He's who I want to be."

"So you watch Fraudbusters?" Fernandez asked.

"I have every episode memorized."

"He's an impressive investigator. From what I hear it's not Hollywood, it's 100% real."

"It most certainly is!" Felix asserted vehemently.

"What do you like about him, Felix?"

"He's never been wrong," the crusader said confidently.

In light of recent events Fernandez could hardly believe he was having this conversation. The irony was so fresh he could bite a piece off and spit it in Felix's face, but he was far too old to be name dropping. He decided to try and use it as a teaching moment.

"Everyone is wrong sometimes, Felix. In fact, the possibility that you could be completely full of shit needs to occur to you at least once a day for you to make it in this life. Had that ever occurred to you?"

"No Mr. Fernandez, it hadn't," he didn't seem to be buying it. Fernandez was most likely fucking up his daydreams of fraudbusting up and down the island.

Fernandez reached way down into one of his drawers. Here was an un-filed file, one Nicole had been gently leaning on him to lose for years.

"I'll tell you what, Felix. Let's try it for three months. We'll see how you do and reassess then. I'll have Simon put together an offer and a contract. In the meantime, here's your first assignment."

Fernandez dropped the file on the desk and went into the kitchen. Felix could barely make out the half-faded writing scrawled in pencil on the cover. It said "The Furniture Man".

All Dressed Up
2009

"Father. Father!" It took Fernandez a second to realize the officer was talking to him. "Hey Father. What's the rush?" His heart was about to explode out of his chest. Fernandez slowly turned around. "Yes…my…son?" An enormous policeman with a bunched up face too small for his head approached him slowly and suspiciously. "Where are you going so fast?" he squeaked. Fernandez cocked his head to the right toward the men's room. "Oh." The man relaxed visibly. He was most likely bored, pulling guard duty outside Henry Delgado's room.

"Nature calls, even for the, apostol-i-call"

Fernandez stuttered out fully realizing how ridiculous it sounded. He'd nailed the outfit, if only he'd had more time to research the spiel. He thought back to when he was an altar boy at Christ the King. Father Jimenez. How the hell did he talk again?

"I'm sorry to interrupt but do you think I could talk to you? It would only take a minute. It's about my Aunt Berta."

This is what Fernandez was afraid of. Dressing as a priest had given him easy access to Henry's room. The downside was an Intensive Care Unit was precisely the kind of place he'd likely be approached by someone needing his "services". He didn't foresee it would be the guard calling up on his divine connection, though. He nodded wordlessly.

"Thank you!" the big man said with considerable emotion. "You see, she suffers so badly, and we all love her so much."

"Which room is she in?" Fernandez cut him off. The killer was still in Henry's room. He didn't have time for this.

"Oh she's not here. She's at home in Orocovis."

"Then what's the problem?" Fernandez huffed out clearly betraying his impatience. "My son, that is."

"She's afflicted with the gout something furious."

"The gout?"

"She's miserable! The part of her foot next to her big toe has swollen considerably. She has become so difficult and testy, snapping at everyone. She's making the whole family suffer along with her. She used to laugh and joke, she's not the same free spirit she used to be," he reminisced wistfully. "The doctors can't help her. As much as I'm ashamed to admit to a man as yourself, of the cloth that is, we even took her to see a Santera."

Fernandez gasped, appropriately. "I know! I know!" the guard blubbered beginning to fall apart. "I'm guilt stricken, believe me!"

"Ok, ok, ok, bow your head!"

Fernandez unzipped his hand bag, the first compartment, which didn't contain his secret camera. He produced a Bible and placed it on the back of the man's planetary head, slowly nudging it downward. Scanning the corridor, he noticed people were beginning to stare. Not good. He hadn't been to church in years. Just remember one prayer, for Christ's sake, he thought. Any prayer.

"Bless us, O Lord, and these Thy gifts, which we are about to receive from Thy bounty, through Christ our Lord. Amen."

"Father isn't that what we say before we eat?"

"Yes yes, of course," Fernandez rebounded. "I just needed to warm up. Ok, here we go, are you ready?"

"Yes Father."

The guard's head remained bowed. They were attracting more and more onlookers. What's more, Fernandez could see through the long thin rectangular window in the door to Henry's room. The killer was watching too. Good, he thought, as long as his attention is off Henry for the moment. Good.

"Oh my God," he began again. "I am heartfully sorry for having offended thee, and I detest all my sins because of Thy just punishment…"

The guard began to break down and cry. Jesus Christ, Fernandez thought. He backed off the guard and edged toward the men's room while still reciting the prayer.

"But most of all because I have offended Thee my God, Who is all good and deserving of all my love…"

The guard began to moan with guilt.

He dodged two orderlies rolling a gurney, and finally got his hand on the doorknob just as the guard collapsed to one knee.

"I firmly resolve, with the help of Thy grace, to sin no more, and to avoid the near occasion of sin."

He stood back to the door, had one last look around the corridor and pushed.

He was in.

"Amen!"

"Amen!" came a yowl from the hallway.

The men's room was small and cold. The door had no lock. There was only one stall. Fernandez hurried inside and closed the latch. The stall was clean. He sat down to catch his breath, scratching furiously at his fake beard and removing his fake eyeglasses.

Generally, Fernandez prided himself on his ability to stay cool in the presence of criminals and assorted riff raff, but the guy in Henry's room was a whole different level of lunatic.

His name was Rafi. He was a sniveling rat-faced psychopath. Fernandez had already seen what he was capable of a couple days before. To think, because of the itchiness he'd almost left the beard at home. It had positively saved his ass, since Rafi hadn't recognized him.

"Fernandez you're a fucking genius," he muttered.

He returned the Bible to the bag sure he'd gotten more than enough footage to satisfy Delgado's family. Satisfy was an odd word to think in this situation. Surely they'd be satisfied to know the truth, and they'd be somewhat satisfied to know Henry was not extorting money from them again as he genuinely lay dying right there in the ICU. But satisfied their brother and son wasn't long for this world? Relieved at the prospect of being unburdened of this world-class screw-up once and for all? How do the bereaved cope with such schizophrenia? To love someone incorrigible, then breathe so much easier when you don't have to deal with them anymore. How do you handle the guilt? Did being rich make it easier? These questions were for hardier souls, or perhaps for the prostrate policeman he could still hear whimpering outside. It was difficult for Fernandez to relate. He liked everyone in his family; there weren't any drug addicts, assholes, or lunatics.

He banished the thoughts from his mind. This was no time for reflection, and Rafi was a huge problem. He had clearly tricked the staff into thinking he was part of Henry's immediate family, but in reality he was a stone cold killer sent by the Ramon cartel. In fact, considering the events of the last 48 hours, Fernandez was almost sure it was Rafi who'd put Henry in here. Henry's case was not being treated as a cut-and-dried accident, hence the police presence.

But why? Fernandez had overheard the doctor tell Rafi that

Henry's lungs were on the verge of failing. He had two, three days left max. Was he here to witness the end or hasten it? More likely he was there to ensure Henry didn't wake up and blab to the cops before he died.

Fernandez once again pushed the thoughts aside. As much as he wanted justice for the Delgados, first things first. He'd been hired to do a job, obtain visual proof that Henry was actually sick and not once again trying to rip off his family back in Jersey. This he had done, and pulled off his first disguise in his career without a hitch. He was so pleased he started to give voice to the pop song that had been running through his head the last couple days.

"Finally the time has come," Fernandez contentedly hummed as he unzipped the second compartment of his hand bag, the one that housed the tiny pinhole camera. "Let's just dance in the sun. Everybody grab someone and …and you gotta be fucking kidding me!"

He stared into the second compartment in horror. The light wasn't on! The power indicator! He was sure he'd saw the little blue light when he turned it on, and the red one that showed it was recording. Had he accidentally switched it off when taking the Bible in and out? The camera was basically just a wire, there was no readout, no timer, no way to tell until he attached the USB to a computer and watched the footage. "Fuck!" Fernandez said a little too loud. Did it record or not? This was a one-time thing; there'd be no second chance. He couldn't take the risk that the camera had been off.

"I have to go back in," he whispered with a shudder.

Four days previous, Fernandez was eating lunch at his desk and watching Burn Notice on Netflix when he should have been organizing his case reports for invoicing. It was a mind-numbing task for which he was an adept procrastinator. Everyone else but Simon was out, and he was at his desk in some kind of trance with his eyes rolled back into his head. Fernandez thought of throwing some paper clips at him, but was quickly distracted as the show was getting good.

In a particularly exciting scene, Michael Westen and Fiona Glenanne were attempting to affix a large C-4 frame to the side of a building in order to gain access to the records of an unscrupulous company filing fraudulent Medicare claims on behalf of unwitting South Florida retirees. As the two set about their work, Westen did the usual voice over explaining spy stuff to the audience in the simplest terms possible, in this case the dangers and intricacies of explosive door breaching, accompanied by a percussive, neo-Jan Hammer bed track. It was a trademark device of the show throughout it's seven seasons and Fernandez couldn't get enough of it.

"Man, that's so fucking cool," Fernandez breathed as the wall exploded across his computer screen.

"I didn't realize invoicing was so exciting," Nicole appeared out of nowhere and Fernandez quickly closed the window on his computer. "Language!" she reprimanded while pinching the back of his arm.

"Ow!" he yelped. "You're aware it's lunchtime?"

"If you're at your desk you're working."

"Yeah but…" the phone rang and Fernandez used the opportunity to get out of the conversation. "Gonna have to take this, since Simon's across the universe right now. Covert Intelligence, we uncover, you discover," he sang into the receiver.

"Hello? The connection isn't clear. Is this Covert Investigations?" a woman's voice asked from the other end.

"Covert Intelligence, ma'am," Fernandez winced.

"Oh. May I speak with Fernando Fernandez please?"

"Speaking."

"Hello Mr. Fernandez. My name is Sylvia Delgado, I was given your number by Paula O'Connell. I believe you did some work for her recently?"

"Oh yes of course!" Paula O'Connell was a pragmatic, hard working 52-year-old woman who ran the production department at a large bond-rating agency on Wall Street. She had contacted Fernandez because she'd become concerned about her husband Walter who seemed to be spending an unusual amount of time, and not to mention a good deal of her money, in Puerto Rico.

Two years previous Walter O'Connell had lost his partnership at a prestigious Manhattan personal injury firm for doing cocaine on the job. He vehemently denied the charge all the while asserting his shifty partners had pushed him out. After this disgrace, Walter, an avid deep sea fisherman who took the majority of his vacations in the Florida Keys or Caribbean, persuaded his wife that the best way forward for the two of them was to invest in a brand new sports bar in San Juan. "Touchdown" would be the first bar in the resort area of Condado to feature NFL ticket thereby ensuring a steady stream of puffy red Yank clients who couldn't bear to miss their Sunday game while on vacation.

After hemorrhaging money for a year Madeline demanded to see some progress, and for Walter to account for all his money and time on the island. Walter texted Madeline a photo of the facade of the completed Touchdown in all its glory. When she proudly showed off the shot of her Caribbean investment to Manny, a native Puerto Rican who worked in the mailroom, he sadly had to inform her that it was a shot of a famous Criollo restaurant in Fajardo with the name Touchdown clumsily photoshopped over the original sign. That's when Madeline got in touch with Fernandez.

Within two days, Fernandez had managed to uncover that no permits had been filed, no licenses had been bought, and there was no sign of Touchdown in Condado or anywhere else on the island. He caught up with Walter on the back streets of Miramar near Parada 15, chewing on his own teeth and in the care of a blond transsexual named Gigi. Madeline immediately filed for divorce.

"How is Madeline these days?" Fernandez asked.

"She's actually fine, moving on," Sylvia said happily. "She's dating a guy in the cast of West Side Story."

"You don't say." Of course she is. "How can I help you this fine day, Ms. Delgado?"

"I'd like to talk to you about my brother Henry. I want to hire you to find him."

"How long has he been missing?" asked Fernandez becoming interested.

He was strange among P.I.'s to relish the challenge of a missing person case. They were difficult and expensive, but the rewards were worth the trouble. It certainly made his heart feel good in a way finding a cheating drug addict husband in bed with a tranny couldn't.

"Well, he's not technically missing," Sylvia hemmed. "He might be in a hospital, only we, my family that is, are not sure where."

"I'm sorry I don't quite follow you, Ms. Delgado."

"It's kind of a long and sordid story," Sylvia sighed.

"Oh, I like long and sordid stories," he smiled deviously at Nicole motioning toward his computer screen. She left the room.

"Ok," Sylvia let out a long breath. "My brother has basically been a problem since he was born. We grew up in Isabela with my other brother and sister. My father and mother came from nothing but they established a small guesthouse on Jobos Beach before we were born. By the time we were kids, it had grown enormously."

"Wait a second," Fernandez interjected. "Delgado? As in the Casa Delgado?"

"Yes! You're familiar with it?"

Fernandez indeed was. Casa Delgado was a high end golf resort on the west coast of the island. It was a quiet, unassuming, but mega rich place you had to look hard to find. There was no casino, no riotous pool bar with Reggaeton blasting your ears off. There was, however, a world-class restaurant and golf course. It was the kind of place that catered to wealthy gringos and Europeans who wished to relax and stay well under the radar, and it was priced to stay that way. Fernandez had once stayed there, given a free weekend by a grateful client. Nicole loved it but his girls were bored out of their minds. The pool didn't even have a slide.

"Yes, my family and I spent a weekend there once."

"When?" asked Sylvia.

"Last year, I forget exactly when."

"How was it?"

"Nice. A little more high-end than we're used to but we had a good time."

Fernandez was impressed Sylvia Delgado still had her mind on customer service in the midst of family crisis, but then again it stood to reason, often a character trait of the successful in the hospitality industry. He'd once known a restaurant manager who returned to work two days after his wife tragically and suddenly died of a heart attack. Fernandez simply couldn't imagine how the man could take complaints about cook temperatures seriously while his wife was lying in the morgue. "Yes ma'am I'm not saying I don't believe you made a reservation for 8:00, excuse me one second, it's the other line. Oh, she's clear for burial, thank you Inspector Sanchez." Was business really that important? The show must go on, he supposed.

"I only ask out of curiosity. I haven't been to Casa Delgado since my father sold it to Radisson three years ago," she revealed.

Huh, still concerned about a place that isn't even hers. That's dedication.

"I only have the reviews on Trip Advisor to go by," Sylvia continued. "It seems they're keeping up the standard my family set. I'm sure it has lost some personality though, less homey, more sterile and corporate. I'm just happy they haven't put in a pool bar, or a friggin water slide. I suppose it sounds kind of sad I still care, but it is my family's name at the end of the day. Old habits die hard."

"Indeed," as he spent most of his time dealing with people who didn't want to talk, Fernandez was content to let her keep going.

"We so didn't want to leave Isabela, but my father wanted to position himself to be able to retire in the states. He was getting tired of the hard work."

"Hard work?"

"I'm sure you know what it's like, Mr. Fernandez, in the hotel and restaurant business. I don't have to explain it," she chided.

"Of course."

"Dad took a managerial position with Caesars and we moved here to Atlantic City. Henry stayed home."

Jesus Christ, Fernandez thought. Tired of hard work so he moved to a job in a casino in Jersey. To each his own, he guessed.

"Henry didn't want to trade Jobos and alcapurias for the Jersey Shore and cheesesteaks?" Fernandez asked playfully.

"Well, when I say he stayed home it's more like he wasn't invited to come with us. My father had cast him out. It was the fourth time. I said Henry was a problem. He'd been into drugs since he was thirteen. He routinely put us through hell. I don't know if you've ever seen that show, Intervention?"

"Can't say that I have."

"You get to a point where everyone has to agree that if the addict doesn't surrender and seek treatment, everyone cuts contact, basically removing his safe harbor. Henry had three interventions. He never put up a fight and perhaps that was the most annoying thing."

"How do you mean, Ms. Delgado?"

"It's like there was no internal conflict. He loved dad's money and his lifestyle. He'd just say anything and go anywhere with his tail between his legs. Then he'd come back, stay clean for a few months only to jump right back on the wagon. Like I said, no conflict. He didn't think he had a problem."

Fernandez didn't even know what he was supposed to be working on yet. She was volunteering so much personal information to a stranger, basically. They hadn't even discussed price. It started to give him a clear picture of the Delgado family dynamic. He'd seen it before. Where old money was inaccessible and insular, new money tended to advertise their problems in public where they'd fester like an open wound. No boundaries, easily infiltrated, everyone knew their business. When they failed, they tended to fail spectacularly.

"He went to Passages in Malibu, that was the first one," she continued. "It's where Mel Gibson went. Then he went to Crossroads in Antigua, then Thoroughfare to Light in Maryland. That was a Catholic one. Dad didn't know what else to do at that point."

Fernandez wondered if all rehab facilities had road-oriented names.

"All these places aren't cheap, Mr. Fernandez, as I'm sure you can imagine. Dad wanted the best for Henry and spent a considerable amount of money ensuring this. Crossroads alone cost 25 grand for four weeks."

"Phew," Fernandez exhaled. She was building up to the reason she called by making excuses for her family. She felt guilty. The kind of person who feels they could always have done more.

"So I take it Turnpike to Light didn't work out either if he'd been shunned a fourth time," Fernandez observed.

"Thoroughfare to Light," Sylvia corrected. "And no, it

didn't. Dad decided no more interventions, no more cushy
facilities. He basically told Henry to get out. Three months
later we moved. Henry made his way to San Juan and wore out
his welcome with a list of people. Eventually, he was reduced
to begging at traffic lights and we're coming to the reason I'm
calling you, Mr. Fernandez. In the past three years my father's
resolve has never faltered, but I can't say the same for my
mom."

There's always one in the family, Fernandez thought. How
far can you really be pushed that you actually turn your back on
a child? A child with a problem, nonetheless. For all the crap
he had so far heard about the Delgados, they were clearly a
loving family in a bad situation. Funny, Fernandez knew people
in his life that could give two shits about their parents, and
parents who could give two shits about their kids. Families like
this tended to produce hard and loveless people, but people
who were a lot more resilient to life's travails when they flew
the nest. Then on the other side of the coin you have Mama
Delgado, who would probably volunteer to do time for Henry.

"She was helping him out?" he predicted.

"Yes, unbeknown to my father. Twice in the last three years
Henry has gotten in touch with my mother and played her like
a clave."

It took him an extra second to decipher this convoluted
English-ism.

"He told her he was sick and asked for money, and she
obliged."

"And you found out he wasn't sick."

"Of course he is," Sylvia explained. "Sick from coming
down off smack, or from whatever he picked up out there

under the Baldorioty Avenue bridge. The intervention people make it quite clear, if even one person caves this doesn't work. It's like," she searched. "It's like the whole family is sick, you know?"

"You're all addicted to helping him."

"Exactly!"

Fernandez had heard this line before. The addict and the family locked in a death roll all the way down. He wasn't sure if he bought it.

"Both times he took the money and disappeared. Now he's popped up again. He says he's dying. Dad found out, he's got my mom on lock-down, and he's not forking over a red cent. But I talked to one of Henry's friends yesterday. I know I sound like a putz, but I think he might be telling the truth this time. I'm his sister. It sounded bad. I don't even know who this friend is. He must have dropped the phone..." she began to cry.

Fernandez gave her time to collect herself.

"Even if he is using his real name there's the HIPAA laws to contend with. I've been on the phone all night and I've gotten nowhere. If he really is dying we need to help him. Dad's just not buying it, he's been burned too many times. I figured if you found Paula's husband so quickly you could find Henry. Only we don't have much time, as I said, it sounded really bad. It needs to be now."

A totally different situation, Fernandez thought. Walter O'Connell had been gacked up and splashing money all over town like a jackass. Finding an anonymous drug addict in the hospital was another story entirely. Even with his connections he'd likely encounter the same results as Sylvia. It might be a better idea to dump this task on his staff and for him to proceed directly to the street. Here, Fernandez did have a few things going for him. The wheels began to turn in his mind. As a child of privilege Henry may have enjoyed a high profile amongst the other junkies. There were a few hot spots in San Juan that could yield immediate results as they tended to jockey for position on four or five key street corners and intersections. Sylvia also had mentioned the Baldorioty de Castro Ave., the main east-west expressway that linked San Juan to the airport.

"You mentioned the expressway. Was that just for dramatic effect, or do you have reason to believe he's there?"

"I hear things from people," she said dejectedly. "You can't completely shut yourself off, Mr. Fernandez. A few friends have seen him around there. They call to see what we're doing. It's embarrassing. They don't know how much we've already done."

"Ok, I understand. Ms. Delgado, we haven't talked price yet. I'm carrying quite a heavy caseload at the moment, for me to drop everything..."

"Money isn't an issue, just please hurry. A photo will do nicely, something to show dad. If he's dying, we need to be with him. Despite everything we still love him very much," her voice began to break again.

"Ok Ms. Delgado I 'll be in touch as soon as I know anything."

Fernandez hung up the phone and for the first time regretted firing Felix, as this was one of the few things he was good at. He came in full of procedure and theory but was absolutely inflexible when it came to learning on the job. In the case of finding Henry Delgado it was simple. Fernandez would only have to provide him with a script and a list of hospital phone numbers. Hospitals couldn't technically give out any patient

information, but there sometimes was a way around this if
you called up impersonating a relative. You had to speak with
confidence and pretend you knew the patient was already there.
Then you could try a variety of things, say you were disconnect-
ed from his room phone, or even more simply say you forgot
the room number. Either way you'd find out if the patient was
there or not pretty quickly. Especially if you could put on a
gringo accent and act genuinely confused, which Felix could do.
He would have enjoyed it as textbook detective work. As it was
now, he'd have to pass the job to Simon. And Simon was going
to have a problem with it.

Nicole came in with a cup of tea. "What was all that about?"

"A woman from New Jersey wants me to find her dying
brother in the hospital but she's not sure where he is," he
explained.

"New Jersey?"

"Yeah. Do you remember the lady whose husband I found
with the transsexual?"

"How could I forget dear," she deadpanned.

"She connected us! Guess my reputation is starting to
spread far and wide."

"People know good work when they see it," she leaned
down and kissed him tenderly. His chest swelled up with pride
and emotion.

"We're going to need to jump right on this, Nicole. Simon.
Hey Simon! Break-time is over, the ashram is closed man."
He laughed too quickly, realizing he might have burned up his
recent goodwill in a matter of seconds.

Nicole eyed him reproachfully. She's always taken a keen interest in Simon's spiritual practices and theories. She'd taken his

recommendation for a yoga teacher, and even accompanied him a couple times to his meditation group in Rio Piedras. She was a vegetarian, and follower of some Hindu beliefs. But that's as far as it went and Fernandez was glad. At the end of the day his wife was practical, raised in a solid working class family. When Simon went too far, she'd politely and delicately disengage from the conversation with an air of respect.

Fernandez was the opposite. If he was talking to a perfectly normal person at a bar who all the sudden started spouting theories about how the moon landing was faked Fernandez couldn't help himself but to start poking holes in the "argument". He'd come to see the value in Nicole's technique, though. She was able to deftly guide the conversation back to a sensible topic by getting the person off their particular hobby horse without making them feel stupid in the process. It would reduce animosity in the workplace if Fernandez were to adopt this approach. It didn't do any good for him to challenge Simon as his employer.

It certainly didn't do any good for Fernandez to refer to his outfit as a "sari" as well.

"Simon?" he prodded gently.

Simon opened his eyes just as the rotating fan blew up his billowy linen clothes around his head. He eyed Fernandez over his black rimmed glasses. "An ashram is Hindu."

"Pardon?"

"An ashram is Hindu. I was practicing Vipassana, it's a Buddhist technique," he explained.

"You don't say?" Fernandez knew the conversation was about to take a turn into the irrelevant and pointless.

"It's the practice of watching your breath rise and fall."

"To make sure you remember to keep breathing?" he asked. Nicole cleared her throat as a warning.

"It eventually leads to insight," Simon went on. "Once you pass through the jhannas."

"That's really interesting Simon," said Fernandez making a clumsy attempt to butter him up. "But I have something I need you to do right now that is of the utmost importance. Now, I know we don't usually involve you in the investigatory process, but this is a job I need done right...for which I want you to apply your... unique skills and special attributes."

Relieved to have successfully completed the sentence, Fernandez continued while looking at the ceiling with his hands behind his back as Simon eyed him suspiciously.

"I need you to call all the hospitals in town. We are looking for a patient and it's urgent."

"The hospitals aren't going to tell me that information," he said mechanically.

"I know," Fernandez realized he had to choose his words carefully. "You're going to have to get creative."

"Creative?"

"Yes."

"You mean lie," Simon breathed.

"Listen, you're just going to have to do a little light fibbing for the greater good," Fernandez explained as Nicole came to his side.

"I won't break my precepts," Simon announced.

"What?"

"The five precepts dear," Nicole explained. "One of them is

a prohibition against lying."

"I never lie," Simon said. "It's bad enough that I unwittingly shelter such behavior by working here, so I will not outright..."

Fernandez stood up and walked over to Simon's desk.

"Simon, we are looking for a guy who may be about to die. His family desperately needs to know so they can help if they can. I think, that in the big picture, stretching the truth might be ethical in this situation."

"Ok. What's his name?" Simon relented.

"Henry Delgado."

Simon paused for a second considering this.

"Is it the same Henry Delgado from the hotel family? The junkie?"

Fernandez nodded.

"Well, that's a shame," Simon said dejectedly. "The last I heard he was doing quite well." He sat down and took off his glasses, rubbing his eyes against the island sun melting through the Miami shutters.

"Why Simon, I had no idea you ran in those circles," Fernandez played. "No, but seriously, how do you know about this?"

"He was one of the people we were helping out. My meditation group does community outreach, charity work, you know?" he explained. "It's sad because I would have considered him one of our successes. Wait! Why is he in the hospital? Was it a relapse?"

"I think that sounds like the safe bet, but you never know, Simon. Could be anything." Damn it was a small island, Fernandez thought.

"He'd kind of fallen through the social work cracks. His family has a lot of money. I don't know, maybe there wasn't much sympathy. It didn't matter though, at that point they weren't helping him at all. He could have been from the projects like the other ones."

"And the last you heard he was all right?"

"Yeah," Simon exclaimed innocently. "We'd gotten him group housing and a job. At the year check-back he was doing better than we'd ever dreamed. He had a car, a nice one, a black Toyota Highlander. He had money too, in fact. At first, we figured his family was helping him again but he said no, he'd picked himself up and done it all on his own."

"That's a hell of a turnaround, but not impossible." For the first time Fernandez had to consider options other than drug abuse for Henry's sickness. Maybe good old fashioned social work and good Samaritanism had succeeded where the cushy high end and vapidly named detox resorts hadn't. More likely that without family support, Henry had truly hit rock bottom just in time to get scooped up by Simon and the Buddha Brigade.

"Where was he last living?" Fernandez was beginning to hope this would be easier than combing all the hospitals trying to dupe the staff.

"I'm not sure. He'd left the group home, obviously. He seemed to be affiliated with a restaurant in la Placita, Santavida or something like that," Simon explained.

"Affiliated?"

"I don't know if it he was involved business-wise, or he just liked the food. But he was installed firmly at the end of the outside bar. All the staff and patrons knew his name."

"Thanks Simon, you may have made this a hell of a lot easier," Fernandez said getting up and grabbing for his car keys.

"Do you still want me to call the hospitals?" he asked hopefully.

"Yes. As a matter of fact, can you do a gringo accent?" Fernandez asked.

"Yeah" Simon sprang from his chair. "Check it out." He squinted and cocked his head to one side. "Are you talking to me? Are YOU talking to ME? I don't see anyone else in here."

"That's really good," he backed out the door. "Stick with Spanish for now, though, ok?"

In 1910 the government of Puerto Rico zoned off a parcel of land in Santurce specifically for the establishment of a large Plaza del Mercado (Market Square) to serve the citizens of San Juan. Originally a sprawling, two-level complex the Plaza del Mercado quickly became a bustling center for commerce and city life. Kiosks on the ground floor featured produce from all over the island while the second floor housed a butcher and various government and medical offices. Ringed by warehouses and a few lunch counters, the plaza was remodeled several times over the years but always operated as a business district. It was a ghost town at night.

Then in the 1990s, faced with increasing crime and steady urban decline, the government decided to embark on a series of revitalization initiatives aimed to turn the Plaza into a hot nightspot and tourist destination. Re-zoning the area and redirecting traffic on the weekends allowed for the Placita to skirt open container laws (which were never really enforced anyway). Restaurants and bars set up shop in the high ceilinged warehouses which once contained plantains and yucca, and the whole area quickly became a thriving, weekend pedestrian zone full of dancing and drinking.

Even with the tourist dollars pouring in, and some high-end restaurants setting up shop on the fringe streets, Placita still retained it's authenticity and grittiness. It was the kind of place more adventurous tourists would ask their hotel concierges to direct them to, so upon returning home to Philadelphia they could boast to their friends they had hung out with "the locals".

The Santavida Gastrobar was one of the two or three places that had sprung up to fill the missing high-end cuisine establishment category. The reviews had been favorable and public opinion was positive. When Fernandez arrived to find Henry Delgado, the place had been open for a year.

The purveyors of the new restaurant had the foresight and luck to include a parking lot on the premises. Although it was tiny and completely jammed on the weekends, only navigable by a crack team of valet parkers, it was a godsend for any restaurant in Puerto Rico where parking is generally impossible.

Fernandez arrived midweek, and after the lunch rush, so the place was empty except for an ostentatious Escalade with gold rims and a BMW Roadster, both impeccably washed and detailed. He felt self conscious ambling into the lot with his un-sexy gold 2004 Toyota Sienna. Nondescript and secretly kitted out specifically for surveillance jobs, the mini van had served him incredibly well in the past. But he made a mental note, not for the first time, to buy a cooler car at some point in the future for these kinds of situations. As it was he looked like he was on his way to Chuck E Cheese with the kids. He could already see he'd attracted the attention of some well dressed patrons at the outside bar, obviously the owners of the two high end jobs he was pulling in next to.

The windshield of the Sienna was tinted at 20 percent, so Fernandez could spend a bit of time taking in the scene. No one could see what he was doing unless they walked right on top of him. He immediately noticed some pricey after factory modifications on the Escalade, besides the gaudy and useless gold rims. All doors had ballistic steel overlaps, and he couldn't be 100% sure but it looked like ballistic glass as well. The thing was a fucking tank, Fernandez thought. The guys at the bar were transporting some Reggaeton group or they were drug dealers. Either way they looked big time and they were becoming antsy. He got out of the car and tried to look as dopey as possible.

Fernandez sidled up to the opposite side of the bar, it was midday hot and the wooden overhang didn't provide much relief with the sun shone directly overhead. The interesting patrons were bunched together where the bar curved in toward the bathrooms where there was more shade. Fernandez gave them an "I have no idea what's going on here" smile.

"Buenas," he said.

"Buenas," one of the seated guys mumbled. Then he made an inaudible comment and they all chuckled.

Fernandez was satisfied. He could tell immediately they didn't perceive him as a threat. In situations like this, he reverted mentally to all those years he worked in I.T. and put on the personality of the friendly guy in tech support. It was a technique he referred to as "turning on the nerd."

What could possibly be amiss at the office? No guns. No drugs. Just a normal days work partitioning the server and assigning IP addresses. But it allowed him to take everything in, while these guys are probably thinking he was there to service the POS system.

There were four of them. Two seated and two standing in protective postures behind with a vantage point that encompassed the entire bar, the parking lot, the street, and the Baldorioty expressway whizzing past about half a block from the end of the outside bar deck. Between the deck and the highway, there was a half basketball court in sort of a low lying gully. Fernandez could hear kids playing, shoes squeaking, the hollow bang of the ball against the backboard, but couldn't see them. The two standing, clearly hired muscle, would take turns looking over the side of the deck at the court about every five minutes.

One was big and stupid looking with a kind of open-mouth gape. Fernandez fought off the inner obsessive desire to grab a napkin and wipe the slobber out. The other was more interesting. If he was a bodyguard he didn't fit the part at all. Stick thin, he stood no taller than 5'5". While the two seated men laughed and enjoyed their cocktails, and Drooly stared vacant eyed at the pretty cars traveling the highway, this guy was looking right through Fernandez's soul. He could see three visible knife scars on his rat face from the other end of the bar. For a man of his stature to be counted on as a bodyguard, he must surely be a fucking maniac.

Fernandez smiled another unassuming smile and turned away. The guy kept looking at him with his dead black eyes.

"Can I help you sir," the bartender asked.

"Yes, a Medalla please. Are they really cold?"

"Of course they're cold," the bartender hissed, annoyed he was having to work in the lull between lunch and dinner. He handed the beer to Fernandez leaving fingerprints in the ice crystals on the surface.

"Oh that's perfect!" Fernandez exclaimed. "I hope my mouth doesn't get stuck to it, ha ha ha!"

"Whatever," the bartender turned away and started screwing with his cellphone.

Fernandez took a big slug and risked a glance at the mirror behind the bar. To his relief, he saw Rat Face going to check on the basketball game again. He began to wonder why exactly was he so on edge. He reminded himself that he was just an everyday person looking for someone who hung out at this restaurant. What had pricked his Spidey sense so? Had he reason to fear these men? His gut told him that everyone had reason to fear these men.

The two thugs were on secret service level alert. All of them were dressed in black but where the guards looked like they were wearing jumpsuits, the two seated patrons were dressed business casual, but with some clearly expensive labels. Versace? Dior? Pricey but low-key. The subdued effect was somewhat ruined by the sunglasses the guy furthest from Fernandez was sporting. He mused the ridiculous pair of diamond encrusted Dolce & Gabbanas probably cost more than he'd made in the last three years. You can take the boy out of the hood, he thought.

A waitress appeared and laid down two plates of what looked like ceviche in front of the men. As she tried to walk back to the kitchen, Sunglasses playfully pulled her back by the belt loop. Fernandez couldn't hear the conversation but could see her strained smile. Inappropriate. He flirted with the confidence of a man who wasn't used to being ignored. The girl remained polite, giggling at the right times. Fernandez could see her face. Fear. Rat Face gave him another look from his position behind the girl and Fernandez promptly began admiring the bar's Scotch selection.

"Selena, go get Pancho," the other guy suddenly piped up sounding irritated.

"Ok!"

Selena clearly was thankful for the excuse to extricate herself from the situation. She disappeared quietly into the kitchen. The two men began studying their plates without eating, in some kind of urgent conversation about the ceviche.

"Hey can I see a menu?" Fernandez asked.

The bartender let out a heavy sigh, retrieved a menu, and handed it to Fernandez with a look on his face like Fernandez had asked him for a ride to the airport.

"Thanks buddy!" Fernandez remained cheerful.

The bartender went back to his cellphone. This guy is going to be a pain in the ass, Fernandez thought. Impossible to get information out of the straightforward way. He started considering his options. There were only the waitress and the drug dealers. Given the current situation, it went against his gut to just flat out start asking questions about Henry Delgado.

Pancho came out in a huff with a concerned look on his face. He shouted something over his shoulder to the kitchen but continued walking. A plump man with clothes too tight for his body, Fernandez guessed he was the manager. He looked tired and stressed, and more than a little frightened as he approached the men at the bar. Selena must have decided to stay in the kitchen.

"What's up, Tony?"

The one without the sunglasses was named Tony.

"What can I help you with?" Pancho was trying hard to sound casual.

"I want you to taste this" he said. Before he could respond Tony roughly and unceremoniously picked up a chunk of raw fish from his plate and forced it into Pancho's mouth. "What do you think of that, huh?"

Sunglasses giggled.

"It's ceviche, Pancho. Unless the shit is fresh you can fucking kill someone. Have you been serving it like this?"

"I'm pretty sure it's fresh," Pancho stammered.

"Don't fucking contradict me, you fat fuck. I know what's fucking fresh and what's fucking not."

Tony used the f-bomb with the accuracy of a shotgun. Moron, Fernandez thought. He was thinking of ordering the ceviche too, dammit.

"Of course Tony, sorry."

"It's gotta be cured and served the same day. If I go back there and find out this shit has been sitting around, Pancho, you don't want to know, man. Get your shit together. You're the manager!"

"Yes Tony, it won't happen again." Pancho scurried off into the kitchen. Fernandez could hear some muffled yells as Pancho began getting his shit together.

These guys clearly weren't just customers. Whoever they were they had the whole place running, that was for sure. They could be investors, owners, using the place as a front. It could be a vanity project. It could be anything. Fernandez thought about what Simon had said about Henry having been "installed" at the end of the outside bar and realized the whole thing was getting more complicated. He couldn't help but think of the sequence in Goodfellas where the gangsters take over the restaurant and the poor manager has no choice but to let them run amok. Tony was, however, expressing concerns about food quality and customer safety, so regardless of the situation he clearly had some kind of personal stake in the success of Santavida.

"What can I get for you sir?" Pancho's epic chewing out had shaken the bartender out of his complacency.

"Not the ceviche," Fernandez smiled.

"No," the bartender said gravely.

"I'll just have the fish tacos."

"Sounds good. Another beer?"

"Not yet, I'm still working on this one, thanks."

The bartender turned around to ring in the order. Fernandez decided to use the tension Tony created to his advantage.

"Hey so how long has this place been open?"

"About a year," the bartender said uninterestedly.

"What exactly is a Gastrobar anyway? I can't say I'm familiar with that word."

"I don't know," he said growing testy again. "A gastronomic bar, I guess. A place where you can get food and drinks."

"That's usually called a restaurant."

"Well, there's all different words for restaurant, bar and grill, bistro, diner, eatery. Maybe they were just trying to come up with a new name."

"They?" asked Fernandez.

"The owners," he said impatiently.

"Ah! And have you been here the whole year and a half?" Fernandez asked.

"What?"

"Have you been working here since the beginning?"

"Yes, it's only been a year though I told you."

"Oh sorry, just slipped my mind. I'm forgetful. I've never been to a Restobar before. Can I have another beer? Is the food ready yet?"

"Gastrobar. Uh, yeah here," he reached into the cooler and produced another Medalla. "I just rang the food in man."

"Just sounds kind of unappetizing to me," Fernandez continued.

"Then why did you order them?" the bartender asked getting more and more confused.

"What?"

"The tacos."

"No, I mean Gastrobar. The name. It's got "gas" in it. Reminds me of flatulence or something, ha ha! Can I have that beer?"

"I just gave it to you!"

Fernandez looked down at the beer in surprise.

"Oh, you did! Hey, I'm looking for someone who used to work here. I don't think I should have ordered the ceviche."

"I thought you ordered the tacos. Yeah...ok, right, who are you looking for? I've been here for the whole year," he said confidently. Fernandez had talked him into a whirlwind and he was searching for the center.

"Hen..."Fernandez cut himself short as he lost the bartender's attention. Something urgent was happening at the other end of the bar.

"What the fuck is he doing here?" Tony exclaimed.

All four men were looking through the window at a busboy who'd just emerged from the kitchen with a stack of clean plates. He turned on his heel and walked back inside, obviously scared shitless.

"Rafi, go get that fuck."

Rafi (Rat Face) was already on his way to the kitchen before Tony got the words out of his mouth. After he entered Fernandez heard a scream accompanied by a loud crash of dishes. Thirty seconds later Rafi emerged, smirking.

"Hey, hey you. Dude!" Tony yelled at the bartender.

"Yes?"

"Did Pancho hire that fuck?"

"I really don't know, sir."

Rafi returned to the group wiping his hands. Fernandez could see through the window the unfortunate busboy stagger from the kitchen with a puffed up left eye, where he had obviously been punched. A crew of cooks stood in the kitchen doorway. The bartender stood glued to his spot. No one moved.

"Pancho, get the fuck out here!" Tony yelled.

"Guess he's gonna need a new busboy," Sunglasses joked handing Rafi a wad of napkins. All four men laughed, calm, obviously accustomed to this level of violence. Fernandez was cool too, but decided to continue to play the part.

"Shouldn't we call someone? He just punched your guy in the face!" he asked the bartender excitedly.

"Be my guest," came the response. Now Tony was looking at the two of them, no doubt deciding whether or not Fernandez and the bartender were going to be a problem. He could tell the bartender was about to shut down again and go into mind your own business mode. Fernandez understood. How else could you work at a place like this? He had to act fast or he was back to square one with the guy.

Pancho emerged from the dining room, seriously rattled and carrying two new plates of ceviche.

"Tony, I'm sorry. I'm sorry," he said as he put the plates down. "I had no idea who that guy was. He's just a busboy. I hired him yesterday. He's out. I promise."

"You just gonna leave him there?" Tony asked surgically prodding the replacement ceviche.

"Of course not, Tony."

Pancho signaled the cooks who collected the busboy and brought him back into the kitchen, putting a bag of ice on his swollen face.

"I swear I didn't know," Pancho continued to blubber.

"Just don't let it happen again. Go away," said Tony. The new ceviche had apparently met his standards and he became more interested in eating than talking.

The bartender was withdrawing to the back corner of the bar and reaching for his cellphone again. Fernandez went for it.

"So do you know that guy?" he asked.

"No way man. I have no idea who he is."

"No, I don't mean the guy with the plates."

"Who?" he huffed, impatience combined with fear now produced exasperation.

"Henry Delgado," Fernandez said.

Improbably, he smiled.

"You want those guys," he motioned to Tony and his crew. "Hey Tony, sorry to bother you, but this guy is looking for Henry Delgado."

All four faces looked up at Fernandez simultaneously.

"Go over there and talk to them," he said wickedly, managing to unburden himself of the troublesome customer and deflect the attention of the gangsters all at the same time.

"No problem!" Fernandez smiled, staying as cool as a cucumber. No need to arouse any suspicion in these guys. He jumped off his barstool and walked over to the dangerous group with the eager openness of a Jehovah's Witness.

"Hi fellas. I hope that kid is ok! The bartender told me he's really clumsy, falling all the time. Incidentally, I'm looking for Henry Delgado. The bartender said you know him?" he said extending his hand in friendship.

Rafi came to intercept him halfway down the bar.

"Rafi, chill," Tony waved him off. "How can we help you?"

"I'm looking for Henry Delgado. I heard he worked here," Fernandez reiterated.

"We heard you the first time, Tubby. He's not here today. What do you want?"

"Do you know where I can find him?"

"Yeah, we know where you can find him," Sunglasses said with a smirk. Drooly started chuckling vacantly.

"At least for now."

"Stop." Tony growled menacingly. "Take it easy with the

fucking Cuervo."

Sunglasses shrunk into his chair. Clearly Tony was the Big Shot.

"Rafi, I told you to take it easy. Fuck's wrong with you guys today?"

During the last exchange Rafi had squared up toe to toe with Fernandez, preventing him from getting too close despite Tony's instructions. Although he only came up to Fernandez's chest, the unwavering glare from his empty eyes combined with his cut up face was intimidating as hell. Fernandez knew lots of guys with short man syndrome. Clearly, Rafi's way of overcompensating was by busting open people's heads.

Fernandez tried to draw a connection between these men and Henry. They were on edge. Was it because he was asking about Henry? It certainly stood to reason that, given their line of work, they were probably always on edge. Simon said Henry was "affiliated" with the restaurant. That was the perfect word to describe this crew too. Upon mention of his name the bartender immediately directed Fernandez to Tony. Was that Henry's ticket off the street back into the mainstream? Drugs? What was his connection? He needed to prod but it was getting dicey.

"It's kind of urgent," Fernandez said.

"I'm sure it is. Look, the shop's closed. Go eat your tacos, or go to Llorens," Tony directed his attention back to his ceviche.

The shop's closed. Llorens. Llorens Torres was the biggest housing project in the Caribbean. It was also a well known drug point. Did they think Fernandez was here to buy drugs from Henry? The drug trade on the island was highly organized, with discrete purchase points run by individual cartels. You usually didn't buy drugs at a restaurant. Sure there were independent sellers, there always were, but these guys didn't operate like that. Fernandez could tell the kind of money they had was cartel money. They were big time. Point bosses or higher. Maybe they were underlings of the actual Bichote. The shop is closed. If Henry was selling their drugs out of Santavida, it's highly possible these are the guys who put him in the hospital.

He'd lingered too long.

"Why the fuck are you still standing here asshole?" Rafi hissed slipping his hand around the back of Fernandez's neck. "He told you to leave." The two men looked up from their food, Tony wasn't telling Rafi to back off this time. His grip tightened. Fernandez had to think quick or he'd be kissing the bar in no time. What did Simon say? What was the fucking car?

"Hey! Let go! We made an appointment last week. I've been at a flatware convention in the States since then."

"Flatware Convention?" Drooly mewed.

"Yeah, Cutlerama, it's in Duluth, a city in the northern state of Minnesota, extremely cold climate. It's the largest silverware convention in the Western Hemisphere. I sell cutlery but I specialize in forks," Fernandez explained.

"Henry wanted to buy some forks?" Rafi asked, finally letting go of Fernandez sore neck.

"Jesus," Tony spat.

"There's plenty of forks here already," Drooly volunteered helpfully. "I was just in the storage area upstairs, there's got to be 50 boxes or more. Pancho told me he won't open new ones unless he has to. If the waiters drop them in the trash he makes them fish em out..."

"Are you finished, Dennis?" Tony asked irritatedly.

"This is all extremely interesting," Sunglasses joked.

"No no no, this had nothing to do with business," Fernandez continued. "That's just where I was in the meantime. I'm supposed to meet him here. I want to buy his Highlander. He put an ad on craigslist."

All four men visibly relaxed. Dennis still looked confused.

"Flaco. Listen," Tony spoke slowly. "He's. Not. Here. He's never going to be here. So take your forks, your Highlander, and leave."

"Ok man, no problem," Fernandez said finally breaking Rafi's grasp. "I tried to call him, he's not answering his phone." He backed away quickly.

"Why don't you ask his boy Emerenciano where he is," Sunglasses said with an outrageously gay accent. They all began laughing.

"Ok, Emerenciano! That's great guys. Thanks for the tip." Fernandez stopped and began scrutinizing the place settings on one of the tables.

"Say you guys are using some really low end stuff. If you ever want to upgrade to some higher quality cutlery just give me a call." He pulled out his wallet. "Shit I gave out all my cards in Duluth. You know what, I'll come by later and drop one off. Thanks again guys."

He went immediately to the parking lot and realized he'd left his food uneaten and his tab unpaid.

Fernandez pulled out of the Gastrobar, jumped onto Baldorioty Avenue and pointed the Sienna westward toward the old city. He needed to think and often found long, meandering drives to be the best thing. Simon was no doubt still working on the hospital list so he decided to give him a call.

"Simon. Fernando. How are things going?"

"Nothing yet boss. I haven't been able to call but four or five. I keep getting placed on hold for very long periods of time. It's frustrating."

"Well, why don't you try monitoring two or three lines at once?" Fernandez suggested.

"What if someone answers when I am already talking to someone else? Or what if all three answer at the same time?" his voice betrayed pre panic.

Fernandez felt the irritation swell up. Simon was undoubtedly a smart guy but there was a type of smart guy that just had no common sense whatsoever. It came from over-thinking. He really was more suited to the academic environment, where not committing to anything was virtually a religion. But Simon had left his job at the university and somehow landed with Fernandez at Covert Intelligence. Fernandez never got the full story of Simon's professorial fail. Nicole knew it. It was actually Nicole's cousin Celina who'd recommended Simon for the job at Covert after his unceremonious departure from academic life.

All Fernandez knew was that it had something to do with Simon routinely emptying all classroom furniture into the corridor in order to have his students in a circle, following some cutting-edge and alternative teaching method. Fernandez wasn't sure if his technique got him fired, or the fact that he managed to completely block the hallway with desks and chairs on a regular basis.

He was, of course, initially skeptical about Simon, taking him on as a favor to Nicole. But as time passed Simon had proved his worth. The only downside was that every once in a while something like this would happen.

"Then just hang up on the other two and continue talking to the one you are speaking with," he explained.

"How will I remember which one is which?"

In a managerial position, you simply couldn't continue to give explicit instructions to someone like Simon or he would never learn. You had to allow them autonomy and let them assume the risk. An extremely smart person that develops the confidence to think for himself could become your best employee and well worth the extra investment. The down side is they will make mistakes along the way, and Fernandez wasn't running a Pizza Hut. A mistake today would mean too much.

"Simon, get a sticky note out. Write down which hospital you are calling on which line. When someone answers, hang up on the other two and cross off the line that's been answered so you know you've talked to them already. Got it?"

"Yes, ok, that makes sense. No problem."

Fernandez was about to hang up when he remembered the last thing the drug dealers said.

"Hey Simon, do you know if Henry Delgado is gay?"

"What!"

"Just answer the question."

"Well, no not really. We didn't get that personal with him. I suppose he could be, as much as anyone else, that is."

"Do you know anything about a friend of his called Emerenciano?"

"No. It doesn't ring a bell," Simon answered apologetically.

"Ok thanks. I'll be back to the office in a little bit. Call me if you have anything."

He was stopped at a red light on the causeway that bridged Santurce and the Isleta de San Juan, where the old city stood for almost 500 years. Viejo San Juan was guarded back in the day by two massive fortifications and a wall that enclosed the entire city which positively bristled with canon emplacements. Now, Fernandez mused, it was one of the biggest tourist destinations in the Caribbean, its narrow streets routinely clogged with doughy white cruise ship alighters in search of piña coladas and assorted coqui-themed souvenirs.

He mentally checked himself for being bitter. For better or worse, tourism was seriously important to the island at this point in its history. While the old city was truly beautiful and an historic landmark, he couldn't help but wonder why most tourists never ventured beyond it's walls. Why someone would come all the way here just to go to the same Johnny Rocket's they could have gone to at home? Beyond the resorts and casinos there were places inside the island that were truly magical, tiny town squares with their churches nestled high up in the mountains, or wide isolated beaches that seemed as if they hung on the edge of the world. Perhaps is was for the best that we keep those things for ourselves in the end, Fernandez thought.

He continued through the Puerta de Tierra which led right up to San Cristobal's fortress and the walls of the old city. He decided to continue up the steep incline that led to El Morro, the older of the two fortresses. As he crested the hill, the sun was setting behind its ancient hulk. He could see a couple of ships moving out to sea, so far out he couldn't make out which type they were. Their reflections were dull and black in the fading light. Turning back down the hill he took care around a throng of locals and tourists starting to appear around the bars and shops for happy hour.

Ok, back to square one. Time to stop the colonial reverie and start thinking about the case.

Where was Henry Delgado? He was hooked on drugs, working the traffic lights, rehabbed by Simon's Buddha group, employed (maybe) by a drug cartel, and now apparently lying half dead in the hospital.

By the way Tony and his crew acted at the restaurant, it was obvious they were less than happy with Henry. The certainty with which they'd spoke, "We know where you can find him." "He's never going to be here." It sounded like they knew Henry was in the hospital. What's more, seemed to get a kick out of it. Were they showing exasperation with a hopeless relapser? (Most people around here didn't buy the notion of addiction being a "disease," they just thought the idiot had a choice and should know better.) Or was Sunglasses tipsily boasting they'd taken him out?

Fernandez realized his impetus had shifted. This was all irrelevant. As tempting as it was to speculate, it was not what he was hired to do.

If Henry was involved with someone named Emerenciano, it was unlikely Sylvia Delgado and her family knew about it. He could very well be the "friend" that had called Sylvia, but she didn't sound like she thought he was all that important. Otherwise they would have just gone directly to the boyfriend and not needed Fernandez's services. Also she would have told Fernandez about Emerenciano if she knew, considering the urgency of the situation. Sylvia didn't seem stupid enough to leave that kind of detail out.

Emerenciano. Jesus, what a name. He'd used Datasledge with

only one name before, but that's when he had days and weeks to analyze and purge the results. The database package pulled from all kinds of public records to give you addresses, phone numbers, possible associates, etc. A search for Jose Rodriguez in San Juan could yield 10,000 people, but Emerenciano? How many could there be? Figure a set age range, residence most likely in the area. If he was lucky enough to get a recent address he'd have something to work with tonight. There wasn't much time. He pulled over and grabbed his phone.

"Simon, it's me again."

"Still nothing boss."

"I understand. Listen, I need you to stop what you're doing right now."

"Ok."

"Go to my workstation and pull up Datasledge."

"Emerenciano?"

"Exactly. Let's start with San Juan, that's about all we have for now."

"Ok, give me a second."

Fernandez could hear the secondary sounds of Simon negotiating his computer.

"Let's see, start, data...sledge, username, password," Simon whispered agonizingly. "Ok is that E-M-E-R-E, or E-M-E-R-A?"

"Try E first," Fernandez started thinking he should just go back to the office and do this personally, since he was 100 times faster. Every permutation and misspelling of a name had to be input and tried. According to Spanish naming convention, every man, woman and child in Puerto Rico had two last names, and sometimes a middle one as well. What's more, when a woman got married, sometimes they'd jettison their mother's last name and replace it with their husband's. Other times, the woman would marry in the states and take the husband's last name, then come back to Puerto Rico and slap her old last name in there as well.

Say we were looking for Leslie Garcia Jimenez in Carolina. It's possible the key information would reside in the report for Leslie Garcia De Ramos (having married Manuel Ramos). But let's say Leslie Garcia de Ramos was in a rush in 1998 when she applied for her pharmacy reward card and filled out her address incorrectly. You could spend all day following up leads and realize quite suddenly you were beating your head against the wall.

At the top of every Datasledge profile in huge letters it reminded you of this: "The Public Records and commercially available data sources have errors and are never free from defect." Each report produced a mountain of old phone numbers (usually land lines) addressees, PO Boxes, associated persons. Somewhere in the deluge names and numbers there almost certainly were the subject's mother, the subject's father, wife, brother, business partner. But it was impenetrable to the uninitiated, like a doctor quickly going through an entire chart to find the one possible reason to suspect cancer. It had taken Fernandez years to master it, there was no crash course. He was banking on the extremely unusual name of Emerenciano, and Simon knew enough to read the pertinent information on the screen. After the events of the last few hours, something in Fernandez's gut told him he didn't have time to go back to the office.

"Shit, get off. Get off!" Simon yelled. The dogs were on him again. Nicole must have just let them in. "They won't get off of me!"

"Put the phone on speaker," Fernandez said tersely. There was no time for this grab ass shit.

"Oh gross, he licked me in the mouth! Ok, you're on speaker." Simon spat out what was presumably dog drool.

"Dogs! Get the fuck off of him!" Fernandez thundered.

"Ok, they're gone now," Simon huffed. Fernandez could hear Nicole protesting his language in the background, but she was certainly too busy corralling the chastened animals to reprimand him. Why they only listened to him Fernandez had no idea. He tolerated them, but ignored them most of the time.

"I've only got three Emerencianos in San Juan."

"Nice!" Fernandez grinned excitedly.

"What does a "D" mean again?" Simon asked.

"Deceased."

"Ok, I've got two Emerencianos in San Juan," Simon said dryly.

"Even better. Let's start with their ages."

"24 and 87."

"I don't think I'm rolling the dice saying our hotel princeling was most likely with the 24-year-old Emerenciano," Fernandez joked.

"I think that's a safe bet too," Simon agreed. "You're not going to believe this."

"Try me."

"Under possible associates?"

"Don't tell me Henry Delgado?" Fernandez's pulse quickened. It was never this easy, even on Burn Notice.

"Bingo," Simon was getting into it too. "And! We've got an 'S' next to his name. That means shared address right?"

"You're learning Simon. What's the year?"

"January 2008 to March 2009."

"Holy dick, that's just a couple months ago!"

"You're still on speaker," Simon warned. Fernandez could hear Nicole ranting in the background, but she was far enough away to be pretty much inaudible.

"It's in Miramar, kind of borderline between the nice and not so nice parts. 15 Calle Hoare."

Fernandez was about five minutes away from the area. He looked over his shoulder to make sure the box with his hat and ID were still in the back of the van.

"Good job Simon." Fernandez hung up and gunned the minivan down Baldorioty Avenue.

The affluent community of Miramar hung at the far west end of Santurce, sandwiched in between Isla Grande airport and the "not so nice parts". If one was to travel west to east along Avenida Ponce de Leon, one would find high end boutique markets and smart after work wine bars which gave way, quite suddenly, to street corners clogged with prostitutes of ambiguous gender and strip clubs that were actually brothels. This was the real San Juan, according to some, fighting gentrification with a size 13 stiletto heel. The area everyone complained about but missed when it was gone. As in every city, the intrepid artists and restauranteurs who dared to set up shop in these climes marked the beginning of a golden age, but inevitably the beginning of the end. Fernandez gave the area a good 10 years of cultural renaissance before Walmart and Olive Garden moved in. The artists and restaurants that stayed would no doubt prosper, but always have to defend themselves and their motivations against the hardcore. The hardcore, on the other hand, would move on to the next area. There always was a next area.

Calle Hoare was smack dab on the borderline. One block to the west, a multiplex theater. One block to the east, an area affectionately dubbed "tranny corner". Fernandez drove right past number 15, smoothly pulling the Sienna to a halt in front of a corner bodega blasting Bachata as the locals caroused outside and drank 10 ounce beers.

He put on his Island Delivery hat and clipped the fake laminated credentials to his front pocket. The fact that he didn't have a uniform wasn't a problem. The major US shipping companies were so swamped with packages from the mainland they often subcontracted work out to locals. He looked more than legit with the hat and ID. More than once at home, Fernandez had been woken around midnight to encounter a deliveryman in shorts and t-shirt requiring no more than Fernandez to confirm his name before dropping off a package.

Number 15 looked like it had two residences, the main house, and a studio-like affair, the entrance of which was along the right side of the building. The second floor was abandoned and decrepit. As with most private homes, a protective iron fence separated it from the street.

"Helloooo! Emerenciano! Package!"

A shirtless middle aged man emerged from the house with a huge smile on his face.

"Yes sir, good evening. What can I do for you this fine

afternoon?"

A talker, Fernandez thought. Nice.

"I have a package here for..." he looked down at the box and itched his nose at the same time "Emerenciano Dmmnnguez."

"Oh I'm afraid he doesn't live here anymore. He moved out a couple months ago."

"Jeez Louise! This is my last darned delivery of the night. Who would have written down a wrong address? Must not even be that important. I really get chewed out when I bring these things back to UPS. You wouldn't happen to know where he went?"

"No, sorry sir. He used to rent from me the efficiency right there, but he moved out after the thing with his boyfriend. I don't know where he went."

"Damn. Thing with his boyfriend? Do you know where his boyfriend is?"

"Dead, probably." The man motioned him closer to talk right through the fence slats. Fernandez had encountered a bored blabbermouth with nothing to do, and he was going to let him cluck as much as he wanted. He put on the same naughty intrigued face he'd seen his grandmother use at the hair salon as a child.

"I think he was some rich kid into the drugs."

"The drugs?"

"The same. Emerenciano wasn't having it. He was a hard working boy with two jobs. My God, how they used to fight. Into the night, the whole neighborhood could hear. Those guys used to think it was funny," he motioned to the group outside the Bodega.

"What happened next?"

"One night it was really bad. I think rich boy tried to lay hands on Emerenciano. Emerenciano is small, but built. You know how those gay guys work out all the time."

"Oh yeah, totally."

"Emerenciano was raised in the hood too. The rich kid came running out screaming. Emerenciano kicked his ass real good. I think he broke his arm. The next morning Emerenciano came to me crying and said he wanted out of the lease. I said no problem. It's always easy to rent around here."

"That's really something. Do you have his phone number? I'd really like to get rid of this package."

"No, but he works at that restaurant. He just started. He came by last night to say hi."

"Which restaurant?"

"Right there," the man said. "He's there right now. I can see him through the window. Look." He smiled and waved. Fernandez turned around to see a restaurant not one block from where they were standing. Through the glass storefront, in the dining room, stood a short, built young man in a black apron and white shirt. He was waving and smiling back. Jesus, Fernandez thought. What's with all the fucking preamble? Some people really had absolutely nothing to do and nowhere to go.

"That's Emerenciano," the man said triumphantly.

"Ok, thanks so much sir," he turned toward the restaurant.

"There's another gay couple across the street you know," the man hurried after him. "But these ones liked to fight. One night the dude went running down the street with his ass hanging out and the other dude had a strap..."

"Ok! Thanks so much sir!" Fernandez yelled over his shoulder. He was already halfway down the street when the man had reached the limits of his iron perimeter and could go no further. He removed the delivery hat and ID, and threw the empty parcel into an overflowing trash can nearby.

The restaurant was called Eclectic. It was a cute, well lit bistro that couldn't have sat more than 30 or 40 patrons when full. When Fernandez walked in there were more staff then guests. Tuesday night was notoriously slow, and the owners had probably anxiously overstaffed their new restaurant. He could see Emerenciano gossiping with a cluster of identically dressed waiters near the service bar. Eclectic was hip and modern. Every wall was adorned with local artwork and sculpture that probably cost a fortune.

Upon entering, he was quickly pounced upon by two host-esses eager to do something.

"Welcome to Eclectic," they recited in unison then looked at each other embarrassed. Clearly a hierarchy was yet to be established.

"Hi, I need to talk to Emerenciano, he's right over there," Fernandez gave Emerenciano a friendly wave and indicated he'd like to talk to him at the empty end of the bar. The waiter came forward warily, short, handsome, and sharp.

"Hi. Do I know you?"

Fernandez kept his P.I. license on a lanyard around his neck. When speaking with the general public, he usually kept it hid-den because when people saw it they'd clam up instantly. There were certain situations, however, where the license worked to his advantage. This was one of them so he took it out.

"My name is Fernando Fernandez. I'm a private investigator.

I was hired by Henry Delgado's family. I was told you might know where he is?"

"No way." The young man immediately adopted a defensive posture.

"I promise you I am not going to hurt Henry. His sister's name is Sylvia, they grew up in Isabela. His father started Casa Delgado. He got a job in Atlantic City and they left Henry behind. I'm sure he probably hates them, but the family claims Henry hasn't been all that charitable with them either. There's always two sides to every story, Emerenciano, you know that."

As Emerenciano listened his face softened.

"Look, they just want to know if he is really ill. They want to help him. So do I."

He sunk down onto the bar stool and looked up at Fernandez with wet eyes.

"I suppose it doesn't matter now. Yes, I know where he is. He's at Ashford Presbyterian. I had him taken there. He's in the ICU."

"So it's pretty serious."

"Yes it is. I've been trying to get in since then. The bigoted assholes wouldn't let me, even after I told them he's my boyfriend! They said only family."

"Look, can you get out of here for a second so we can talk?"

Emerenciano's manager said it was fine as there were no customers. There was a row of closed shops on a patio adjacent to the multiplex. Fernandez and Emerenciano sat down on the edge of a planter.

"So Henry is ill. His family thinks it was an overdose." Fernandez explained.

"Oh, he was back on drugs," Emerenciano said matter of factly. "But that's not why I kicked his skinny ass out."

"Oh?"

"I was willing to work with him. But at that point he started to work as a confidant to the local cops, and that's just asking to get killed. He put himself and me in danger. That is also why I couldn't stay at the apartment."

"Henry was a police rat?" Fernandez did not see this one coming, at all.

"Yes! The 'fight' was incidental," Emerenciano said making air quotes. "It was just the last straw. Henry had been honest about his past. When I met him he was clear eyed and kind of apologetic. He was proud too."

"About finally getting clean?"

"Yeah," the boy looked up. "You've done your homework, haven't you?"

Not nearly enough, Fernandez thought, still trying to compute the police confidant into the equation.

"Henry kept his work on the down low but I always suspected what he was doing. When you grow up around here...you know?"

"Of course."

"That kind of work was not suited to someone like him. He was a little rich boy playing drug dealer, and he was an addict on top of everything! He told me his sobriety was sound because every day he faced the ultimate challenge. That's as far as it went, that's the only clue he gave, but that's how I knew what he was doing."

"So he relapsed?" Fernandez prodded.

"We've all had our problems. He started selling their drugs out of Santavida to finance his habit, but at the same time, he started working as a confidant to the police. He placed himself in the most precarious situation. I told you, Mr. Fernandez, Henry had no idea the kind of people he was dealing with."

He stopped to consider something. "Remember Sean Penn in Carlito's Way?"

"Oh yeah, totally," it was one of his favorites.

"He was like that. Some privileged puss in way over his head. The cartel doesn't give a shit. I'd look in the mirror and just see collateral damage. I loved him, but I know how to take care of myself. That, and the police work. I know when to get out of a situation, life's too short and I've already had more than enough pain, man."

"I understand. So you said he was in the ICU."

"Yeah. He showed up at my place the Saturday before last at three in the morning and collapsed on my patio. He was totally beaten up, and getting more swollen by the minute. He was delirious but kept saying Tony did this to him. We waited it out through Sunday and he just got worse and worse. So I called his police contact and had him come to take him to the hospital. The guy knew. The cop, he knew the cartel did this. That's why he didn't want me to go with them to get help. After they left, I called his sister, because he had told me she was the only one he still had some faith in, and told her."

"I have to get in the hospital," Fernandez surprised himself by saying this out loud.

"Can't you just tell them? His family?"

"That's not good enough. The old man doesn't believe any of it. He's going to need proof."

"I can't say I blame him. Henry can be a devious bastard. It's all the drugs, man. Anyway, I don't know what good money will do now."

"He's that bad?"

Emerenciano nodded his head tearfully.

"Mr. Fernandez, at this point I think you're just working to give them some closure. Hopefully they'll get down here in time. I can help you, though. I have the name of the doctor in charge."

Fernandez wasn't able to get hold of Henry Delgado's doctor until Monday morning. He informed Fernandez it was likely Henry didn't have more than a couple days to live. Although he was appalled at the Delgado family's hesitance, he sadly explained that he couldn't give Fernandez permission to visit Henry in the ICU. He gave him the name and number of the hospital director "in case he felt moved and gave him a special pass".

The call to the hospital's director didn't go any better. The best he offered was to grant Fernandez admittance on the coming Friday, and that was way too late.

Fernandez started to think about the personnel allowed to visit patients in the ICU. It was a Catholic hospital. Nurses, doctors, maintenance people, some suppliers, nuns, and... priests.

In the hospital bathroom, Fernandez checked the camcorder once again. The blue light was on. For sure it was on now and the second one glowed steadily red, as in "recording" red. He zipped up the hand bag and prepared to return to Henry's room. Damn the beard itched. Fernandez scratched furiously at it then realized he'd scratched so hard the left side had become slightly unstuck.

"Fuuuuuck!" he whispered clenching his fists, knuckles white.

The restroom was still empty. He left the stall and examined his face in the mirror. The beard was slightly bulging and he could see his skin beneath. He pressed hard and the remaining adhesive held but only barely. He'd have to be careful.

"What are you worried about?" he said to his reflection. It was true. If Rafi recognized Fernandez what exactly was he going to do? Bust a priest's nose open against the EKG machine in a crowded hospital with a policeman outside? Beat him within inches of his life like he did with Henry?

There was so much internal damage the doctors had basically given up on Henry Delgado. Fernandez had learned all this yesterday from one of his contacts at the SJPD. That's why the pious cop was stationed outside. Henry's hospital stay was labeled as a murder attempt on a police confidant.

He gave one more firm press to the beard and left the restroom. The guard had finally managed to compose himself and was standing at his post again. Fernandez walked up to him and put his hand on his shoulder.

"My son, please allow me to enter once more to assuage this poor soul."

"I thought you were finished father. With all due respect, I'm not supposed to let anyone in."

"My son, as I prayed for your family and yourself, you would not allow me to pray for this poor fellow anymore?"

"I don't know father."

"My son, this man's soul is right now in your hands. If I don't get in there, we could be risking an eternity of damnation! With snakes! And flesh being flayed! And...other... similar things!"

The mortified officer promptly opened the door and followed Fernandez in. Rafi was nowhere to be seen. Henry had been sat up and moved awkwardly on his side. His current position made it impossible for Fernandez to film him with the hand bag at his side in any natural way. With a dramatic flourish he slowly drew the hand bag over his head with both hands.

"Oh My God..." he began.

"Aren't you going to take the Bible out?" said the guard.

"No. It is still effective through the bag. Don't question me!" Fernandez reprimanded.

Fernandez began rocking back and forth.

"AVE MARIA!" he chanted in a loud monotone. The guard dropped to his knees behind him and crossed himself.

"Gratia plena, Dominus tecum. Benedicta tu in mulieribus, et benedictus fructus ventris tui, Iesus. Sancta Maria, Mater Dei, ora pro nobis peccatoribus, nunc, et in hora mortis nostrae. Amen."

"Aaaameeeeennnn," the officer sang.

"Thank you my son. You shall be rewarded and reap these ample fruits in the hereafter," he touched the guards head and bolted out the door, only to come face to face with Rafi.

"I was looking to buy some forks, cabrón," the murderer spat.

"I don't know what you are talking about, my son."

"Don't give me that shit. Who are you, really? What the fuck are you doing here?"

"Foul language is a venial sin, my son."

"Let's take a walk, father." Rafi gripped his arm savagely. "We're walking out together, nice and easy. Keep smiling or this is going in your fat ass." Rafi revealed the top half of a syringe in his pants pocket. Probably for Henry, Fernandez thought.

"You can't do that here."

"No one will ever know," Rafi hissed.

A doctor pushed past them to check on Henry.

"Excuse me doctor." Rafi's grip tightened but Fernandez pushed the two of them right up into the doctor's face. The three were in such close quarters that Rafi had no wiggle room. Annoyed, the doctor tried to back off but his back was to the door of Henry's room.

"What? Can you give me some space please?"

"I'm sorry. This man was just telling me that he found some of the hospital's property and wants to return it."

"What do you mean?"

"Right here." Undaunted, Fernandez reached down into Rafi's pants pocket and pulled out the syringe.

"What is that? What are you doing with that?" the doctor demanded. "Where's the damn cop? Hey! Officer!"

Rafi split down the corridor and Fernandez walked briskly in the opposite direction. He could hear the cop and the doctor arguing and he turned around.

"He ran down that way my son," he shouted.

"Father, wait there, where are you going?" The cop was already in a full sprint after Rafi with the doctor trailing behind him yelling "Call security! Dammit, code red!"

"I have mass at five," Fernandez called back, ducking into the stairwell.

He had never run downstairs so fast. He felt the priest's robe billowing around his legs and wondered if it could work as a parachute if he fell over the rail.

Within minutes, he was guiding the Sienna out of the parking garage and into the blazing afternoon. He turned off Ashford toward the ocean, took the priest collar out of his shirt and ripped the itchy beard off his face. As he passed by the emergency entrance, he could see Rafi pinned to the sidewalk by four cops, one with his knee jammed down hard on his temple. They were cuffing him as the doctor stood by examining the syringe with a group of nurses. He patted the hand bag, safely in the passenger seat.

"That's that."

"You got the video file, Ms. Delgado? And my report?"

"Yes, thank you Mr. Fernandez. We sent your office the last payment already," Sylvia's voice was weak though the receiver.

"I'm so sorry."

"Don't be. We're on our way to the airport now."

"Your father too?"

"Yes."

Fernandez thought hard about what to say next. The restrictions of his job were clear. He'd investigated what they'd asked for and provided the Delgados with his findings according to their request. This was as far as he could ethically go. He was burning to tell them the truth about Henry, and the cartel.

"Ms. Delgado?" it was bound to be all over the newspaper. They were going to find out.

"Yes?"

"Things aren't what they seemed with Henry. That's all I can say. You'll find out as soon as you land."

"Things were never as they seemed with Henry, Mr. Fernandez. Nothing could take us by surprise."

"I see. I'll be available if you want to meet, of course."

"I'll be in touch. Good bye."

"Have a safe flight." Fernandez hung up the receiver. The office was dark. Simon had long since gone and his girls were asleep. The two dogs lay curled up at his feet.

"They like you so much, Fernando," Nicole appeared in her nightgown. "Why don't you like them?" She sat down on his lap.

He let the question hang. He looked out at the moon behind the palms. The frogs were in full chorus "Co-qui! Co-qui! Co-qui!"

"You know, that was very resourceful of you today."

He'd told her nothing of Rafi or the cartel.

"You turned that around lightning fast, and you really helped that family out. And you're working without an assistant. I'm proud of you."

Fernandez had been in tight situations before, but nothing like this. The hospital was the first time he'd had his life directly threatened. Of course, Nicole knew there were risks involved with this job, but he'd kept all the details of the last 48 hours from her deliberately. Thinking about the assistant's remark, he was kind of glad there was nobody else to worry about in this case.

"Helped them out?"

"They'll be reunited, even if only briefly. Father and son. It means a lot, and you made it happen."

Fernandez found it difficult to find the up side. Perhaps, Henry had been dead to his father ages ago. Perhaps he died the second his father realized his only son would take a path so different from his own. The first joint, hit, shot, a teenager huddled in the concrete ruin of some abandoned vacation house near Jobos Beach, or in the janitor's closet of his father's Grand Resort. His father, the man who came from dirt only to fight his way up and provide a standard of living that produced a boy the antithesis of himself. Was it the upbringing or was in the genes? Maybe there was something faulty in the Delgado line that would have produced the same results regardless of money and opportunity. Clearly Sylvia was fine. Maybe money had nothing to do with it at all, except that it made the fall all the more public. No one would have speculated so if the addict had been Emerenciano, and no one would have expected the genes to be anything less than faulty.

"I suppose." He let it stand at that. Sylvia Delgado had found him through Paula O'Connell. No doubt others would find him through Sylvia. Did that mean the future held more syringes, beatings and head bustings?

"There was an answer for the assistant position in the classifieds. I will call back and make an appointment for you to interview her," said Nicole, completely unaware of his train of thought.

"You know what? Let's give the whole assistant thing a rest

for now. The workload is not that heavy yet. I will tell you when I'm ready for another one," Fernandez told her, thinking about the new risks involved.

"You ready for bed?" Nicole asked.

"Yes."

Flight to Nowhere
2009

Alberto Santiago was bored. Really bored. His work in the airport control tower was about as fun as sitting through a time share presentation. Every once in a while, there was some excitement, but for the most part the planes flew themselves nowadays.

The night was perfect for flying. A full moon loomed over the horizon, dazzling all in its glory and flooding the runway with an eerie, sort of supernatural glow.

"This is a night for pilots" Alberto thought, kind of wishing he was one of them. He missed flying. He still got together with his old buddies, but they all had new stories. All he had was "last Sunday this 727 is over the marker when this dog wanders onto the runway and you'll never guess what happened next." It wasn't the same.

Not after his high blood pressure and pacemaker prevented him from going up anymore. At least he was involved somehow. Being an air traffic controller was as close as he could get to the action without being in the cockpit.

He went back to his musings about the moon. A moon like this made everything clear. Night flying could be tricky, especially for inexperienced pilots. People who didn't fly could not understand just how easy it can be to lose track of what's up and what's down. Spacial disorientation killed many, as the sea became the sky for some poor bastards who tried flying solo and without instruments in the dead of night. However, for an experienced airman flying tonight would be a breeze, even without computers.

"Las Americas Tower, La Bonita 3 5 4 is ready for takeoff."

The metallic voice over the radio got Alberto out of his reminiscences and into the action. Guerra was ready for take off. But his flight plan was not.

"La Bonita 3 5 4, wait, we don't have your flight plan."

"My flight was scheduled for seventeen hundred hours, and then it was changed to twenty one hundred hours."

"La Bonita 3 5 4, yes, we have the flight plan pending the time change. Wait."

"Acknowledged."

"La Bonita 3 5 4, line-up and wait Runway 01. Cargo airline traffic to cross the runway."

"Line-up and wait Runway 01, La Bonita 3 5 4."

Alberto double-checked the UPS airplane's turn, and waited until he had landed safely over on his assigned runway.

"La Bonita 3 5 4, cleared for takeoff Runway 01."

"Cleared for takeoff Runway 01, La Bonita 3 5 4."

Tirso Guerra was en route to Miami, Florida USA. His flight plan was straight forward. He did this run many times before, and was an experienced pilot that could do it again in his sleep. His Cessna Jet was gorgeous – it had just been featured in a trade magazine. All in all, Alberto had no reasons to worry as he gave the pilot the necessary information for its controlled ascent.

Alberto always envied Guerra just a little bit. I mean, the guy was a millionaire. Born in Cuba, owner of a hardware empire with headquarters in Miami, he was a well respected businessman all over the tropics. Here in the Dominican Republic Guerra had kept a huge house, businesses, hangars, and a big part of his life.

Watching the tiny jet lazily disappear in to the blackness, Alberto Santiago wondered, not for the first time, what it must be like to be Tirso Guerra. All the properties, all the businesses, and above all the freedom and money to be able to fly yourself between them at your leisure aboard your own personal jet. When and where he decided to go, he went. Just like that. Tirso Guerra was a man unhindered by lines on the map. To Alberto, It was almost as if Guerra didn't follow the rules of men. A little envious? No, Alberto was a lot envious.

Then the Cessna's transponder signal vanished. Alberto looked down at the radar in astonishment. It was simply gone.

He immediately went into emergency mode and tried everything he was supposed to do to communicate with Guerra, following protocol to a t.

Within one minute the tower was swarming with people trying frantically to get the plane back into reality. Nothing worked. The Emergency Localizer Transmitter never activated.

Not even three minutes into its flight, Guerra's plane had vanished into thin air.

The sun began to touch the tips of the palms in the west. In less than an hour it would be dark and the beach would change hands. The trunk of a rainbow appeared far down the coastline toward Piñones. An offshore squall kicked up and suddenly the entire ribbon was revealed, as if painted across the sky by some giant extraterrestrial hand.

The rainbow firmly asserted itself, dominating half a horizon dotted by countless kite-boarders getting in one last session before they headed home to eat, party, work out, or do whatever it was normal people did. The crazy woman who sold the horrible jello shots to tourists was about to call it a day too, taking off her Panama hat and leaning against the sea wall.

A father threw his son up over a wave, the squeal of glee lasted only a split second before he plunged into the water. The little boy bounced back up like there was a trampoline on the bottom and threw his arms around his father's neck. Both went down in a giggling jumble.

All the radios had long since been taken home. All the coolers had been emptied and left their drippy trails to the street. The only sound that came to Fernandez's ears was the crash of the shore break, the whistle of wind through the palms, and the light piano jazz from inside the hotel. It was a glorious Thursday evening. "Pre social" as they say in Puerto Rico. Magic hour.

Fernandez had come to pay a visit to Julio Gonzalez, but had found the bastard had stood him up. It wasn't the first time. Fernandez wondered once again if it was rudeness or senility. In Gonzalez's case it was probably both. He'd salvaged the trip by walking to the Hosteria and taking a seat at the beach bar. Ceviche and beer. Unless something came up, there was nothing scheduled for the night, no surveillances. Interference International had him quite busy for almost a year now and tonight it was time to relax.

"Here you are sir, another beer?"

"Yes please." He dove into the citrusy dish as the bartender magically produced a frosty bottle from nowhere.

The outside lights came on and the hotel began the switch from sandy to elegant. From his seat at the bar Fernandez could see the kite boarders leave the water and begin packing up their gear. He couldn't resist a chuckle, thinking of his second assistant Vicente. The guys were built like gymnasts.

"What were you thinking, man?"

The momentary reverie made him realize that as much as his fortunes had improved professionally in the last year, he'd still not managed to find a good assistant.

"You know it could be a sign of madness." A woman was looking at him from the other side of the short bar. Fernandez hadn't seen her sit down.

"Excuse me?"

"Sitting out here alone, talking to your food."

"Oh sorry, I was just thinking of something."

"What were you thinking of?"

"An old friend of mine tried that," he motioned toward the guys on the beach. "Didn't go so well."

"What happened?"

"He got dragged across a reef and stepped on a... excuse me, who are you?"

"Jocelyn," she smiled. She was a bit older than Fernandez. American, blond.

"Hi Jocelyn, I'm Fernando. Are you on vacation?"

"Yes I'm alone, I'm leaving tomorrow."

Fernandez knew guys that made this a lifestyle. When you live somewhere people come for vacation it was basically like shooting ducks in a barrel. There was a certain kind of person in this world that checked their ethics at arrivals. He didn't sit around self satisfied thinking he was better, it just wasn't his style. Life was already complicated enough.

"So, did you enjoy your stay," Fernandez asked trying to sound as sexy as the clerk at an information desk.

"Yes but I'd like to go out with..."

Just then his phone mercifully rang. He looked at the screen, it was Dirk Saban.

"Sorry Jocelyn, I have to take this. Dirk!"

"I bet you're sick of hearing my voice, Fernando."

"Don't be silly, what can I do for you?"

He looked up and Jocelyn had already turned her attention to a couple of businessmen sitting down in the lounge. She was sending off such a relentless vibe that the two immediately stopped conversation. The younger man looked like a deer in the headlights, such a sure thing he was mentally making his mind up whether or not sleeping with her was a good idea even before they'd said two words to each other. The bartender smiled and shook his head. Same shit, different night.

"Well Fernando, this is kind of a big one. I'm not going to dick around, this is the biggest thing I've sent your way so far. It's going to require your undivided attention," he explained.

"I'm intrigued Dirk."

"It's for Alliance Insurance."

"Ah."

"Alliance is my biggest client. They've got a piece of everything here. I don't have any ego about this, Fernando. When these guys say jump, I fucking leap. You know you've indirectly been working for them before."

"I've been trying to forget. Jay Lauderdale still won't talk to me."

"Well, regardless, Alliance requested you specifically for this. It's funny, this whole thing goes back to around the time we had our little meeting with Lauderdale. That's when the plane disappeared."

"Plane?"

"It's a long story. Last October a man named Tirso Guerra took off from Santo Domingo airport on a night flight to Miami. After only a couple of minutes into the flight he vanished off the radar. He never arrived in Miami and neither himself or the plane have ever been recovered."

"Let me guess, he had a big policy."

"Three of them, as a matter of fact, totaling 30 million."

"That's a shitload of money in the DR," Fernandez whistled.

"That's a shitload of money anywhere. Now clearly I'm not asking you to strap on oxygen tanks and find the plane, but I need you to check out a few things where you are in Puerto Rico. Guerra had several businesses there and there are already a lot of red flags. Alliance Insurance seems to think there's something fishy about the death certificate too."

"They have a death certificate? For a missing person?"

"After like 5 or 6 months, exactly. The whole thing is a disorganized mess, no one we talk to at the Civil Registry seems to know what the hell they are doing, they never call us back, when we call back they forget that they'd talked to us or tell us something completely different only to go back to the original story when we remind them. I don't get it. People seem to talk simply as a domestic exercise without any regard to the actual meaning behind the words."

"That sounds about right Dirk," Fernandez laughed. "In my experience over there they will just talk you in circles. You're not going to get anywhere unless you flash some cash. Most of the time remarkably little. Most people have nothing."

Just the day before the superannuated Gonzalez had recounted a case to Fernando of two men in San Pedro de

Macoris. They'd killed a man for his cellphone and then sold it for 300 pesos, about seven bucks.

"That's why I'm thinking I'm eventually going to need some boots on the ground, someone who knows the customs, and can speak proper Spanish for Christ's sake. I got a whole international department and no one who can communicate with these people. Depending on what you find we may have to send you there. Do you have anyone over there you can coordinate with and trust?"

"Yeah, I have a ton of people in the Dominican Republic," Fernandez lied while smiling uneasily at the bartender, confessing his guilt to the only person around. Jocelyn was now laughing with the two businessmen in the restaurant. Someone had to be the unseen moral authority for life to make sense and Fernandez cast the young man behind the bar in the role of the unwitting surrogate. He didn't have anyone in the Dominican, but that didn't matter. He could find someone.

"Great. Tirso was a real piece of work. He had millions. Companies in Miami, Dominican Republic, Puerto Rico and doing business with India and China. There are rumors of all kinds of questionable business dealings. He might have seriously been underwater, no pun intended."

"And Alliance thinks this was all a scam and he's still alive."

"It's a distinct possibility. I don't know if you remember the 70s and 80s in South Florida."

"The Cocaine Wars," Fernandez guessed where Saban was headed.

"Right. There are still isolated landing strips in the Everglades, and that's just assuming he went ahead with the flight plan. I believe Tirso was an experienced pilot. He could have disappeared anywhere in South America or the Caribbean. Some of those countries aren't exactly on the ball as I'm sure you know. No offense."

It was like Saban still didn't understand Fernandez was an American citizen.

"None taken."

"Just start by digging up all the info you can over there. Obviously we're going to need to get our hands on a physical copy of that death certificate at some point. Get in touch with my office to get the info on the beneficiaries. You know what to do Fernando, I don't have to tell you your job."

"What kind of plane was it?"

"A Cessna 501, registered to Hurricane Hardware in somewhere called Caguas. I believe that's the headquarters of the family empire. It might be a good place to start."

"Sounds good Dirk," Fernandez was already busy researching the crash and the aircraft specs on his laptop. "I'll be in touch in a couple days."

"Thanks Fernando. I know I can count on you." He hung up the phone.

Fernandez quickly discovered the jet sat five passengers. Usually a plane of this size required a crew of two, but Tirso had bought the SP model, specifically designed for a solo pilot. Newspaper articles all confirmed what Saban had said, that the plane disappeared minutes into the flight to Miami. US Coast Guard turned up nothing. The Dominican Republic Navy had also come up empty handed after an "extensive search".

The quotes were added by the Aviation Safety Commission in their report. There was a fine line between prejudice and pragmatism, and in a matter of life or death usually all bets were off.

Fernandez had taken two vacations in the Dominican Republic and understood the quotes, or at least was prepared to forgive them. All the confusion Saban recounted was true. But it was also a place of fierce and ragged beauty. The kind of place where watching the people go about their daily business made you wonder what in the hell you were so stressed out about in your own life. The mopeds carelessly shooting out from all directions, the roadside bars selling open beers to thirsty drivers while still behind the wheel, the traffic lights which were apparently completely optional, all made Fernandez realize in a moment of grand epiphany on the road from Santo Domingo to Punta Cana that the weight we felt in our daily lives was completely self imposed.

Perhaps fate had fixed it so a country couldn't have it both ways. If you want this careless lifestyle it shall be purchased with corruption, injustice, and bureaucratic ineptitude. You won't be able to count on the cops, you won't be able to count on the hospitals, you won't be able to count on any government agency, and if you wanted security you'd have to purchase it for yourself.

The irony was that the populace was used to this and by and large spent their entire lives not expecting to count on anyone. It was only the uptight First-Worlder who wanted things done correctly. Which is why this adventurous person should be very clear about what he is getting into when he leaves the posh comfort of his all-inclusive Disneyesque mega resort and casino. Go with a local or don't go at all. You're off the grid and in a reality where people will kill you to sell your smartphone for seven dollars.

"Now what have we here?" Fernandez said aloud.

The bartender came guardedly forward and inspected Fernandez's ceviche at a distance, thinking Fernandez had discovered something inedible and foreign.

"Is there a problem with the food sir?"

"Huh? No, no problem son. Just looking at something online here.

Fernandez had bounced through a few links in news stories on the disappearance and found himself on a photographer's website. His portfolio showcased mainly aircraft. The homepage was dominated by a large photo of two men standing on a landing strip in front of a Cessna 501. In large letters under the photo was written R.I.P.

"Tirso Guerra, I presume."

A brief eulogy by the photographer appeared underneath:

"To my good friend Tirso. This is a photo of you and I in happier times. You were taken from us too quickly. It is such a tragedy your plane was lost and could not be recovered by the US Coast Guard or Dominican authorities or even the Navy. You are surely lost forever to the sea."

Fernandez couldn't help but laugh out loud.

"You've got to be fucking kidding me."

The eulogy concluded:

"I am heartbroken that we will probably never find your remains. Rest in peace old friend, in the bosom of the Caribbean."

"What an asshole," he said shaking his head at the screen.

"Suspicion is your default position." It was one of Simon's little rhyming adages that so irritated him. He was angry that it had leapt to mind so quickly, stirring up doubt and robbing him of his burgeoning excitement for the case before it had even begun.

Had the conversation with Dirk already convinced him that all parties were lying through their teeth? Was this good or bad? Weren't most people he came into contact with lying through their teeth? Why would they even be coming across his radar then? They inhabited the meeting point of the Venn diagram, one circle said honest, one said criminal, and in the middle there was "maybe I can get away with it" or "scum".

All Fernandez knew was his gut reaction to the two men on the screen before him. They were a couple of fucking liars. One very big important fucking liar, and a sniveling little shit liar ineptly trying to create a lame smokescreen. It pissed him off, the self satisfied Johnny Depp looking art school boy. Actually thinking he being clever and throwing someone off the scent with his stupid website.

"You're gonna have to do better than that, cutie pie."

He finished up his ceviche. Vacation apparently over.

Tirso Guerra Jr. fidgeted uncomfortably in his seat when the muscle-bound waiter in jean shorts brought him his club soda with lime.

"Here you are sir, are you ready to order?" the good looking young man smiled.

"No, not yet, thank you," Tirso spat tersely.

"Ok, just let me know." The kid turned on his heel, unfazed.

Tirso Jr. watched his tight rear recede into the kitchen then realized what he was doing. He was irritated, flummoxed, and supremely uncomfortable. When he asked his brother Alex to pick the meeting place he should have known he'd choose the most flamboyant restaurant in the universe. A member of the "do whatever you want but just stay the hell away from me" brand of tolerant heterosexual, Tirso Jr. was unfamiliar with this area of South Beach and traversed the distance from car to diner as if it was a minefield. He envisioned himself a walking t-bone steak like in a Bugs Bunny cartoon, with salivating homosexuals behind every corner ready to pounce.

The fact that he was fat, slovenly, ugly, balding and broke didn't seem to matter. He took for granted the subconscious and Cro-Magnon idea he belonged to a higher species of human, and even the dregs of his kind were coveted by the brightest of theirs.

Had he been of a less Narcissistic and more observant nature he would have seen life in this neighborhood happily going on as usual, unperturbed, not interested in or needing his input in any way.

He saw Alex enter and "gayly" kiss the waiter on the cheek in recognition. The waiter pointed in Tirso Jr.'s direction and the two exchanged a giggle as Alex turned to approach the table.

"Hello straight-boy-central. Do you think you could look a little less comfortable?" Alex rebuked as he sat down.

"I'm not used to this area."

"Clearly Tirs, don't worry though. I had a talk with Alan. I made him promise not to try and grab your butt. It'll be tough considering your animal magnetism but I think he'll be able to control himself."

"Very funny," Tirso said uncomfortably, deciding whether or not he was serious.

Alex and Tirso Jr. looked as dissimilar as twins could pos-

sibly look. Alex, lithe, in shape, healthy looked as if someone
loaded a picture of Tirso Jr. into photoshop and applied a filter
called "less ugly and fat and more appealing". Tirso's ill-fitting
white dress shirt was open at the collar one button too many
and his hairy chest exploded outward. His gut spilled over his
grey slacks, portions of it were visible through the strained
material. Alex found himself feeling sorry for the poor shirt.

"Can you just calm down?" Alex asked. "Do you want to go
somewhere else?"

"No we're fine here. Order something."

"What about you?"

"I'm not hungry."

Alex looked at his brother and immediately understood.
Tirso's jumpiness wasn't entirely due to the restaurant or
neighborhood. His perennial hangover made him tense and
irritable in the light of day, basically counting the seconds until
five o'clock when he'd have his first drink. This little exercise in
restraint allowed him to see himself as not an alcoholic. Alex
never lectured his brother. After all, how many people lived like
that? A lot more than would care to admit it, he guessed. Tirso
owned it and faced it. The fact he did so was one of the few
appealing things about his personality.

"Why don't you get a mimosa or something? If you calm
down you'll get hungry."

"It's too early Alex, besides, it's good if I don't eat so much,"
he explained patting his gut.

"You know I never see you eat. How are you so fat?"

"Booze has a lot of calories."

"So you don't eat all day, have a drink at 5, your appetite

comes roaring back, you go over to Versailles and devour a palomilla steak with a trough of rice and beans, wash it down with a Sambuca then go directly to sleep."

"Rinse and repeat."

"That's why you are fat. I'm just worried about your health, that's all."

"There are more direct threats to my health right now than rice and beans, Alex. Threats with guns and bad attitudes who don't like waiting for payment. That's what we need to talk about."

Hungover, uncomfortable, being harassed by the mob for gambling debts again, Alex now fully realized the severity of his brothers nervous breakdown.

"I talked to Alliance Insurance this morning."

"And?"

"They said the claim is still under investigation."

"Fuck! It's been a year. We have the death certificate, what's left to fucking investigate?"

"I honestly can't say. I mean, officially, the paper says he's dead. I guess we are just in a holding pattern until the insurance people decide to hand out the cash."

Tirso went white and stared blankly at his brother. He was dumbfounded Alex could be so callous in light of his impending execution.

"Do you realize the enormity of what you just said? How can you be so nonchalant about this!"

"I'm just saying…"

"Well don't just say! I'm happy for you that you have money

and your wonderful little gay life is all in order."

Alex looked down, realizing he must have really pissed his brother off. Tirso only went into this area when panicked and infuriated.

"I'm in deep shit, Al. I need that fucking money." Tirso's eyes were wide and haunted with terror.

"Like yesterday!"

"Well, I'm guessing it's a little more involved than that," Alex began with as much sympathy as he could muster. "Tirs there's no body, no crashed plane parts, no nothing. I mean, I know Dad's gone, but they don't just hand over that kind of money overnight."

The dissimilar twins sat looking at each other in silence. After awhile, an uncharacteristic look of reproach crossed Alex's face.

"You know honestly I don't know what you were thinking?" he said.

"What do you mean?"

"You played this like you're still down there, in DR. This isn't like getting one of your cop buddies to fill out a fake accident report cause you got hammered and ran your car into a tree. This is a massive multi-national company. You did this to yourself, you and that pet lawyer of yours jumping the gun on the death certificate. You know..."

"Look," Tirso interrupted. "If they end up sending anyone over there we'll have Duarte deal with them. You can't have a better reputation than him. He told me he'll be able to explain why the certificate was expedited, that there were special cases. I trust him completely. He made it sound like it wouldn't be a problem at all. We all just have to stick to the story and not arouse any suspicions."

The last three words came out more or less as a yell. The suspicions of all the surrounding tables were getting aroused. The waiter approached them but Alex flashed a smile that told him everything was ok.

Tirso said the last sentences like they were a mantra he'd been rehearsing for a year. As if the dogged and enthusiastic recitation would eventually just make it true. It had to be true, in his case there simply was no other choice. He wasn't squared away like Alex, and he didn't have all encompassing passions like his sister Patricia. Both were far more responsible than their fuck-up brother. Although Alex wouldn't scoff at 10 mil, he seemed like he could take it or leave it.

But Patricia was a different story. In a way she needed the money just as bad as he. Only instead of using the 10 million to make a problem go away, she was going to use it to start some problems of her own. Anyway, that's how Tirso Jr. saw it. It was difficult to understand his sister's motivations, as it became difficult to understand his father's shifting preoccupations as he got older. All Jr. wanted was a big house with a pool bar, and to not be in serious debt to dangerous people all the time. Perhaps not panicking about money gave you the time to manufacture other interests. Maybe this explained Patricia's political ambitions.

"And when it's all over, you think she'll still lie low?"

"I don't give a shit Alex, she can take a boat to Cuba with a huge sign that says 'I've come to kill Fidel' and get it reported on every news station in the world. By that time we'll have the money."

He slammed his hand hard on the table, again creating a disturbance.

"You know for someone trying to lie low you sure are making a lot of noise."

"Just stop bringing this shit up and making me more nervous than I already am. Everything is going to be fine. We'll have the money soon."

Tirso Jr. got up and downed the remainder of his club soda in one gulp

"Then I'll get these maniacs off my back once and for all."

Fernandez left for Caguas right after lunch. The southbound afternoon rush out of San Juan always started a couple hours early on Friday. He needed to avoid the crunch of people eager to start their weekend ahead of time. Still about halfway down route 18, in the vicinity of Rio Piedras, he hit a 15 minute snag. When he reached the obstacle and found it was someone receiving a ticket, both cop and motorist were way off the road and not obstructing traffic in any way, he could have screamed. Rubbernecking was an epidemic.

Traffic on the island was every bit as terrible as Miami or DC. In fact it was worse. In the States there was always an alternate route, another interstate or turnpike. Failing that the surface roads were well maintained. In Puerto Rico there simply wasn't the room. Every highway was all part of the same circulatory system, a blockage usually had a knock on effect for miles in every direction. If you got stuck, you could be stuck for hours.

Your only option was the "old road". This is the road people used before the highway system was implemented. It was usually two lanes, uneven, and roadblocked by traffic lights that may or may not be working every 100 feet. So you'd sit there on the highway in tense, swelling anger that couldn't vent in road rage because road rage could easily get you shot. Failing that you always could stop caring.

Deep down Fernandez knew that, while counterintuitive, this was the far more sensible option. Most would think that this would come easily "in the islands". But Puerto Rico was Caribbean and it wasn't. For all the beaches, nightlife and partying, it still had an urgent and nervous imprint from the United States. That pressure to succeed, to do.

In his travels to the US and other parts of the world, Fernandez constantly found himself confronted with the Caribbean stereotype. When people heard he worked out of Puerto Rico their eyes would widen and they'd invariably say something like "wow that must be nice." Some said this with a voice tinged with jealousy and reproach, almost like an accusation of cheating at life. Like the only places serious life was occurring were cold, unhappy and dark.

Vacation was a frame of mind, and people painted his whole island with the memory of their two weeks of careless fun in the sun. The fact that people worked the same shitty jobs and were subject to all the pressures of living life and being human regardless of the climate seemed lost to them. Once at a conference in Dublin a detective named Rory McIlvanney, as Irish as they come, called Fernandez "Detective Daiquiri".

There were islands that were significantly more laid back than others. Saint Maarten and Aruba sprung to mind. But not here, at least not when driving. As Fernandez passed the "obstruction" he saw a young lady in the lane to his right almost stopped. She was wearing headphones and had broken off mid-text to gawk at the cop giving a speeding ticket. He wished for a second that he had a bottle of piss, then sped off.

He was on his way to Hurricane Hardware, Tirso Guerra's flagship business on the island. The morning had been busy and he'd uncovered a few things about the old man in the sea.

Tirso's businesses in Puerto Rico were in shambles. Hurricane Hardware was teetering on potential bankruptcy, and had requested extensions for filing financial reports each of the last five years. In addition, there were no less than six cases against the company currently in civil business litigation. A call to the headquarters in Caguas resulted in an endlessly ringing line.

Interference International had provided the names of all three beneficiaries, Tirso's children Patricia, Alex and Tirso Jr. They also reported that the family claimed Tirso had called them right before the flight and said he would be late due to problems with the plane. Out of the three, Interference International only had a number for Alex. Fernandez called but it was inactive, possibly indicating he was off the island.

Homeland Security and the Coast Guard confirmed there had been no changes in the case and no further investigation on the US side.

He pulled off the expressway outside Caguas and doubled back northward taking the old road. Hurricane Hardware's main office and warehouse lie beyond a cemetery and a dilapidated taco stand at the end of a pitted and destroyed street 2 blocks off the main thoroughfare.

Even from a distance, Fernandez could tell that all was not right. The massive parking lot lay empty, the guard post as well. The automatic gate was apparently frozen half open with not enough space for his car to get through. He parked in the dirt and continued on foot, wedging himself through the gap in the fence. After a quick glance around, it was clear the place was deserted.

The large bay doors for loading and unloading lay open and Fernandez could see inside the warehouse. There was some stock on the higher shelves but the place was mostly empty. Tucked around the corner of the right side of the loading dock there was a pedestal fan that was running, pointed toward a small stool. He approached and found some reading material under the stool, a couple old magazines and todays paper. Someone was here. Deciding that honesty was the best policy, and unsure of what specifically he even was looking for anyway, Fernandez made his presence known.

"Hello in there! Is anybody here?"

Nothing. He ventured further into the warehouse.

"I'm here from the insurance company. Hello?"

The second floor perimeter on the south end of the building was a line of windows. He could see offices on the other side of the glass. He caught a side view of a small old man in a security guard outfit. He hadn't heard Fernandez through the window. He was in a cubicle hunched over a computer, flustered and obviously struggling with something.

Fernandez cautiously climbed the steel stairs leading to the mezzanine. Upon entering the office Fernandez could see the old man at the far end with his back to him, obviously still unaware of his presence. And he was armed.

"Sir?"

"Shit almighty!" He jumped a foot into the air and spun around.

"Don't shoot," Fernandez said with a smile and hands up.

"Son, you scared the ever-loving crap out of me," he said

breathlessly.

"I'm sorry sir! I called before I came but no one answered. I'm from Alliance Insurance, I was hoping I could talk to the manager here, or whoever is in charge."

The old man fell into the office chair behind him, grabbing his chest and breathing heavily.

"Are you ok? Here, let me help you."

Fernandez saw a small canteen off to his left and got the old man some water. There were no plastic cups so he had to wash out a coffee mug that looked like it had been sitting around since the Clinton administration.

"Here you are."

The man drank while Fernandez fanned him with an interoffice mail envelope. He let out a long sigh and finally had calmed down.

"I'm so sorry, Mr...?"

"Burgos."

"Mr. Burgos."

"No, just Burgos, son."

He untucked his light brown shirt and began dabbing his forehead. Everything else about him was impeccably groomed. Uniform pressed and clean, security badge gleaming, Fernandez could even see his face staring back at him through Burgos' black shoes. Even though he might as well be stuck in some Siberian outpost, he was a man who clearly still took pride in his job.

"Burgos, I called out a couple times when I walked in as to not alarm anyone."

"I can't hear a damn thing up here," he laughed. "You know I could spend months here not seeing a soul and the second I decide to come up here to do this you walk in," he pointed to a digital camera on the desk. The line was attached but he'd obviously been trying to plug the USB into the computer with no luck.

"Having trouble?" Fernandez asked.

"I just want to print out some pictures of my grandkids," he admitted, somewhat embarrassed.

"Let me guess. The modern technology that's supposed to make life easier isn't making life easier."

"You said it. My daughter-in-law said it was easier than going to Walgreens. It sure doesn't seem easier to me. I kind of feel like an idiot," he laughed again.

"I know how to do it. Do you want some help?"

The old man eyed Fernandez suspiciously, but then a huge smile burst across his face.

"Sure, thank you that would be nice."

Fernandez sat down at the computer and attached the camera.

"I just have to figure out what printers are working. This place always been such a ghost town?"

"No," a hint of sadness crept into his voice. "Not always. It didn't happen overnight either. I used to think it was just a phase, but I'm not so sure anymore."

"Where is everyone?"

"Laid off, re-assigned, a lot of people were forced into long vacations and just didn't come back. There didn't seem to be anyone to talk to, anyone in charge since the boss left us."

"You mean Tirso Guerra, right? So all this happened in the last 10 months?"

Burgos' eyes narrowed and he took a step backward.

"What do you know about it?"

"It's my business, Burgos. Now that he's gone someone has to unravel this whole financial mess. He had policies on several of the bankruptcy security processes pertaining to the fiduciary climate as well as several offshore banking entities," Fernandez bullshitted. "It's quite routine."

Burgos nodded in understanding.

"We just have to get all this in order to find out what goes to his kids, so they are alright financially, you see?"

"Those fucking kids, excuse my language Mr., what's your name?"

"Fernando Fernandez. Not a fan of his kids?"

Burgos looked around the office and relaxed again. He sat on the desk next to Fernandez as he worked. His feet barely reached the floor.

"Those kids could have saved this place if they just took an interest. The twins were useless, one's a drunk and the other one is a fashionista. I don't think there's anything bad about that myself but Tirso did. Either way neither one of them was gonna run the company. We all thought Patricia would step up, now she was a smart one. Just like her old man."

For a moment Fernandez felt a twinge of guilt, plying Burgos for information. The old man was lonely and bored, starved for someone to talk to.

"Look at all these, I love them."

He leapt off the desk and went over to a wall lined with

framed pictures. Most of them were of Tirso Sr. and Patricia deep-sea fishing. Patricia got older as you walked down the hallway toward what Fernandez guessed were the executive offices. In the first two she was a giggling little girl on her father's lap, then a serious but still smiling teenager, the last few she was a confident woman with her arm around her father, on equal footing.

"These are great. Do you mind?" Fernandez held up his smartphone indicating he wanted to take some pictures.

"Don't see why not," Burgos responded.

"Was this his boat?"

"Yeah, it was incredible, massive. The two of them were peas in a pod, they used to fish everywhere. The Florida Keys, the Dominican coast. They basically lived on that boat, it was called Revenge," he drawled slowly and evilly.

"After the Tennyson poem?"

"Not sure about that. I think it had more to do with Castro."

Fernandez began to see a blurry picture coming into focus. Tirso Sr. was born in Havana in 1939. He knew that much for sure. Beyond that he'd not the time yet to delve into his family, but Tirso was of a certain age and social class that one might be excused in making several unpleasant assumptions about his past.

The best Fernandez could guess Tirso had begun building his Caribbean empire in 1968 or 69, the early 70s at the very latest. As he would have been too old for Operation Peter Pan, he could have come to the US during the first wave of exiles right after the revolution, or the second wave in 61. The freedom flights were also a possibility. The fact that his boat was called Revenge made a lot of sense.

"A troop transport for when the counter-revolution came?" Fernandez joked.

"Nah," the old man laughed. "Tirso wasn't like that. Well, not when I first knew him. He had a chip on his shoulder about his family losing everything, of course."

"Who wouldn't?" Fernandez concurred.

"He didn't understand those people in Miami though, those loonies in the Everglades training to overthrow the regime. He was more down to earth. His revenge was being successful. That's what the boat meant. He felt his success as a 'capitalist pig' was the biggest poke in their eye he could deliver."

"Why didn't he name the boat 'Capitalist Pig' then?" Fernandez joked.

"Yeah, he should have," Burgos laughed.

"At first, you said. What happened?"

Burgos let out a long, sad sigh and looked down the row of pictures. The sun dipped into the outside window and was partially obscured by a craggy and overgrown peak. It cast a shadow of a past gone forever over his face.

"You were good friends." Fernandez could tell Burgos must have been more than a regular employee.

"Yes, back in the old days. I took this picture as a matter of fact. It's at Tirso's place in St. Croix. Right outside of Christiansted."

"That's a hell of a view," Fernandez observed.

The picture was the only one on the wall not on Revenge. It showed Tirso and Patricia on an opulent balcony overlooking an incredible ocean sunset.

"I don't know, Mr. Fernandez. When Patricia went to College

in New York things started to change. She had some political ideas Tirso started to get really excited about. I didn't go to college, I don't know anything about that kind of thing. All I know is he started coming around less and less, and now..."

Burgos motioned around the abandoned office with his hand.

Fernandez began trying to piece together how this all fit in. Political ideas? Statistically speaking at a Western university one was more likely to develop an anti-Western stance, especially a rich kid who'd grown up under the very umbrella of the West's affluence and security. It's just what usually happened. Had Patricia made her father do a 180 and got him to rally against the imperialists? Given what Fernandez knew of Cuban men of Tirso's age and history, this seemed extremely unlikely.

There was another possibility though. Post 9/11 there was a new vein of liberalism and rationality coursing through the system. One accepting the evils of the past but not embracing the easy dogma that the US and the West were the cause of everything wrong with the world. Had Patricia tugged at her father's heartstrings and got him to take a more active role against totalitarianism? Is that where all the money went?

There were too many new questions now. Whatever was going on here though, it was getting more complicated than a greedy family looking for 30 million to save its ass.

"Do you want me to print all these pictures, Burgos?"

The old man returned to the desk.

"Yes please."

He pulled out the first page from the printer and examined it with a frown, waving the flimsy copy up and down.

"What's this?"

"You have to buy photo paper," Fernandez laughed. "Sorry about that. Maybe it is easier to go to Walgreens. Burgos, is there anyone else working for Tirso at all? Is there anyone I can talk to maybe in a management capacity?"

"Mr. Nuñez, that's his office. He shows up from time to time. He spends most of his time at the other office in Guaynabo. There are still a few employees there."

Fernandez left Burgos with his crappy photo printouts and went into the office. He grabbed the business card of Osvaldo Nuñez, Vice President Hurricane Hardware, off the desk.

"Do you mind if I take this?" he asked coming out.

Two minutes later Fernandez was sitting in his car calling Mr. Nuñez.

"Hurricane Hardware, how can I help you?"

"Osvaldo Nuñez please."

"Speaking."

He decided to go right for the jugular.

"I'm looking for Tirso Guerra."

Nuñez didn't miss a beat. No change in voice, no confusion as to the identity, nothing. Fernandez could have been calling about a faulty paint roller extension pole.

"He's not in the office right now."

"Do you know where I can find him?"

"With whom am I speaking?"

"My name is Fernando Fernandez, I work for Alliance Insurance. I'm investigating a claim regarding Tirso Guerra."

"He's fish…" he replied too quickly and rigidly, then he swallowed his own tongue and coughed on it.

Fernandez could hear Nuñez put the phone down. There was some muffled conversation, he couldn't make out if the man was talking to someone else or himself.

"What? He's a fish? What kind of fish Mr. Nuñez? A mackerel?" Fernandez pressed on, mockingly.

"No…"

Nuñez then sputtered his way through a couple of false starts. Fernandez remained dead quiet. When he'd finally managed to construct a sentence it came out as an oral book report in front of the class.

"Tirso Jr. is currently in St. Croix on a fishing trip with his sister Patricia."

"Tirso Jr.?"

"Yes of course Tirso Jr.," he'd regained a modicum of composure and authority. "The family will be home in five days and they will call you then. I'll pass on the message, goodbye."

With that he hung up the phone.

Two minutes later Fernandez was taking the scenic route back to San Juan in order to mull over what just had happened when he received a phone call. The number was blocked.

"Is this Fernando Fernandez?" the voice shot through the phone before Fernandez could even say hello. It belonged to a woman hurried and supremely irritated, like she'd been chosen an unwilling spokesperson.

"Yes."

"This is Patricia Guerra. I understand you are looking for my brother. He's here in St. Croix with me, but otherwise engaged at the moment. Can I take a message?"

Fernandez was not at all surprised that Nuñez had forwarded information on his call so quickly. He was, however, surprised at the hurriedness with which this Patricia person wanted to squash any further questions.

"I was just told by Mr. Nuñez I would have to wait for a week for your brother's arrival to San Juan, Ms. Guerra," Fernandez responded coolly, pulling his minivan of the road into a service station not wanting to talk while driving.

"Well, anyway, we are here now, and the fishing is good, so we may stay a little longer."

"Fantastic. I hear the Yellowfin is great this time of year. Do you guys use a 50 or 80 pound outfit for that?"

"Huh...I," Patricia was momentarily fazed but snapped back into pressing mode quickly.

"Listen, Fernandez, what's all this about?"

"You called me, ma'am," Fernandez observed.

"An associate informed me that you were asking about Tirso. What do you want?"

"I'm investigating your father's life insurance claim."

"Still! In Puerto Rico! Why?"

A woman obviously still very upset about the loss of her dear father, Fernandez noted sarcastically. Best to proceed with caution, she might go to pieces with grief.

"We're just following standard procedure Ms. Guerra."

"It's been almost a year! What's the deal? What else is there to find out? His plane is gone, he's gone, he crashed! Why are you keeping the money from us? And what the hell are you looking for in Puerto Rico?"

"I know you are clearly grieving terribly, Ms. Guerra, but

cases like this can sometimes go well over a year. It's quite a lot of money and we need to make sure we've dotted the i's and crossed the t's if you catch my meaning. Ha ha!" Fernandez laughed the laugh of an unconcerned bureaucrat in an attempt to infuriate Patricia all the more. The woman seemed on the verge of exploding.

"Look, we told them everything we know. He called us and said there was a problem with the battery, then he crashed. My poor, poor father..."

Fernandez wanted to puke.

"I will call you to set up an appointment when I get back to the island," Patricia said with final authority.

"I wanted to talk with your brother. I can swing by his house in the town of Dorado."

"You can swing by all you want. You'll find the door closed, Fernandez. You can, however, talk to me. I will call you," she spat the last four words out slowly. "We will set up an appointment and I'll tell you whatever you need to know. Thank you."

Fernandez was left at the service station, hung up on twice in five minutes. Saban was right. The whole thing stunk like backed up sewer on Ponce de Leon Avenue. He needed to be informed of everything that had just transpired. Fernandez knew he'd be headed to the Dominican Republic very soon. But he had to get in touch with someone first. He looked down at his phone, pulling up his photo of Burgos' photo.

"St. Croix, huh?"

Bill Morales was born in the island of Vieques, a small territory of Puerto Rico just off its easternmost shore. He moved to

Spanish Harlem with his family as a young kid and got drafted to fight in the Korean War when he was 18, and then again for the Vietnam war. He had been in the famous 65th Infantry unit. He survived his war months unscathed physically but like so many others fell through the cracks upon his return to the States. He'd been determined to push forward with life regardless of the memories and thoughts that plagued him. A forward thinking therapist had explained to Bill that thoughts and memories couldn't actually hurt him, the fear he was experiencing was simply unpleasantness. His ability to navigate the anxiety he felt on a daily basis hinged upon his ability to discern this difference between danger and discomfort.

He charged back into life in New York armed with this and similar therapeutic mantras. Sometimes they worked, sometimes they didn't. The fear was intense, it would gnaw at him particularly at night, an old crone just out of sight as he slept waiting to wrap a bony hand around his neck and strangle him until he went mad. At these times his therapy seemed like a paper shield against an overwhelming onslaught. He'd stand his pathetic ground as all the minions of the Inferno raged and cackled around him. Awake in bed he'd be certain the psychologists couldn't possibly understand the wave that engulfed him. Because if they did they'd see how frail and inadequate the coping techniques they were teaching him actually were. Like yelling into a hurricane.

He would think of them, at home, rich, comfortable, sane, and he'd hate them. Then he started to hate everybody. The man walking his dog before dawn, the policeman casually bantering with the driver through the open bus door, even the homeless drunk all seemed more legitimate than him. They all had their place, they all were getting on with their lives and the worst part about it was that it all seemed so effortless. He'd wonder what he was fundamentally missing, and despair.

He'd worn two wives out with this crap before he realized a person couldn't rely on someone else to save them. They'd both been in love at first, and by definition interested and sympathetic. But Bill didn't get any better, and they both realized to their horror he was going to harp on the same themes indefinitely.

With two marriages disintegrated and middle age breathing down his neck, Bill decided he'd been taking life and himself entirely too seriously and he was ready to return to the land of his birth. He left for Puerto Rico determined to never look back. Thinking it fit in with his island plans he took a job as a food and beverage manager at the Courtyard Radisson in Condado.

After one year he found himself burnt out from working 60+ hour weeks. Needing a break from his break, Bill moved again to the smaller island of St. Croix in the USVI. He was determined not to make the same mistake again and took a job with the least responsibility possible. He became a taxi driver.

The night demons became less frightening, he even considered making friends with a few of them.

Gradually, unexpectedly, he found himself waking up in the morning enthusiastic about the coming day. He made friends, the kind who'd shout at him as he drove his taxi by. He stopped being jealous of people for living their lives because he'd finally started living his. For the first time since the service, he was not unhappy.

On St. Croix he made his own schedule; when he didn't feel like working he didn't work. He shuttled tourists between Frederiksted, Christiansted and the airport by day and carted around dignitaries, social types and politicians at night. On an island of 50,000, there weren't many cabs. Without even asking,

Bill Morales became the eyes and ears of St. Croix, his finger firmly on the pulse of every shady business deal, every back door political negotiation, and every cheating spouse. It was an occupational hazard that would simply require earplugs to avoid.

Drama not being part of the prescription for his new, stress-free life, Bill generally let the information go in one ear and out the other, laughing. At times he used what he knew to help out people he respected, but mainly spent most of his free time at the beach or at bars near the boardwalk.

There was one exception, though. There was a Private Detective, a fellow Puerto Rican who struck up a conversation with him from the airport to his hotel, arriving to the island for a surveillance. A friendship was born that day, and a new spark in Morales' low-laying life. A way to bring back some excitement, without the worries. He became the P.I.'s guy on St. Croix. He called every once in a while with a new case, and Bill helped him out. It had been a while since the last call, though.

On a particularly glorious afternoon he was in Cane Bay draining a Budweiser at a place called the Sandbar, embroiled in the difficult decision of whether or not his financial situation was such that he could remain draining Budweisers and not work the coming shift.

"What d'ya say Bill? Making the hard decisions ain't ya?" Shelly the waitress called from the server station at the other end of the bar.

"You know me too well, Shelly."

"Go to work, ya lazy bastard," she taunted. "How else ya gonna take me out one day?"

She smiled through her tight braids and turned back to deal

with her customers. Bill shook his head and wondered how serious the young girl actually was. This wasn't the first time. Was it flirting? Shelly was 23, beautiful, but hard all the way through. He'd seen her cleverly and ruthlessly dispatch so many men since she'd started at the Sandbar he knew to keep his distance. Plus he was old enough to be her grandfather.

The other waiter Julio came up behind him.

"Why on earth is she so nice to you? If I get a grunt of recognition it makes my shift."

"I have no idea," Morales admitted.

"Maybe she thinks you're complicated?" Julio offered.

"I am complicated, and it's incredibly overrated. Well, better get to work if I'm gonna take Shelly out!"

Morales grabbed his 65th Infantry Unit cap from the bar and pulled it on. These days it was generally good for a free drink here and there. As he made his way out to the parking lot he was startled out of his Shelly-themed daydream by the text alert on his phone. It was from Fernando Fernandez, his P.I. friend, and it was long.

"Seriously? I'll be a son of a bitch."

When he finally digested the load of information he decided it was just what he needed, and definitely a more interesting way to spend this night.

"Ok, let's try this again," Fernandez said as he pulled into Parque Barbosa.

For the second night in a row Fernandez was paying a visit to Julio Gonzalez. This time he'd received verbal confirmation beforehand that he was actually in his office. He'd originally needed Gonzalez for the routine task of notarizing an affidavit of process service, but now that had taken a back seat. Fernandez had been given the go ahead by Dirk Saban to continue the investigation in the Dominican Republic and he wanted to pick Gonzalez's brain before he left. The old lawyer had a practice there for years.

He was a little apprehensive, planning to discuss an ongoing investigation with the talkative Gonzalez. He pacified his nerves with the knowledge no one really took the crazy old fucker seriously.

"Sorry about yesterday, Fernandez. I completely forgot."

"Don't worry about it."

"You got the papers?"

Fernandez handed over the affidavits. Gonzalez looked through them and began stamping angrily, in a mood incongruous with his mismatched Hawaiian shirt and Bermuda shorts. The old man could have stepped right out of the cruise ship boutique, but his sun-leathered skin betrayed his residence.

"How much this time?" Fernandez ventured.

"Fernando, don't piss me off, ok?" He irritatedly went back to his stamping.

"Shit, must have been a lot. You know when I bought you that iPad for Christmas I thought it would be an excellent tool for work-related activities," he laughed.

"What could be more work-related than making money?"

"Offtrackbetting.com?"

"Nah, I was in Canóvanas."

"And I was here waiting for you at the Hosteria," Fernandez

scolded.

"I said I was sorry. You gotta cut me some slack, Fernando. I'm getting up there, you know."

"I don't buy that for a second, Julio. You've always been an inconsiderate bastard, and now you can't just blame it on senility."

Gonzalez looked up from his desk and gave Fernandez an evil smile. He looked like a wicked spider. It was a smile that indicated beyond a shadow of a doubt to Fernandez that all his marbles were firmly in the bag.

"What motivates you, old man?" Fernandez asked.

"Ass," he replied. "And money."

"Aren't these supposed to be your Autumn years? Why not just call it a day? Horse losses aside, I know you have enough."

"Fernandez…" Gonzalez pushed back from his desk and slowly stood up, looking interestedly at nothing, no doubt sorting through a lifetime of dubious wisdom and deciding which portions to impart. Fernandez prepared himself for another poignant, albeit insane lecture.

"Fernandez, destination is an illusion. Purpose is all that matters."

"Oh Jesus," Fernandez exhaled.

"I operated a firm in the Dominican Republic for a long time."

"I know, that's kind of why I…"

"Don't interrupt. My partner Juan and I made a lot of money. We had the world at our fingertips."

"The world?" Fernandez scoffed.

"Beloved by women," he continued undeterred. "I was neck deep in tits and ass Fernandez. Quality ass too, classy society kind of skirt."

Fernandez couldn't help but snicker. Gonzalez's slang belonged to a different era. He sounded like he should be hanging out with Sinatra and Joey Bishop.

"Then one night at 3 am I get a call. Juan's dead, shot through the back of the head by some daffy broad's husband. I started thinking of all of my indiscretions and I panicked. You think it's bad here? Someone could make me disappear over there in about two seconds, and unless one of my friends or relatives was willing to push and grease that would have been fucking that. Done."

"And as you told me before your family doesn't much care for you," Fernandez remembered.

"Exactly. There was a certain thrill to living in a country without a net, it's liberating at first, especially coming from the States. On the surface you think you see people really enjoying their lives the way God intended."

"Which God Julio?" Fernandez pulled an innocent and confused face pointing with one hand to Gonzalez's painting of the Dome of the Rock and the other to the statue of Saint Michael.

"You know what I mean. But the thing is as soon as the tide turns against you, as soon as you wander into 'fucked' territory, the whole place changes. People don't look as friendly anymore. Suddenly you're nobody's business. There's no recourse to the law. You can yell and scream all you want but you'll get no sympathy from anyone. Bad luck is like catching a disease, it doesn't matter at all how it happened or how innocent you are. Do you see what I mean?"

"I think so."

Fernandez watched Gonzalez as he rooted some dust out the corner of the picture frame with his pinky finger and flicked it into the trash can. For all his bluster and 'indiscretions' the old man really did have the knowledge of years. Fernandez secretly loved listening to him go on like this. He felt he could sit there all day. There was also something strangely soothing about his voice. At times like these it sounded like the patter of water dripping from the roof and hitting the pavement after a storm.

"Anyway. My point was..." he stopped and seemed genuinely confused.

"I think you finished."

"No," he searched and searched. Fernandez began to be slightly concerned, and regretted his senility remark deeply.

"Was it that like Juan you can go at anytime so you might as well keep doing what you enjoy," he offered.

"Nothing that cliche," Gonzalez rediscovered his line of thought. "What I mean is that working towards something, the something itself is an illusion. You never get there. There has never been one person on this planet that achieved what they wanted and then just shut down and sat back like a pig in shit. They may want you to think that, particularly the materialistic and shallow, but although they'd admit it to no one they are still worried about something. It's our condition not to be satisfied. It's impossible. It would mean death. That's what I'm saying."

"Christ, Gonzalez, you sound like my assistant the Buddhist."

"Well anyway that's what I learned in DR watching people, particularly poor people, busy themselves. It might sound like

I'm setting you adrift, but the drive and goal are just excuses to find things to do during the day. Like notarizing these papers for you, imparting to you this wisdom…"

"Unasked for," Fernandez deadpanned.

"In the distraction lies life. I fully intend to keep doing this until I drop," he finally finished.

"Or get shot in the back of the head."

Gonzalez laughed and looked out his grubby window where he had a partial view of the beach. Fernandez could see along his line of sight the same father and son he'd seen the evening before in the water. The boy was jumping up and down, flapping his hands a little too excitedly and making strange noises.

"Those two are here everyday like clockwork," Gonzalez observed. "There's something up with the little one."

"Like what?" Fernandez asked.

"I don't know," Gonzalez said. "He's a doll though."

He sighed heavily and returned to his desk. For a second it seemed to Fernandez like he was going to reach for his iPad, but decided against it.

"We all just do the best we can," Gonzalez concluded.

"Not all of us Julio, otherwise I wouldn't have a job and I wouldn't be here today. I'm glad the Dominican Republic is fresh in your mind. I'm headed there tomorrow and I need your help with something."

"Sure no problem, most of the ones I knew would probably be a little too old for you though."

"I'm serious Julio. This is the biggest case I've ever worked. There's a ton of money at stake."

Fernandez explained everything he'd learned so far, leaving out particulars and names. He could tell by the look on his face that Gonzalez was probably familiar with the aircraft disappearance from the news but was letting him maintain his air of secrecy as a courtesy. When Fernandez had finished Gonzalez didn't miss a beat.

"You didn't need to get in touch with Morales, unless you're just curious, but it doesn't matter if Mr. X is dead or alive. The death certificate is illegitimate. They bought someone off. Just get a copy from the Civil Registry. Bing. Bang. Boom. You're in there like swimwear."

"You're sure?"

"Of course! In a disappearance like that it's a five year minimum before they can pronounce him dead. These greedy bastards couldn't wait that long? Did they really think Alliance wouldn't check?" he marveled.

"Maybe they thought they could get away with some kind of special dispensation or something? If they could get some official to vouch for them? The family has a lot of influence," Fernandez offered.

"Nah, even over there the law is the law in a matter like this. They just were stupid enough to think they wouldn't check thoroughly," Gonzalez explained. "Like they're just gonna hand over 30 million. Idiots."

"I find it difficult to believe anyone could actually be that stupid."

"Or desperate for cash," Gonzalez shot back. "Welcome to island life. Just get your hands on that certificate. Be careful though."

"I always am," Fernandez said getting up then stopped for a

second. "What do you mean exactly?"

Gonzalez looked as if he was about to explain calculus to an orangutan.

"You've got a powerful family you are going to be depriving of a lot of money they clearly are doing anything to get their hands on. You've also got the party or parties that issued the bogus certificate. Exposing them would place their jobs in jeopardy and make them liable to prosecution as well. Don't catch bad luck is all I'm saying."

"Yeah but unlike you I've got a few people who will be irritated if I disappear."

"I know that Fernandez, but what good will it do you then?"

About 5 minutes after Aguadilla disappeared from view Fernandez could see another land mass under him through gaps in the dense cloud cover. It looked the same but different.

"Can I take that for you sir?"

Fernandez stared down at his half empty water bottle and unopened bag of blue tortilla chips.

"It's about 45 minutes from gate to gate sir," the flight attendant smiled. "We'll be landing shortly. I have to take that."

"Of course. I'll probably spend more time in customs than we did in the air," he said and handed the stuff over.

The terrain below him was jagged and bushy. Hispaniola was on the continental shelf, the same as Puerto Rico. The topography was essentially identical, but in his current situation it looked anything but familiar to Fernandez. Ten minutes before, when looking down at the interior of his home island, he saw green mountains, easy winding roads whose corners hid friendly bars and restaurants. He saw children swinging from rope swings into the river at El Yunque. He saw happy old men playing dominoes and drinking beer in Isabela town center. The land that lay below him now looked nothing of the kind. It looked like a dusty wasteland full of people who wanted to kill him.

He laughed as he realized how easily Gonzalez had managed to get into his head. What was he looking at exactly on the eastern approach to the Dominican Republic? Some of the greatest beaches in the Caribbean. Starting in the 70s Punta Cana had become a major worldwide tourist destination and now boasted countless high end and all inclusive resorts. From the plane the area looked like a golden rim, the dangerous part Fernandez was contemplating lie just beyond. Most coming for the fun would only see it at 65 mph through the hotel van's window.

The real island now came into view. Higuey, La Romana, San Pedro de Macoris, the human raw material factory that fed the resort engine. How many would think it was fair? Or was it as he'd suspected before, how many would even expect it to be fair? In a way, people like that were the most dangerous.

If the system is supposed to work you can bitch about it being broken. You could basically spend your life bitching about it being broken, waiting to get yours. When you ultimately didn't you'd become bitter and die, rooting for some fucking football team that never wins. But that's as far as it went, that's the worst that could happen. You'd be dead but you hadn't killed or affected anyone else. Your all encompassing gripe against the rest of the world was now silenced in a yawning abyss of indifference. Nobody cared about you.

A society that told everyone they were important produced

well-behaved citizens because they tended to spend their whole lives waiting for something to happen. Such brilliance eventually must be rewarded no?

No.

The land which the aircraft now began it's approach was no such place. Come to think of it, Fernandez mused, neither was most of the world.

If you were never told you were important you didn't expect the game to be fair. If you didn't expect the game to be fair you realized you had to make things happen.

There were good and bad ways of making things happen. Fernandez's business dealt with the bad ways, the good ways were not his concern. There were only two things that might intimidate one away from choosing the bad way. First were the ethical ramifications, represented in this part of the world by the Catholic Church. Second was the law. Both were identical in as much that they motivated by fear of reprisal, one supernatural the other terrestrial.

If you didn't buy religion, or at least weren't too bothered by it, that left the police. And the police in the Dominican Republic were just as likely to rob you too, or at the very least ask for a bribe. So what kind of example does that set?

Get away with whatever you can and get paid.

Fernandez was now wading into a pool of such people without a life vest. There were Tirso Guerra's children, possibly Tirso Guerra himself, maybe some officials, lawyers, could there be air traffic controllers, who knew at this point? A knot of miscreants. People who had possibly done some very bad things and were undoubtedly prepared to continue this policy to either get paid or save their ass.

And Fernandez was willing to bet none of them were ever told they were important.

As the capital came into view, Fernandez allowed himself a glance at the ocean off Boca Chica. He imagined Tirso at the bottom, his plane and his person still intact sitting upright on a low, sandy plain. Tirso was calmly operating the controls, trying to take off out of the sea, oblivious to the fact he was hundreds of feet underwater. The scene was wispy and ghostly white. As soon as the jet touched down it evaporated into bubbles.

Bill Morales could see a middle-aged, white haired man gesticulating wildly in the wheelhouse. His shirt was soaked right through in the brutal afternoon heat. The woman he was talking to took mercy on him and activated the retractable bimini to give him some shade. It didn't seem to improve his mood. He sat down in the captain's chair exasperated and covered his face with his hands. The woman put a sympathetic hand on his shoulder.

If Morales wanted to hear what they were saying, he'd have to get in closer.

He'd casually parked his taxi in front of the marina's convenience store. In full view. There was absolutely nothing odd going on here, just a cabbie innocently waiting to pick someone up. He'd purchased a bag of Doritos and was munching on them to complete the disguise.

When Fernandez told him about the Revenge, Astor Marina was the first place he'd checked. It berthed some of the most opulent and unnecessarily large watercraft in the Caribbean. He'd trawled the docks the previous night only to find the boat in question empty and locked. He gave up and went back to the

Sandbar to enjoy more flirting from Shelly. When he returned the next afternoon, he could immediately spot the arguing couple in the elevated cockpit.

Fernandez had briefed him on the particulars. If the angry man was in fact Tirso Jr., his story would seem to check out, but the guy seemed to be much older than he thought Tirso Jr. would be. Morales realized the only way he was going to be any kind of help to Fernando was if he could get some information, and that was going to be tricky. Between his cab and the Revenge lay a treeless, empty parking lot and a stretch of sun-soaked gleaming white dock. For the amount of attention he'd be drawing to himself he might as well be dressed up as a pirate with a parrot on his shoulder squawking "pieces of eight! pieces of eight!"

Then he saw it. The lower level of the dock extended behind the store. He could circle round back and jump down. At water level, his approach to the Revenge would likely be obscured by the other large vessels closer in. He could then hide behind a large storage box he saw next to the boat. Thing was he wouldn't know for sure if he'd be invisible until he was visible. He sat munching and deciding if he wanted to take the risk.

"Don't do anything stupid, Rambo," Fernandez had warned him the night before. "Just stay out of sight and see what you can see. I'm not expecting anything, Bill. These are likely desperate people and there's is absolutely no reason to risk your ass, ok? Any information would be helpful at this point."

"You got it, Sherlock," Morales had replied. The two had spent their entire relationship referring to each other as fictional characters and Morales was quickly running out of detectives.

The man was up again, talking agitatedly. The woman steadied him, likely afraid the man was going to go overboard. He didn't look armed. The woman was in a swimsuit and running shorts. Of course there was the possibility of a gun on the boat, but Gonzalez's gut feeling was the two weren't dangerous in the traditional sense. Besides, they were in broad daylight and there was a manned Coast Guard cutter moored at the end of the westernmost dock.

Having devoured the Doritos he bought a sandwich and Coke from the shop. He was just a guy who liked the water and was looking for a shady spot to eat his lunch.

"You guys got a bathroom?" he asked the attendant.

"Yeah, it's around back. Here's the key."

Morales unlocked the bathroom, opened the door and let it close. He left the key on top of a pile of cinder blocks and jumped down to the dock's lower level. Immediately he realized he was right, the larger boats completely blocked the view. He easily made his way to the storage locker of the boat alongside the Revenge, sat down and quietly unwrapped his sandwich. The woman spoke softly but the man was loud and clear.

"Do you think these people are asking around just for the fun of it? You guys fucked it all up! Idiots," he didn't yell, but was forceful, in a scolding kind of way.

"It wasn't me, it was Junior!" she said apologetically.

Morales left the Coke can unpopped and took a mayonnaise filled bite of the soggy sandwich. Not Junior then, who was this guy?

"Couldn't he wait a little longer? Christ, a family is not supposed to give up hope on a disappeared father in as little as five months!" the guy said. He sounded to Morales like a man astounded by incompetence.

"It's done, we have no choice but to move forward," the

woman explained calmly.

"And now what have we got? The whole thing's blown, dammit we should have told them."

"Stop beating yourself up, please. You couldn't have known he would have been so staggeringly moronic. I'm surprised myself," she said.

"I should have known, the lush," the man sighed with supreme resignation. "We could have handled this better, you've got me all whipped up about this project. I should have been paying closer attention."

Morales became aware of the putter of an outboard motor far off in the distance. A small boat appeared around the headland, returning from the open ocean. It steered into the channel and seemed to be headed straight for him. There was only one occupant.

"Crap," he whispered and did his best to casually eat his sandwich and admire a large pelican sat atop a piling.

"We don't need this distraction now. There's no time to lose," the man said.

"We can bide our time! All we've got is time because tyranny never sleeps."

"Don't get all philosophical on me, young girl! You know very well what's going on and where we are going. There is most definitely a time stamp on our arrival. All this nonsense is throwing our plans out of whack!"

The small boat was getting closer. Morales realized there was no doubt, it was headed straight for him. The sole occupant looked to be a young man, maybe in his late 20s. He was in very good shape, and obviously very comfortable in the water. Even at this distance Morales could tell he had some cargo in the little boat. Nothing else to do but sit and get as much info before the boat arrived and gave away his position.

"This Fernandez guy," the man in wheelhouse continued. "I have no idea what he's looking for, snooping around. Nuñez said he was in Caguas, that he spent at least an hour talking to old loudmouth Burgos."

"Oh, Burgos," she said wistfully. "What a sweetheart. I miss him. Do you think we'll ever invite him out here again?"

"Not likely, sweetheart. Under the circumstances."

"Five years is nothing. He must have cut some kind of deal with that egomaniac Duarte. A reporter from a high school newspaper could figure it out, to say nothing of an actual private investigator. I think he fucked us all," the woman sighed.

"Nothing to do now but wait it out. Here's our guy Miguel. He will have to go on without us."

Morales could hear the guy jump out of the cockpit and walk up the boat. When he reached the bow he became visible. He was looking at the little craft and its captain.

"What's with this people?" he raged. "He was told to hide the cargo!"

"Hey!" the captain of the little boat was not addressing the Revenge. He was addressing Morales.

"Hello," he responded friendly.

"I am going to need you to move out, man," the young captain threw a line in a well practiced way. It landed at the mooring, right next to Morales' foot. Morales got up and as he took it he couldn't help but notice the young man was trying to stand in a way as to hide the cargo behind him.

"I have some business here," he explained. "Need the

space."

"Patricia, who is that?" the old guy at the upper deck stood staring wide-eyed, now aware of Morales' presence. He was no doubt trying to decide if he'd been listening, and if it mattered.

"Thanks a lot," the man said as Morales tied his line onto the dock. "I still need you to move away, Mister."

"That's ok, I was just enjoying lunch and watching the birds," Morales said nonchalantly.

"I think you can find better views elsewhere." He grinned a sneaky, sort of vicious smile. Morales decided it was probably time to go.

"Hey, Miguel, I need you up here ASAP." the man nervously looked back and forth between Morales and Miguel as he talked.

"We need the stuff, the... repair supplies quickly!"

Morales could hear Patricia moving things in the background, probably making space for the "repair supplies".

"Yes, Mr... Sir!" Miguel shot back at the boat. The nameless guy fixed a firm glare on Morales, conveying the silent message that he was not welcome.

Morales turned to walk back up to the lower dock and made his way to the store. Making apologies, he returned the bathroom key to the attendant, jumped into his cab and immediately dialed Fernando Fernandez. The line was dead.

"Mr. Fernandez, I'm not going to beat around the bush. In the entire history of aviation in the Dominican Republic a plane has only vanished without a trace twice. Once in 1947, and not again until Tirso Guerra's last year. Land or sea, we always at least find something. Always."

Ignacio Arias radiated competence. There was no mincing words, no hemming and hawing to cover his own ass in case he was wrong. Fernandez was already thrown by the Sub-Director of the Civil Aviation Institute's candor. He'd landed prepared for a long slog of double talk and buck passing. If everything went this way, he'd have the case solved by dinner.

"You don't sound convinced then, Mr. Arias."

"I'll get political for a moment though it disgusts me," he winced. "I can't answer that. This is technically an ongoing investigation. I can just give you the facts as I see them. Keep me talking Mr. Fernandez because I have a shitload of facts. As long as you keep asking questions I'll keep answering, so get your papers together and when you're ready, shoot."

Arias smiled, got up from his desk and opened the door to his office.

"Lourdes, I don't want to be disturbed for at least a half hour, ok?

"Yes Mr. Arias," chirped a voice from the other side of the door.

He went to the window. The Aviation Institute was situated right behind the Palacio Nacional. The streets outside were sprinkled with young and efficient looking government employees.

"Is it possible he landed at another airport?"

"Airport? No way, we would have easily found that too."

"Bermuda Triangle?"

"Not taking off from Santo Domingo," Arias laughed

good-naturedly. "He was on runway 1, which faces right out to sea. Ask me about the ELT."

"What about the ELT?"

"The Emergency Locator Transmitter. It's impact sensitive. Very sensitive. So sensitive that sometimes they go off on the runway. Every plane is required some kind of locator in order to receive its license."

"And Tirso Guerra's obviously didn't activate," Fernandez surmised. "Could he have tampered with it or shut it off?"

"You said it, not me."

"Was there a problem that night that would have impeded his visibility?"

"As a matter of fact, that night the full moon shone brighter than most. It was beautiful weather for flying. With the amount of ambient light from a moon like that, an expert pilot could fly without instruments, relying only on sight."

"I spoke with his family. They claim he'd called before the flight and reported a problem with the battery."

Arias turned from the window laughing and muttering a sentence that clearly contained the words "stupid" and "fuckers".

"What was that?" Fernandez asked.

"Nothing. The 501 has two jet engines, and each engine has two generators. After starting the plane the battery is no longer needed. You could throw it out the damn window, the jets produce their own energy."

"So the battery not working could have delayed him but…"

"It wouldn't have been a reason for him crashing," Arias finished. "I know that plane was sound. Hell, he had used it just a couple of days before!"

"Oh? Where did he go?"

"Cuba. Set em up Fernandez, and I'll whack em down."

Fernandez let that sink in for a moment. Here in the Dominican Republic, flying to Cuba wasn't a biggie. But Guerra was a US citizen. That kind of made it a biggie.

"Who was the last person to see him?" Fernandez asked.

"The FBO." He watched Fernandez' eyes go from interested to totally lost. "It's the Fixed-Base Operator, the one who fueled his jet. I interviewed him myself. He said Tirso appeared normal, cool as a cucumber, not under the influence of drugs or alcohol. Nothing."

"Can I ask you a stupid question, Mr. Arias?"

"Of course."

"If this is an ongoing investigation how is there a death certificate?"

"That is funny, isn't it," Arias whispered with mock surprise. He stared at Fernandez for a long second. He looked like a responsible man exhausted from a lifetime of beating his head against a wall.

"I don't have the resources to ever close this case, so to some it's already closed," he explained. "Depending on who you grease and how much you have, that could be good enough here in the land of Quisqueya. There are influential and powerful people who can push things through here just by virtue of their own will. Never forget that, Fernandez. The only question though is how it's all gonna jive with your insurance company. I'm guessing not at all."

"That's why I'm here."

"Indeed. You're not going to have to dig very deep, but that's not the point. There are some particularly nasty critters that aren't going to like being exposed, and they'll bite you without even thinking twice."

"I understand."

Arias' assistant entered the room and laid a styrofoam take-out box and a large, bulky file in front of him. As he opened the box steam wafted up and a heavy aroma filled the room.

"Sancocho?" Fernandez offered.

"Nothing but the best. Here, I had Lourdes make copies of everything," he said handing Fernandez the binder.

"There's audio tapes and videos, the flight plan, pre-flight checklists, audio communications with the control tower, everything. I don't think it's going to be hard to deprive these people of the money; I'm still desperate to know what really happened. But like I said, I don't have the resources," Arias repeated apologetically.

"Thank you so much Mr. Arias. You've been more than helpful."

Fernandez got up to leave. When he was halfway out the door Arias called to him.

"Hey, Fernandez!"

"Yes?"

"Do you like facts about airplanes? Say yes."

"Yes."

"Me too. There's this plane called the Cessna 501. You wouldn't know by looking at it, and not a lot of people know this. In a pinch, given the right pilot, it's easy to land it on the water. Have a nice day!"

He returned his full attention to the Sancocho.

Fernandez wasn't able to quite place the acrid odor that he was experiencing. It was like a combination of sulfur, dust and brush fire. Having spent a nail biting hour negotiating the chaotic streets on the outskirts of the capital, he was finally cruising smoothly on route 4 bound for La Romana. It was an open and easy evening ride, the brand new highway was wide and uncongested. The only stress came from the occasional motorbike buzzing past him like an annoying bumblebee. Not quite big enough to call motorcycle, and not quite small enough to call moped, whatever they were they certainly didn't look spec'd for highway travel to Fernandez.

The smell undoubtedly had something to do with the huge cement processing plant in San Pedro de Macoris, the town and MLB player factory that was halfway between the capital and his destination. Maybe it was also combined with the fires set during sugarcane harvesting. Whatever the source, it was overwhelming even with the windows firmly shut.

La Romana. He'd never been. Like most tourists he'd only driven past, and it had looked like a difficult and confusing place at the time. If the bikes were bees La Romana was the hive. It's streets positively teemed with the things, darting out of blind alleyways and trying to squeeze through spaces you'd think twice about walking through. He remembered thinking at the time the hotel van driver was some kind of genius savant for being able to pay attention to it all and not hit any of them.

And now he was headed there, alone in an economy rental car that wasn't much less flimsy than the bikes.

After his visit with Ignacio Arias, Fernandez had called the

Civil Registry in La Romana. Even with his fluent Spanish he was bounced around and double talked in much the same manner Dirk Saban reported. Only after he stressed he was "conducting an investigation" and threw a bit of gringo into his accent did things start to happen.

"FBI?" the clerk asked.

"Yes, Special Agent Fernandez," he lied.

He was immediately put through to the Registrar and granted a meeting with her assistant at 7:30 the next morning. Clearly when the feds said jump, they jumped. It was dangerous and illegal to impersonate an agent, though. What if they asked for credentials? He decided that if this happened he'd play dumb. From now on, he worked for Federated Bankers Insurance

With one night to kill in La Romana, he was planning on lying low.

Fernandez was mostly impressed with how he fared on the streets. He'd kept the windows open and stayed alert with both hands on the wheel. He'd also taken Gonzalez's advice and not expected people to stop at red lights. He had a couple close scrapes that caused him to groan nervously.

Starting to feel cocky and local he turned on the radio and hung one arm out the window, experiencing that momentary rush of excitement one feels when first tapping into the verve of a new place. Then he turned a blind corner and almost barreled into a crowd of people hanging outside a nightclub. They yelled in annoyance and several approached the car brandishing beer bottles like billy clubs. Fernandez reversed with one hand up, accepting blame.

He wondered why they were so surprised, as they were spilled out into the street in such a dangerous way. But then he realized only a tourist would not know about the corner, and there were no tourists here. So much for going under the radar.

When he finally found his hotel, The River View, he was such a ball of nerves he decided the car would remain parked for the night. The concierge directed him to a sandwich shop across the street for a bite.

When Fernandez walked through the open storefront flies were buzzing around the sticky counter. The shopkeeper quickly grabbed a rag and started to wipe it down, no doubt noticing an unfamiliar face. He was business casual, still in his blazer from the meeting with Arias. Around here, though, he looked like he could have been a Cabinet Minister.

"Sorry, just about to close, sir. What can I get for you?" He pointed to the wall behind Fernandez.

Fernandez turned to see a cruddy, yellow sign boasting about fifty different kinds of sandwich and fruit juices written in pale aquamarine.

"The juice is all natural sir," he explained although Fernandez hadn't asked.

"Do you have beer?"

"No, but I can get you one. Presidente?"

"Yes."

"Jumbo?"

"Yes. I know you guys say it tastes different here in the motherland," Fernandez laughed.

"It sure does. I know the Irish say that about Guinness too. I tried it once, ick, like black soup. Hector!"

An emaciated short man with a face like a wallet appeared out of nowhere. The shopkeeper gave him a sign and he took off down the street.

"He'll get it for you. So you're from out of town?"

"Yes."

"You're lucky you came to the right place. These are the best sandwiches you're gonna get. My name is Diego. If there's anything you need, just let me know."

"Thanks. I'll just have a ham and cheese."

"You got it. Do you want me to turn on the TV?"

"That's ok."

"How about the radio, I can put on some music," Diego searched Fernandez's face, trying too hard.

"Diego no, that's fine. Everywhere else is so loud I like the relative peace and quiet," Fernandez explained.

"Suit yourself," he smiled and went about preparing the sandwich.

After three minutes Hector appeared again. He gave Fernandez his beer and asked for 80 pesos. When he tipped him a US dollar Hector's face lit up like Fernandez had just squared away the rest of his weekend. He looked to the back of the shop, confusingly stuck his tongue out, and ran off. Diego delivered his ham and cheese.

"Buen provecho," came a squeaky voice from the darkness behind him.

Thinking up until this point he was the only patron, Fernandez spun on his stool surprised and found the intended recipient of Hector's rude gesture. The voice belonged to an old woman sitting on the last stool of the counter busying herself with what looked like a crossword. She didn't look up. Fernandez could only describe her appearance as nun-like.

"I don't think Hector likes you very much," he offered.

"He can go fuck himself," she said, her eyes still glued to the puzzle.

"Benedictus qui venit."

The old woman looked up and smiled deviously at Fernandez. She jumped down off the stool and rushed toward him at an alarming speed considering her vintage. He tried to play it cool but instinctively recoiled a bit, and for reasons he didn't understand took a defensive posture over his sandwich.

"Don't mess with me, ugly!" she snapped poking him in the gut repeatedly with a tiny bony finger. Even though Fernandez was sitting she still had to look up at him.

"Easy Mother Teresa," he shot back, lifting his sandwich over his head.

This further infuriated her and she began poking at him harder, staring up at him with a determination that suggested she believed she'd eventually kill him through sheer persistence. Some pans smashed to the floor in the back room and Diego emerged tripping over them and waving his arms in large concentric circles. His mouth and eyes were wide open in shock and anger. It was a look of determination probably invented specifically for the woman, as he didn't strike Fernandez a confrontational man.

"Oh no no no no! No way! Maria Evarista we've talked about this. Don't make me throw you out again."

"It's really alright," Fernandez panted. "She's not hurting me."

"It doesn't matter sir. Get off of him Maria Evarista. Cut it out!"

Diego grabbed for the first thing available, a large roll of pan de agua and tried to beat the woman about the face with it. The roll was too large and soft; it buckled in the middle halfway through his first strike and harmlessly bounced off the top of her head. In defiance she ripped a piece off with her mouth and began to chew it, cackling like a witch. Fernandez couldn't help himself and burst out laughing. Diego wasn't sure what to do.

"He's being sarcastic. He's mocking my fucking devoutness!" she yelled at Diego.

"I truly am sorry ma'am. Look, do you think you can stop poking me now?"

Satisfied with the apology, Maria Evarista relented and spent a few seconds in silence looking him up and down, trying to categorize the stranger in the suit. After awhile she jumped up onto the stool next to him.

"Oh leave him alone," Diego whined.

Maria Evarista ignored him. Diego had already exerted the sum of authority he had in him. She faced downward and looked at Fernandez though the tops of her eye sockets. She looked like a miniature Jack Nicholson.

"What do you need to know, good looking?"

"Excuse me," Fernandez exclaimed, nearly choking on his sandwich. "Didn't you just call me ugly?"

"I know everything in this town. I'm from the mountains but I came here to the big city when I was only nine. I've been here ever since."

"The big city huh? How many years then?" Fernandez taunted.

"Don't be a dick. I know how old I am. You think you come from fancy Puerto Rico, that's right, I know your accent. You think you come from that fancy place and we're just a bunch of uneducated rednecks?" she said confidently.

"You're determined to fight someone tonight, aren't you? Can't a man just sit and enjoy his sandwich in peace? Anyway, don't get all offended on me. Isn't that the same thing you people think about the Haitians?"

"That's different."

"Why?"

"Because they're black, stupid," she explained.

"Of course," he relented. Apparently he hadn't been talking to a black person all along. This was, no doubt, a complicated set of parameters that he had no wish to delve further into. Maria Evarista stayed right where she was, she wasn't going anywhere. For a second he had the automatic urge to hand over some money so she'd leave but decided against it. It would likely insult her further. She was fiercely proud.

"Why do you think I need to know something."

"Because a man like you only comes to a street like this to cause a problem. You're looking for someone or something. You're working for someone rich or important who should have better things to do than harass the kind of people that live around here."

Man she was quick, he thought.

"Maria I'm not here to cause you…"

"No don't get me wrong," she interrupted. "I don't give a shit about any of these assholes. No one in this place has ever done anything for me. I'm just saying, I know the score. Maybe

I know something that's worth something to you, that's all."

She did want money, he thought. But she didn't want it in the form of a handout.

"Ok I'll play along, Maria. I work for an insurance company. I'm looking to find stuff out about a man who used to live here. He had an accident about a year ago," Fernandez explained.

"What kind of accident?" her eyes widened. Diego stopped what he was doing as well and returned to a state of tense nervousness.

"Plane crash."

"Tirso Guerra!" she threw her hands into the air.

"Oh Jesus Christ not again," Diego sighed.

"It was on a night just like this," she shut her eyes and her voice became a quavering drone, like she was delivering a sermon.

"No Maria Evarista!" Diego barked as if he was scolding a child.

"I got the call the very next morning from my sister in the capital," she started wiggling her hands as if conjuring a spell. "He was dead. I was the first to know!" She opened her eyes and looked heavenward, bringing both hands to rest over her heart.

Fernandez couldn't have known the enthusiasm he had provoked, giving the marginalized old crone a second act. He sat back in wonder at the show he was watching. She closed her eyes once more and delicately extended her arm to rest her hand on his shoulder.

"If there's anything you need to know," she whispered. "Ask

me." The last two words were barely audible.

"I'm just looking for friends or family," he smiled at Diego.

She opened her eyes and looked disappointed.

"That's it?" she asked.

"Yes."

"He has a sister in Buena Vista."

In all his research Fernandez had turned up no specifics about Tirso Sr.'s siblings. He'd assumed they were either dead or had remained in Cuba after the revolution.

"Her name is Rosalind," Maria explained returning to the back of the shop and her crossword puzzle. "She lives in the big white house on Las Palmas."

"Thanks."

"Don't thank me yet. She won't let you in. She never leaves that house and never talks to anybody. Good luck, ugly."

Fernandez polished off the rest of his ham and cheese, amazed that the chance visit to a sandwich shop had yielded something. He made a mental note to check in on Rosalind after he visited the Registry and took the remainder of his beer across the street to his hotel. As he settled down on the bed to watch some television, he got a call from Bill Morales.

"Dude, where have you been?" Morales asked excitedly.

"Sorry Bill, it took a few hours to get it set up with the phone company. I didn't want to get killed on the roaming. What's up?"

"Wait till you hear this."

The conversation with Bill had been short, and Fernandez's instructions had been brief. He wasn't surprised the vet still had an ancient flip phone without a camera. Thinking ahead Morales had bought an equally dated disposable camera before their talk. Even though Bill assured him he wasn't threatened by those people in the slightest, Fernandez still cautioned him to keep his distance and take no unnecessary risks. In times of desperation, desperate men were capable of ignoring their programming.

He thanked Bill for his effort but inside bemoaned the lost opportunity. Whoever the hell the nameless guy was, his ass was going to be on lock down inside the Revenge for the foreseeable future. On his way to the registry, Bill confirmed via text that the boat was still there. Fernandez firmly expected it to be gone by the end of the day.

In preparation for his visit to the Registry, he double-checked the camera pack on his hip, making sure the correct lights were on. After the fiasco at the hospital earlier that summer he'd become obsessive about his equipment. This time he decided to go with the recording glasses. It left his hands free, and he thought the glasses added to the Special Agent persona. The glasses were slightly tinted, but not so much as to impair his vision indoors. They gave him the air of cool and casual.

The death certificate was unquestionably fishy. He was going in determined to get information from whoever the Registrar had arranged for him to meet. This was no interview, he was in full interrogation mode. Time to get some answers.

The Civil Registry in La Romana was located in the same building as the police station. As Fernandez approached the plaza in front he found four tight huddles of frustrated people, no doubt waiting impotently for news of their misbehaving relative or friend held within.

Each group featured a woman at the center, either a wife, girlfriend or mother Fernandez guessed, with 3 or 4 friends or family members in sympathy orbit, nodding their heads and occasionally sighing as the source of gravity ranted and gestured toward the adjacent building in anger.

Fernandez wondered, had it been a particularly epic night, or was this typical on any given morning? He got the feeling that in this town, people didn't really need any excuse to have fun.

Inside the station there was an unattended main desk and two smaller ones on either side. On the wall behind hung about 35 terribly self important hand-painted portraits of various uniformed men. In a nation of so many colors they were all white as snow. Instead of "officer" or "sergeant" they all had grandiose titles like "Brigadier General". They stared defensively down, almost daring him to meddle.

This wasn't a part of the United States, there was a different big brother here. This big brother wasn't an overachieving goodie goodie who constantly lectured you, but a bully who punched you in the nuts and stole your lunch money. He was suddenly hit with the highly disconcerting realization that he wasn't dealing so much with an organization of public servants, but with a gang.

All the furniture and paneling was wood and the place reeked of a heavy, musty odor. It felt to Fernandez more like an old library or historical site. Police milled around, completely ignoring him. There was one officer sat behind the left desk looking extremely bored and important. Having spent the morning dealing with the women outside Fernandez guessed he'd be in a great mood.

"Excuse me, I am looking for the Civil Registry."

He didn't look up.

"Sir?" Fernandez persisted.

"What do you want?" he asked still not looking up.

"The Civil Registry, it's in this building. I have an appointment. Can you just tell me…"

"It's not here. That's in Santo Domingo. You have to go to Santo Domingo," he said loudly, with 100% certainty.

"But they told me it was…"

"Look, I'm not going to tell you again. It's not here. You have to go to Santiago."

"What? Santiago?"

The officer made the supreme effort of standing up. He approached Fernandez, gently took him by the elbow, and started nudging him toward the door.

"You're not allowed to be in here, this area has to be clear of civilians. People aren't allowed to wait in here. Go outside and wait in the front with everyone else."

Fernandez looked to the side and inexplicably saw a small waiting area with a water cooler and a television set. There were a few elderly people sitting and some open chairs. Beyond them lie a door that was labeled Civil Registry of La Romana.

"Look man, there it is!" he said pointing to the door.

"No that's another thing. It's in Santo Domingo, you'll have to leave," he persisted. The officer had about pushed Fernandez to the door. It opened catching him in the back. Another officer walked through.

"Let me in, dammit," the new officer said.

"Look, can I go through that door please?" Fernandez asked

him. "I have an appointment."

"That's the Civil Registry. It's closed today."

"It's in Santo Domingo, Fuentes," the first officer continued to assert to the second.

"No, it's right there, Jose," the second explained.

"Did they move it?"

"It's been there for 20 years, man."

"They must have moved it." Jose unhanded Fernandez and went back to his desk muttering. After being contradicted he clearly had no further interest in the situation. And all the sudden Fernandez's presence was no longer a security risk.

"Anyway, sir it's closed today," the second officer said walking away as well. "You'll have to come back tomorrow."

Fernandez then simply opened the door and walked through.

The scene waiting for him inside the Registry was worse than the one outside. People were all over the place, screaming and pushing one another in a desperate attempt to speak to anybody that looked official. Those who were actually employees of the Registry were going about their business, listening to some and ignoring most.

"Special Agent Fernandez?" came a short, nervous voice from the other end of the room. "I'm Carlos Montoya."

He couldn't see Montoya as he was momentarily blinded by the sun pouring through large windows directly in front of him. After his eyes adjusted, a little guy frantically waiving his arms trying to get his attention came into view. He checked the camera again, and made sure it was recording.

Fernandez made his way to Montoya, pushing and shoving a fair amount of people along the way. By the time he got to the other end of the room, he could see that Montoya was sweating profusely in his suit. Fernandez extended a hand. Montoya grabbed it too fast and agitatedly shook four of Fernandez fingers with an apologetic look on his face.

"The Registrar regrets she could not receive you herself as her mother is ill and she is off the island," he explained. Making detailed excuses for high ranking officials, Fernandez began to gauge how important they thought he was. This was delicate. The less said the better. Montoya looked like he was ready to do a whole lot of talking anyway.

"Have a seat please."

Jesus he really is sweating, Fernandez thought.

"How can I help you, Agent Fernandez?"

"First of all, I want to thank you for agreeing to see me in such short notice."

He wasn't prepared for small talk. He didn't answer, he just nodded.

"Well anyway I'm conducting an investigation into the disappearance of a man named Tirso Guerra, and I need a copy of his death certificate."

He stood up fast.

"Give me a moment." Montoya quickly disappeared through a back door. Fernandez was left feeling a little disoriented, surrounded by the hoards of people looking for attention, some of which were looking at him with contempt. He could only guess they were miffed at how quickly he got service.

"Can you come with me?" Montoya was back in no time.

"Excuse me?"

"Follow me."

He led Fernandez out the back of the office and up four flights of stairs. He unlocked the door at the top and walked out onto the roof of the building, motioning to follow him. Fernandez's instinct was that he wasn't in any danger, but he still walked out onto the roof cautiously and kept Montoya between him and the ledge.

"Come, I have your document."

"Why don't you come to me, Mr. Montoya," Fernandez asked. He'd situated himself as far away from the ledge as possible, his back to a large condenser. He adjusted the glasses on his face, as to get a clearer picture of the whole setup.

Montoya looked genuinely perplexed.

"What do you think I'm going to do? I'm the one in trouble, right?" he said walking toward Fernandez.

"Well that all depends," Fernandez played along. "Let's hear it, Carlos."

Montoya lit a cigarette and closed the door leading to the stairwell. He came in close, and handed Fernandez a paper. It was Guerra's Death Certificate, dated five months after his disappearance.

"When Duarte came to me I registered the death, but I didn't register the certificate. Registering the death means nothing legally. You can't do anything with it. I told him in order to register the certificate he'd have to go to the court and verify them under warrant. Honestly, I didn't think I'd see him again after that. When he came back with the correct documents I was shocked, it had only been 5 months. He was able to get it done and what's more, he thinks no one is gonna say shit. The ego is off the charts. He thinks he's invincible."

"You don't mean Felipe Duarte, do you?"

"Yeah, who else? I felt bulldozed the entire time. I didn't feel I had a choice, Mr. Fernandez. It's almost like the President walked in here and started telling me what to do. I couldn't say no. He's totally in bed with half the government, he would have just gotten me fired and put someone else in here. Now I'm probably going to get fired anyway. The motherfucker, I need this job. I have four kids dammit!"

Felipe Duarte was the son of the most prominent and high profile lawyer in the Dominican Republic, a national celebrity. His father achieved his notoriety chiefly by getting corrupt politicians and policemen off the hook. Montoya was right. Half the government and local authorities were indebted to the Duartes in some way. As the heir to the principal actor in a corrupt system, Felipe had carte blanche. Considering his reputation, getting fired should have been the least of Montoya's fears. Fernandez sympathized; the poor guy was in an impossible situation. The President? No. It would have been like one of the Sopranos walked in his office.

"I had to tell Diana, that's what I feel the worst about. Now she's fucked too."

"Diana?" Fernandez asked.

"The Registrar!" he yelled exasperatedly. "That's why she told me to meet with you today. You can help us. I got you the copy but you have to do something for us."

"What do you want?"

"You're an official of the United States government. Even Duarte and his people will care about that. You have to inform the investigation that I was coerced into this by Duarte. That I was scared of losing my job, or worse. It might save our ass. Make something up. Tell them I said he threatened to kill my kids," he flicked the cigarette off the roof and grabbed the top of his head with both hands.

Fernandez kept his poker face. He didn't know what Montoya was talking about when he said "investigation". The man was getting more and more agitated. He was clearly nearing the end of his rope, or maybe considering buying one.

"I'm actually a little confused as to your interest," Montoya offered. "Why are you here anyway?"

"Tirso Guerra was an American citizen and there is reason to suspect foul play considering the circumstances," Fernandez made it up as he went.

"Oh I don't know anything about that. He's just a name on a piece of paper."

Montoya walked over to the ledge and looked down. He swung his arms back and forth like a bored child. A casualness had crept into his manner that Fernandez found alarming. He rushed over and put his hand on his shoulder.

"Don't worry," Montoya smiled weakly. "It's not high enough anyway. What good would I be to my family paralyzed?"

This confirmed he'd at least been thinking about it. Fernandez knew thinking and doing were two hugely different things. Carlos Montoya might be in a hard place, but Fernandez's gut feeling was that he wasn't the type to kill himself.

"Mr. Montoya, I'm not going to lie, I am functioning alone right now. I have no ties to... the investigation," Fernandez quickly changed the subject, prodding for information.

"I don't know if it has started yet. I've only heard rumors that the Central Election Board is going to set up a commission. Listen, Agent Fernandez, I never thought even Duarte had the clout to get those documents. I think everyone is going to go down, even him. Just please tell them what I've said. There's something else I should mention. I'm just going to come right out and say it. He gave me $300 US dollars."

"Well that's certainly not going to look good," Fernandez observed.

"He made me take it. He knew he would have me by the balls when he came back. Look," he took his wallet out of his pocket and started to fish around inside. He produced a piece of paper and pushed it into Fernandez's hand.

"I gave all of it to the church of St. Rose. I didn't want it. Like I said, he forced me to take it."

Fernandez examined the receipt. It had a stained glass window and cross drawing in the upper right corner. The close juxtaposition of the ecclesiastical and terrestrial seemed kind of funny.

"I guess you gotta account for it all at tax time," he said.

"I just want to be 100% honest with you about what happened. It's all there, the entire truth. Will you help us?"

Fernandez felt genuinely sorry for the harried and hunted man who was staring at him pleadingly. What really could he do or say? He reported to Dirk Saban and Interference International. He'd never confirmed he was FBI but he'd let Montoya go down this road of false hope.

"I promise I'll do everything I can, Mr. Montoya."

"Thank you," his eyes were wet and he shook Fernandez's hand vigorously. "Thank you."

Fernandez followed Montoya back into the office, shutting off the camera as he went down.

Fernandez piloted his rental car around the empty streets of Buena Vista. The area couldn't have been more on the other side of the tracks. A quiet and tree lined center of affluence a mere stone's throw from the riotous, moped choked streets. In fact, Fernandez could even see the poor side of town he'd just left through gaps between the houses that didn't have opaque security gates.

In all his travels he could not recall the haves and the have nots ever being in such close geographic proximity. Most of the properties looked like they employed their own armed security guards.

As he neared the end of Las Palmas he spotted the house the old lady at the sandwich shop described. It was Spartan and chalky white. There were no plants or indeed anything living at all from the looks of it. It sat dead and sunbaked, radiating a kind of angry isolation. He eased his car onto the median across the street.

He placed the lapel wired microphone on his jacket very carefully as he wanted to get the best possible audio of the meeting, which he suspected would turn into an interview of the sister. The microphone couldn't be seen, and the wire connecting it to the little recorder in his pocket had to be secured. At this point, he would take no chances, and avoid all risks.

He realized there was no security guard or security system. There was also no way of making one's presence known. It was 9am, and there should have been someone awake by then.

"Hello!"

Nothing. He leaned against the gate to take a look inside the patio. It creaked open. With such comparative lax security he began to suspect the house was abandoned. Then he arrived at a front door, an impregnable iron monolith. The surface was smooth and featureless, there were no handles. Visions of a pharaoh's tomb came to mind. Was one even meant to enter?

The windows on the house looked like the slits on a castle that archers would use. He realized why there was no security, it wasn't needed. The place was a bunker. There was no way in.

Suddenly he heard a loud beep from inside and the door slowly swung open. He realized the tomb comment wasn't far off the mark. Before him stood a skeleton of a woman with her hand on a wall mounted control panel. She was dressed in a similar fashion to Maria Evarista, but even more humble. Just looking at her heavy white dress made Fernandez want to scratch himself. It seemed specifically designed for self mortification. Her necklace looked like someone had fashioned a cross by tying two random sticks together and strung them around her head with a thin, dead vine. Fernandez wondered if the women in town were participating in some kind of competition.

"Can I help you?" Her voice was remarkably smooth and unperturbed. He was expecting a croak or cackle.

"Yes. Thank you ma'am. I'm sorry but the gate was open and I…"

"Can I help you," she repeated.

"I am looking for Rosalind Guerra," he explained.

"You've found her, Fernando Fernandez," she stated plainly.

For the first time he could remember, Fernandez was utterly at a loss for words.

"You better come inside. Don't worry, I'm not going to hurt you. I promise."

Fernandez floated inside the house on a cloud of bewilderment and apprehension. He followed Rosalind though to the living room. The entire place looked like a monastery. She motioned him to sit down on a hard, uncomfortable wooden chair. Fernandez finally found his voice.

"How?"

"I'm in touch with certain entities."

For a second, given her appearance, Fernandez thought Rosalind was wondering into the spiritual. The fact she knew who he was threatened to supremely freak him out, but he calmed.

"Your brother," Fernandez guessed.

"My brother is dead, Mr. Fernandez. His plane crashed into the water off Boca Chica last year. Didn't you know that?" she taunted him.

She got up and retrieved a frame from a table. It was as far as Fernandez could see the only thing that approached an ornament in the place. She handed it to him. It was a black and white photo of girl about 20 and a boy about 12. Behind the two was visible an enormous chalky white house in much the same style as Rosalind's. Upon examination, Fernandez realized that Rosalind's house looked like a half size replica of the estate in the photo.

"This is you and your brother Tirso Guerra, the deceased," he said, trying to get a definite identification for the recording.

"Yes, that's us, in another life," she lamented, although her voice did not betray sadness as much as an old acceptance.

"I miss him terribly and I love him," she continued.

Fernandez handed her back the frame.

"No Mr. Fernandez I am not receiving communication from my brother beyond the grave. Who I am in touch with is of no consequence to you. However, what they have been telling me is of the utmost consequence," she explained.

"What is that?"

"You are in danger. Today, right now as we speak. I'll try and explain. There are three parties who stand to gain a lot of money, correct? The first doesn't care about the money. The second would like the money, but could essentially take it or leave it because it has other priorities. I myself am a woman of other priorities, but mine motivated me to leave the material world and all it's empty temptations a long time ago, so it's well known I am not the fourth party, that in fact, there is no fourth party to share the money with."

"I see." Fernandez was looking at a woman so perfectly wronged by life she'd decided to abandon it.

"This second party I talked about has my sympathy and support. They will get along fine with their preoccupations and causes. Money is instrumental and can be extremely useful if you are ethically sound. Which brings me to the last party, those who need the money desperately and will do anything to get it. This party does not have my sympathy. Call it cruel, but I believe this party must be held accountable for their actions in this life, whatever that may entail," she said.

"And this is the party coming after me?" he asked.

"They don't have the courage," she laughed. "But they could easily find someone who does. Tell me Mr. Fernandez, what do you think of my adopted country?"

He was startled by the change of subject.

"I haven't been here long enough to form an opinion," he lied.

"Ha! Let me help you form an opinion. Until you got here it

was entirely within the realm of possibility that Felipe Duarte could make this happen. He's rich and influential enough to compromise an investigation if there is one. He's got more riding on it than his reputation."

"Tirso Jr. is going to split the money with Duarte," Fernandez guessed.

"But you coming in from the outside is threatening to screw all that up Mr. Fernandez. Do you see what I am saying now?" she smiled.

He began to. Duarte could easily have handled Montoya and the Registrar, and paid off the committee. He could have had people continue to run Saban in circles until the death certificate was proven legit. But now Fernando Fernandez had personally landed and his boots were on the ground. He'd found out what actually happened and was on the verge of making it public.

"Why are you telling me this?" he asked.

"The fact the two of them think they can get away with it offends me," she explained. "I asked you what you thought of this country. I'll tell you that I love it. It's where I feel at home. It might not look it, but it is full of good people who know the right thing but are too afraid to do it. I have no fear of anyone but God. We may not be perfect but we're free. And we're trying, a little at a time. I have to believe that."

"Thank you Rosalind." He shut off the recorder surreptitiously.

"Your next stop should be the airport," she said.

"That's incredible. I mean, the balls on that guy."

"Do you know him, Julio?" Fernandez said into his phone as he drove to Tirso Guerra's place of business in San Pedro De Macoris.

Although he didn't have this stop on his agenda, he decided it couldn't hurt to pay a visit after the morning's events. Rosalind Guerra's warnings notwithstanding, he was curious to compare the state of affairs between his businesses in the Dominican and Puerto Rico.

"Duarte? I had a couple run ins with his father. This was awhile ago, though. He wasn't the man he is today. Well, looks like that's that then."

"Yeah, I just sent the report to Saban. I need something from you though. Rosalind seems to be safe, but this guy Montoya is a fly caught in a fucking spider web. I want to find out everything I can about this investigation. Can you make some calls?"

"Me?"

"Problem?"

"No...I," Gonzalez stammered. Fernandez realized it was the first time he'd ever asked him for help on anything substantive. The old man was no doubt taken aback by the unfamiliarity of feeling useful and trusted. It had been a long time, no doubt.

"What do you need?" The efficient, no nonsense Long Island edge snapped back into his voice. Now it was Fernandez's turn to be taken aback and he couldn't help but smile.

"Something about a committee formed by the Central Election Board to investigate the death certificate. I just need you to verify it's existence and try and get a contact number for me. Do you have anyone you can call?"

"Yes, a friend of a friend like. I'll get to the bottom of it."

"Leave that to me, Columbo. Just get me a number, a name, anything. I don't have the time to be dicking around with the government right now. I'm not walking in there cold. I'll lose it."

He pulled into what his GPS said was the front of Hurricane Hardware's main office in the Dominican Republic. A huge gate impeded his entrance.

"Ok. You're thinking an investigation will solidify Alliance's position?" Gonzalez asked.

"Yeah, there's that"

"I'll do what I can, man. So you headed back?" Gonzalez asked.

"Tomorrow, I want to check something out first."

"Fernando, if it's done and done, what's there to check out? You just most likely took a shitload of money away from someone, and the streets have ears. Don't be a dick. Leave now, you heard what the lady said. Those Dominicans don't just say things for effect," Gonzalez implored.

"You're being dramatic, and you're working me up. I thought a guy was going to throw me off a roof yesterday and he just wanted to talk. Relax, I'm just curious about something. I'll be in touch."

Gonzalez began to protest but Fernandez hung up on him and got out of the car. As he approached the gate to the offices, he started taking pictures with his camera. He brought the regular, tourist-style Nikon Semi-Pro with a photo lens. He snapped away as he took the place in.

The building was a one story, low, industrial type place, looking more like a warehouse than an office. There were almost no windows, only one, simple door to access the place, and no parking spaces in the front. He could also make out a couple of bigger, wider buildings behind the main one, but couldn't quite make out their purpose. The whole complex was painted a drab beige, and it had an air of abandonment.

All of the sudden, his camera viewer showed an unfriendly security guard approaching. An AK-47 hung on his back as he walked.

"Hello there, Sir!" Fernandez lowered the camera and put on his best salesman face.

"What can I do for you?" The guard came to a stop right in front of Fernandez, but a couple of paces back, as if to have space to sling the ugly looking gun to his front and shoot without a problem. There was an equally menacing sidearm on his hip. He must prefer the big guys.

"I'm looking for the manager? The person in charge?"

"Don't I look like I'm in charge?" the guard said threateningly.

"Ok, sir, yes, you certainly do! However, I need to talk to the business manager? The person left in place after Mr. Guerra... left?"

"And you are?"

"I work for Alliance Insurance. We are conducting an inspection of the facilities for the... property liability policy," he said, marveling at how easily the lie came to him in a moment of stress.

"We are closed. There's no one here you can see. Better be on your way." The guard's stance and demeanor had changed abruptly. He'd quickly reached his shit-taking limit.

"Well, are you closed for the day, or are you closed for good..." Fernandez cut himself short when he saw the guard caressing the leather strap that held the gun on his shoulder. He knew the man would shoot him. He could see it in his eyes. He started to retreat to his car, very slowly.

"As I said, we're closed. Good bye." The guard remained stiff as a statue, fingering his gun strap and looking straight at Fernandez as he quickly got into his car and drove away.

Fernandez didn't breath again until he was a few kilometers away from the place. Then, after a couple of deep, shaky breaths, he started to think about what he'd seen, what he'd heard, and what he'd felt. He saw a strange office complex that looked abandoned. He heard nothing except the voice of the guard, who sounded edgy and defensive. Why would a guard be defensive? He was the one with a gun! And how did he feel about the short visit? Like there was something else happening, that was for sure.

He stopped the car when he felt he was far enough away. He started to check the pictures he just took of the place. He zoomed in on one of the pictures of the office building, and could barely make out a couple of cars in the back. So the place was not abandoned after all. He then looked at the other buildings in the photos.

And it hit him. The bigger buildings behind the main offices. They were hangars.

By the time Fernandez reached Santo Domingo, it was a little past 1pm, and he rushed to follow the instructions Gonzalez had texted him while he was in transit. The Central Election Board sat in a huge roundabout dead in the center of Herrera Industrial Park. Even with detailed instructions, he still got lost, driving by the Armed Forces Ministry a couple of times before finding the turn that took him to the place he was looking for.

Fernandez found a parking spot not too far away from the entrance, a small miracle, and ran inside the building only to find it deserted. He guessed the lunch break here was at one instead of noon. The only soul in the place was a lonely guard at a dilapidated desk by the front door, eating a sandwich and looking at a baseball game on a small black and white television.

Verifying this particular guard wasn't armed to the teeth, he approached the man, ignoring the "out to lunch" signed placed on the desk next to the his coffee.

"Hello! Sorry about the timing, but is there any possibility a certain Mr. Leonardo Castro is in the office right now?"

The guard didn't look at him, engrossed in the game and his lunch.

"No."

"Who's playing?" Fernandez asked.

"What's it to you?"

"I'd like to know."

"Where are you from?"

"Puerto Rico"

The guard finally looked up and broke into a devious and condescending grin.

"Damn good ball players over there! But not as good as ours."

"Hey, we got Roberto Clemente, the greatest baseball player in history!"

Fernandez hoped the conversation would not take a turn into a more detailed area as he was not an avid sports fan.

"Yeah, but he's dead. Here, the Tigres are going to flatten El Cibao. Just you wait! They are going to win the championship!"

The man may have well been reciting instructions on how to repair roofing tiles. Tigres? Cibaos? Were those towns? He decided to go with something innocuous.

"Who's on first?"

"Bonifacio"

"Nice," Fernandez breathed easier. "Hell of a player. How about Castro?"

"There is no Castro on the Tigres, man."

"No, I mean Leonardo Castro, the one that works here."

Suddenly, the guard stood up and started to jump, dropping his sandwich on the floor.

"Run! Run! Run for it, you bastard! Go, go, go!"

Fernandez got into it.

"Yeah! Run, run like a bastard!"

"Home run!" They ended up yelling it almost at the same time, Fernandez one beat behind. The two jumped in unison as they gave each other high fives.

"Wooo! So how about Castro?"

"He's having lunch in his office, man. Second door on the third hallway on the right."

The guard sat down smiling and went back to his game.

"Thanks! Woohoo! Home run!" Fernandez high fived the guard one last time before walking over to the hallway area, having no idea what he'd just seen on the screen.

He knocked on Leonardo Castro's door and waited for an answer. According to the information Gonzalez gave him, this guy was straight as an arrow, dedicated to his job, and a stickler for rules and regulations. He was also apparently very religious, and abhorred injustices of any kind. Fernandez was hoping this would help him win some favors for Montoya, who was stuck between a rock and a hard place he didn't deserve.

"Who is it? It's lunch time!" said a muffled voice from behind the closed door.

"This is Fernando Fernandez, Mr. Castro. I'm sorry to interrupt your lunch. Can I come in?"

The door opened to a strong smell of pickled onions and garlic. Leonardo Castro was right in the middle of enjoying a huge plate of mangu with fried eggs, the smell of which permeated the office, and very soon, Fernandez thought, his clothes.

He took a look at the austere surroundings: white walls, very scant furniture, and a huge, black cross on the wall opposite to the door, positioned in a way which you could not escape. The only other adornment was an obligatory picture of the President.

"I got a message form a friend saying you would come by. Come in. I'm almost done here."

Fernandez walked over to the only available chair in the place, a very hard, very old wooden piece that looked like it belonged in a school from the turn of the last century. When he sat his intuition was confirmed, it was indeed uncomfortable.

Castro sat at his desk chair opposite Fernandez, and proceeded to finish his lunch with gusto. Fernandez's belly reminded him it was lunch time for him too. He hoped the noises from his gut were not noticeable.

After what seemed like hours, Castro finished his meal and

put the cardboard plate in a trash can next to him, so that the smell continued to linger and make Fernandez salivate. He swallowed hard.

"Mr. Castro, I..."

"Please, call me Leonardo. I know what has brought you here, son. You come very well recommended! And by people I absolutely trust."

Fernandez made a mental note to bring a bottle of Brugal back to Julio. He owed him big for this one.

"So about the documents from the Registry..."

"That wretched death certificate is a disgrace. I had already started an investigation into the matter, but now that you are here, I will push it forward even more vigorously. We cannot have a company from the US of A filing a complaint because of an illegal document we have failed to deal with! We can't allow an insurance policy to get paid based on a fraudulent Dominican official certificate!"

Fernandez was amazed. This guy seemed to be everything Gonzalez claimed him to be, and then some. Fernandez produced his copy of the death certificate.

"This piece of paper says my insured is dead, and has a very legitimate looking government seal on it."

"As I said, we are conducting an investigation, but I can tell you that certificate will not be valid for long, and somebody here will lose his job."

"Somebody here? Not in the Registry office at La Romana?"

Castro took out a file, and opened it to reveal a whole bunch of papers about Tirso Guerra. There was the death certificate, but also birth certificates, driver licenses, and a photocopy of a passport.

"There was no mishandling of the paperwork as far as I can see. I'm sure Duarte chose to certify the death in La Romana thinking it would be easier to manipulate someone who wasn't working here in the capital. He showed up with the necessary papers and forced some poor bastard to certify the death prematurely. The offices where he got those papers? That's where all hell is going to break lose."

As Fernandez started going through the stuff in front of him, he was relieved to hear Montoya would likely not be fired. However, there was still a certificate on record, and with it the distinct possibility Alliance Insurance could be sued.

"Can I take pictures of some of these papers?" Fernandez asked.

"What? I'm not looking."

Fernandez took his Nikon out and shot a couple of pictures of the driver's license, which was much older than the one he remembered from his own file. He also fired off a couple shots of the passport, because it looked funny somehow.

"So, Leonardo, there is definitely no way this certificate is legitimate."

"Fernando, may I call you that? That certificate is a piece of evidence against a very powerful, very well oiled political machine called Felipe Duarte. The guy's father was a powerhouse, full of clout and the necessary contacts to do what he wanted without fear. I could never touch him. This guy Felipe, however, is just riding in his father's wake. He's pushing all the wrong buttons, and getting people very upset. Now, nobody is willing to do anything about it because of Papa, but this one? This is a major injustice and there is no way I will let it slide. This is my chance to make someone happy," he said, pointing to the cross above his head. "And you, my dear fellow, you are the ticket."

"Me? What did I do?"

"You showed up. You, with your big US bucks, and you big US insurer. If we don't deal with this mess, the feds will. And we can't have that, can we? So, you made it real. Thank you!"

After a couple more pleasantries and an offer to serve as tour guide when Castro visited Puerto Rico, Fernandez walked back to his car in a daze. The whole thing had blown so quickly out of proportion! He couldn't help but wonder what would have happened had he not arrived.

As he sat in his car, he looked at the pictures he took of the documents in Castro's file, and took out his own file to compare. The driver's license was definitely a couple of years prior to the one he had, but the passport? As he looked at it a weird feeling began to creep up his spine. The passport he had on his file was different. Same name, but different picture of the same guy, and different passport number.

Guerra apparently had two.

Fernandez left the Central Election Board and called the airline, but there were no more flights to Puerto Rico that day. After a late lunch at a cafeteria where they served the same mangu plate he just smelled at Castro's, he decided to drive blindly into town and pick the most nondescript hotel he could find, in case somebody was really after him. He sent his latest report to Interference International, including the information on the double passport and the soon to be invalid death certificate, the video and audio recordings and all the pictures. After a light room service dinner, he slept fitfully and was woken at 7:30 am by a phone call from Dirk Saban.

"Jesus, Fernandez, I sent you there to get a death certificate, not to set the whole island on fire!"

"What the hell are you talking about, Dirk?" Fernandez croaked groggily.

"I'm texting you the link now."

"What link?"

"You haven't seen the news yet. There's a fire going on and it has your name on it," Saban said excitedly.

"Would you please speak English?" Fernandez asked.

"Felipe Duarte is all over the place."

Fernandez opened the link on his Blackberry. The headline read "Flight to Nowhere: Prominent Dominican Lawyer Defends His Involvement In Pilot's Fake Death Certificate."

"What the fuck?"Fernandez gasped, astonished.

"I had it translated but I can't tell how impartial it is. I suppose they are presenting both sides to the story," Saban suggested. "Duarte is quoted as saying there's a US agent with a personal vendetta, an FBI funded conspiracy to discredit him and his father. That's why this whole death certificate business came out."

Fernandez looked at the photo that accompanied the article. It showed Felipe Duarte and his eminent father looking directly into the camera, steadfast, determined, and courageous in the face of overwhelming oppression. The family was cunning and connected, that was for sure. They'd cooperated and wasted no time going on the counter-offensive.

"Read it. It says he knows who the Special Agent investigating the case is, and that he will make sure justice is served, and his family name is not dragged through the mud any further."

He quickly scanned the article. Most of what he'd been working on the past few days was there. Tirso Guerra's history, his financial meltdown, Duarte's harassment of the Registrar's office and procurement of an illegal death certificate (he was glad to see this), and the commencement of an investigation by a special committee of the Central Election Board. There was even a small graphic of the plane's disappearance with a red line ending in open sea with a question mark.

Despite the avalanche of evidence, the Duarte family was given an unusually large amount of space to defend themselves and make their case.

"Does the motherfucker own the press too?" Fernandez asked.

"What do you mean?" Saban asked.

"How the hell does he know it's me?!" Fernandez stormed.

"Read the last paragraph."

Fernandez read: "Duarte confirmed he is fully aware of the identity of the person or persons who want to hurt his family's reputation. 'Rest assured' Duarte says, 'I know who had lunch at the Central Election Board yesterday, and I will personally make sure justice is well served in this matter.'"

"Anyway, job well done, Fernando. I got your report, it looks great. If I were you I'd get the hell out of there."

"C'mon Dirk, this is not the time to fly off the..."

Fernandez was silenced by a light scratching at his hotel room door.

"Dirk, give me a moment. I hear something at the door."

He walked over and looked through the peephole. No one. He walked back to the bed and began to quickly gather his belongings.

"Turns out you're right, Dirk," Fernandez said, very matter of fact. "Listen, I'm hanging up on you now because I have to climb out the window."

"Don't joke about things like that Fernando."

"I assure you Dirk this is no joke," he huffed as he pulled the strap from his travel bag around his head. "There's a fire escape outside, it looks a hundred years old but it will have to do. If you don't hear from me in ten I've either fallen or they've got me, do you understand?"

"Yeah buddy, be careful."

"I mean it. Ten minutes, no more no less. If you haven't heard from me call the National Guard! You got it?"

"Loud and clear Fernando. Ten minutes."

"Talk to you soon!" he said cheerfully. As he stepped over the window sill, he heard the unmistakable sound of the lock being jimmied.

Saban was left in Houston staring at his phone in concern. As calmly as he could, he sat down to wait a full ten minutes.

The photo arrived via text message from an unknown number. It showed a fishing yacht motoring out a narrow passage into a sky-melting sunset. The name emblazoned across the stern was Revenge. It was accompanied by a text message.

"It's Bill. I'm sending this from my girlfriend's phone. Looks like our boy has set sail. Sorry Fernando. Hope I can help you out some other time. Where do you think they're going, anyway?"

"Venezuela," Fernandez texted back. "Thanks a lot Bill. You did great. Talk to you soon."

He regarded the photo from the safety of his desk. Morales had truly gone above and beyond this time. He thought for a moment that if the vet wasn't so dead set against returning to Puerto Rico he'd make an excellent assistant, even considering his age.

Simon interrupted his musings by showing him a piece of paper. "This came in today."

Fernandez took the document and scanned it quickly. It was a letter of resignation from the latest assistant wanna-be that passed through his office yesterday. She had lasted a full 24 hours on the job.

"Simon, Yolanda sends her regards and thanks you for a wonderful lesson on how to use the copy machine. Unfortunately, she will not be coming back," this last sentence was said with sarcasm.

"How did you scare this one so quickly?"

"She didn't know the job would entail night surveillances and some weekends, and her boyfriend doesn't approve," said Fernandez, wondering what the hell she thought working as a P.I.'s assistant was going to be like.

Then he started to think about what it was actually like to be a P.I., and the risks that seemed to grow and become more pressing as time went by.

"You look worried." Nicole came in from the girls' classroom.

Fernandez didn't respond. He looked through the doorway and could see the children's' happy and eager faces, his Angelic and Lakshmi, bright and shiny, attentive to Sra. Mendoza's lesson.

"You've had close calls before."

"Yeah but this was different," he groaned.

"Why?"

"I don't know. In one sense it all seems like a show, and then it comes to life."

Nicole looked concerned. Simon was on his way to the kitchen and stopped.

"I spent a long time wanting this," Fernandez continued. "This is going to sound ridiculous but this job is fucking dangerous."

Simon started laughing but quickly zipped up when he realized Fernandez was serious.

"When I was talking to Tirso's sister it hit me, Nicole. The way she looked at me."

"What do you mean, Fernando?" she asked.

"It was like I'd gained admittance to the show she'd been born into, like it or not. She took the fact a man like Duarte existed for granted. There are a class of people who are the basis for the characters, and then there's the masses who think it's all just fiction I guess."

"You know, Gonzalez kept warning me," he continued. "I knew what I was getting into but only in a sense. I always knew there was a danger to myself but now I'm swimming among people capable of anything. I mean anything. And I asked for it. This wasn't catching some jerk off with his pants down. This was screwing up the plans and futures of some very dangerous people. I guess I was wondering who the fuck do I think I am?"

"Fernando, I'd get used to it if I were you. You've turned out to be rather good at what you do and screwing up the plans of rich and dangerous people," Nicole said.

"It's not that. For the first time, I'm worried about you."

"Me?"

"And the girls."

"What about me?" asked Simon.

"No, not you."

"From what you've told me it seems Duarte has his hands full right now. He'll probably be going to prison, and Tirso Jr. is laying low because his involvement has not come up" Nicole offered.

"I know. I know. But what about the next time?" Fernandez asked.

"There you go again. He's in need of guidance," she said to Simon and left the room.

"All you can cope with is now. Bring your thoughts back to the present and…."

"Oh, put a fucking sock in it Simon," Fernandez growled turning back to his computer.

Flowers On His Grave
2013

Ten Caribbean News Cares

Voiceover: We turn now to the curious case of the old man known locally as Beijing Joaquin. Joaquin, an immigrant of undetermined Asian background, died last Sunday in his apartment in Old San Juan of natural causes. He was found by his roommate and employer, Eliza Pelayo."

Pelayo: He was very soft spoken, like he didn't want to ever be noticed. That was difficult because there aren't a lot of Chinese people around here. People tended to gawk at him, the locals, not the tourists you know? Some people called him Mr. Miyagi which I thought was kind of mean, but people didn't mean offense. It was just ignorance. I suppose Beijing Joaquin wasn't much better. His real name was Pan Ji ke. In the 80's a bartender from Trinidad tried to pronounce his name Ji ke, and with his accent it sounded like Joaquin. The name just stuck after that. I don't think he was even from Beijing.

Voiceover: Joaquin became a fixture of the Old San Juan area, and was beloved by residents. One man who knew him was local business owner Chris Marigold.

Marigold: You could set a clock to his movements. He'd leave work and always walk the same route, he'd arrive here at exactly the same time everyday and order exactly the same thing to eat. Then he'd go over to Nono's for two beers and leave for home every night promptly at 9:30. I don't know what he did on his days off. It's just going to be really weird not having him around. It's like a part of the town is gone. We're all going to miss him.

Voiceover: Intensely private, Joaquin has left no clues to his history and no way of contacting any family or friends.

Pelayo: We never talked of that. I brought it up a couple times but he just wasn't that way. I never heard him reminisce or talk about his past. He was very much about what he was doing now and not much else. He did mention once that he had children, but where or who they are I have no idea. It's a shame. If he has family living they really should know.

Voiceover: As part of our Ten Caribbean Cares initiative, we at Ten Caribbean are reaching out to the community to try and find the family of Beijing Joaquin. If anyone has any information as to the background of Pan Ji ke, or any clues to the whereabouts of his family, please call our tip line at 1-800-CAR-ALOT. Because as of now... there is no one to put flowers on his grave.

Dramatic music.
Rain falling lightly on flowers atop a white coffin.
Fade out.

"Jesus, what a load of sappy shit! And the fucking phone number, idiots, half the calls are going to be from assholes looking for a used Chrysler!"

Fernandez stood staring at the fading image on the screen. Then, his mood seemed to change in an instant.

"But, wow. Can you imagine? You die, and there are no flowers for your grave." Fernandez was pensive as he shut off the television, still fixated on the blank screen.

"Are you being sarcastic? It sounds to me like you don't think they are sincere," Erick said looking up from his workstation.

Fernandez shot him a 'not today' look. He smiled and went

back to invoicing. Erick Suarez was the first assistant in the history of Covert Intelligence to survive his three month grace period and be offered a full-time position. It had only taken Fernandez ten years. It was a joke between Nicole and Simon that Fernandez had waited until he found a mini me. Erick, stocky with black hair, indeed looked like a shorter version of Fernando Fernandez. His inclination toward slightly more hip and youthful attire was one of the only things that differentiated them.

Erick had simply shown up to the office one day, unannounced, with resume in hand. Having seen the ad in the classifieds, he was determined not to get lost in the rush of applicants. Although the job posting was anonymous, Erick was somehow able to ascertain the company's identity, not to mention the unlisted address of its unmarked office. When Fernandez demanded to know how Erick got his information, Erick responded that he'd tell him at his one year anniversary.

Fernandez was sufficiently impressed with Erick's ingenuity and audacity to offer him a job on the spot. In one year he'd proven himself everything his previous assistants weren't. Hard working, a quick study, and willing to learn. For the first time, Fernandez had an assistant he could trust to fly solo, and this enabled him to increase his caseload.

In the four years since uncovering the Tirso Guerra scheme, Fernandez's profile had increased dramatically. The ever present stream of work from Dirk Saban and Interference International was now, due to numerous television appearances and newspaper articles, augmented by a flood of local requests, much of which had to be turned down. Erick couldn't have shown up at a better time.

Erick's anniversary dinner was held at Papayas in Ocean

Park. Fernandez was finally able to ask him how he'd managed to show up on his doorstep a year ago.

"I saw you on TV, you were being interviewed on WAPA," Erick explained. "You used the word 'detection' in describing what you do. You used it four times. I found it odd. Something about it didn't seem correct. Like, it technically makes sense but most people use it differently."

"And?"

"And the same word appeared in the classifieds ad twice. I remembered Covert Intelligence from the show. After that it was easy. I just took the chance that it was you."

"Well at least someone remembered the name," Fernandez laughed at the time.

Now Erick was six months into his second year with CI and comfortable enough with Fernandez to take a few liberties now and then. His opinion was also becoming more and more relevant.

"I know it's cheesy, but if you think about it, it probably wouldn't be that hard," Fernandez ventured.

"What?" asked Erick.

"Finding the old man's family. We could do it easy. It would be great publicity."

Erick knew they were snowed under, but he also knew the boss was always looking for ways to get the company's name out there. Fernandez sat down at his desk and began to stroke his chin, obviously intrigued.

"You know that's a really good idea," he conceded after a long moment.

"What's a good idea?" Nicole had just come into the room.

"This old Chinese man died…" Erick began.

"We don't know he was Chinese," Fernandez corrected.

"Ok, anyway this Asian guy died in Old San Juan and the news is trying to make a public interest story about it. He's kind of a mystery. They want to find out if he has any relatives so they can let them know what happened," Erick explained.

"He might have children," Fernandez continued. "They are playing up the tragedy angle, like he died alone and his children will never know what happened to their father."

As soon as the last words were out of his mouth, Fernandez experienced that sick realization the he'd just unintentionally been an ass. It was one thing to purposely wander into insensitive territory fully prepared, and another thing entirely just end up there through sheer stupidity.

He looked up and his wife was staring hard at him. He'd directed the remark towards her with such oblivious casualness, he thought for a moment she might be questioning her most basic assumptions about him and their relationship. What did he really think of her? How could her sensitivities and boundaries be so far from his mind? In a way, challenging her directly on the subject of her own father would have been far less damaging. Now, he just came off as a prick.

The unspoken exchange had only lasted a few seconds but Erick caught it fully. He'd already seen Fernandez extract enough information from uncooperative people to know when heavy things were going unsaid. Erick was vaguely aware of what had happened to Nicole's father and the simmering domestic conflict that was always just below the surface. In times like these he entertained the idea that the firm would be better off with a proper office instead of a home-based one.

"Nicole, I didn't..." Fernandez faltered.

His wife opted to pretend the whole thing didn't happen.

"What? Please continue," she said tersely.

"Anyway, I had the idea that we should offer our services," Fernandez explained. "For free of course."

"I think that's a fantastic idea," Nicole said turning on her heel and promptly leaving the room.

Fernandez looked down and was silently cursing himself. Erick didn't let him beat himself up for long.

"That lady, Pelayo, she was on Calle del Cristo. I'm sure of it," said Erick.

"That's the street with all the little tourist shops."

"Yes, and I know the exact one she's standing in front of."

"Go down there and see what you can dig up and I'll try to get in touch with the station," Fernandez said getting heavily out of his chair looking defeated.

Erick could tell this was a time bomb in his relationship. Fernandez had plenty to distract him from the Furniture Man, but it was clearly an irreconcilable knot in his stomach. When professionalism collides with family, you either suck up your principles and back down, or create a mess. Were there special cases or was everything a potential challenge to one's totalitarian dedication? Erick didn't have the answer but he knew this was a fundamental crux in someone's life for whom work was everything. In order to continue the charade of normalcy, there were certain things you simply had to let go. But was Fernandez even able to let go?

Marriages ended this way. Erick's parents' had.

Fernandez slowly made his way through the kitchen towards

the back bathroom.

"I'm kind of low on enthusiasm right now, Erick. I think I feel a headache coming on."

Erick emerged from the parking garage under the huge totem pole and was met with a wet gust of wind that had swept in right from the Atlantic. The old city to his back, he surveyed the scene before him. To his left stretched the wide barren causeway that led up to the half-millennia-old citadel of El Morro. The massive lawn that lay before it was filled with children running, playing, and flying kites. He turned away from his intended destination and approached the low city wall to his right to do what he always did whenever he came to Old San Juan, look over the edge at the neighborhood below.

La Perla was more or less a lawless pirate island hanging on the edge of history. Originally established outside the city walls as a neighborhood for non-whites and servants, it had in recent years become an epicenter of drug activity. Ramshackle houses bunched together and clinging to the rocky shoreline looked ready to fall into the sea at any moment. Erick stood atop the ancient Spanish wall with his back to one of the richest neighborhoods in the Caribbean and looked down into one of its poorest. They were separated by literally a matter of feet. You simply did not go there unless you knew someone. Even the police didn't go there, unless they went 200 at a time with a helicopter the Coast Guard and the FBI.

La Perlans existed in a fishbowl, the entirety of their small neighborhood was visible from the wall. This is what Erick, and so many others, found so fascinating. It was such a dangerous place yet it was on full display. You stood at the top, looked

down, and watched day to day life play out in an entirely different dimension to which you had no access. It was an ethereal
experience, like remembering a dream. He lingered briefly,
watching a massive Royal Caribbean liner make her way out to
open water, once again marveling at the dissymmetry.

Turning back the way he came, Erick made his way across
San Jose Plaza and found the steeply descending Calle del
Cristo. He passed the bar Nono's referenced in the news story
on his left and pictured the old man sitting at one of the high
tables visible from the street, conducting his nightly ritual. The
boutique in front of which Eliza Pelayo was standing when she
was interviewed lay on the right side of the street about two
blocks below.

Erick felt a desolate, day after kind of feel as he walked.
Then he remembered the cruise ship he'd just seen steaming
out to sea and realized the particular area he was entering was
experiencing the fallout after a tourist exodus.

The store had an open front, above which hung a large
polished wood sign that read "Parakeets". As he approached he
momentarily recoiled under the pan flute barrage but pressed
on. Inside the store Erick found exactly what he expected:
more polished wood knick knacks, colorful and tropically painted personalized signs, and insanely overpriced perched wooden
parrots hanging everywhere. The back wall was apparently the
religious area. Buddha statues (fat and slim) of increasing sizes
and prices, busts of Ganesh and Vishnu, and row upon row of
those glass prayer candles featuring Jesus, Mary and a variety of
Saints.

In the center of the store he found the source of the mellow
onslaught, where the featured CD was displayed next to the
boom box. It was a very relaxing compilation of songs by

Strawboy called "Tidal Islands". Next to the CD lie several copies of a book written by a local professor that claimed to reconcile all world religions and science. Erick picked it up, it was about 100 pages.

"That's a very interesting read," came a familiar voice behind him.

He spun around to find TV's Eliza Pelayo.

"Actually I haven't come here to buy anything. I was looking for you," he smiled disarmingly.

"Me?"

Pelayo had her grey streaked, barely kempt Earth Mother hair tied back in a ponytail. Stray strands shot out all around the circumference of her head. She wore a crystal in a dragon claw around her neck and smelled pleasantly of Myrrh incense. She smiled at Erick broadly and he knew right away he was dealing with the friendly breed of hippy rather than the sanctimonious one.

"Why on earth would you be looking for me?" Her voice quavered and her eyes screwed up into a look of genuine good-natured confusion. Erick realized she was much older than she seemed on the television.

"I saw the report on Ten Caribbean. My name is Erick Suarez," he proffered his hand.

"Oh yes, I'm still so sad," she took his hand and looked down. "It's not the same place without him."

"So Joaquin worked here with you?"

"Yes. I own this building. He rented an efficiency from me upstairs," she explained.

This was extremely expensive real estate, Erick thought.

Too expensive to be supported by a tchotchke shop, however overpriced. Pelayo was likely independently wealthy and the store was her pet project. Either that or the building had been in her family for awhile.

"Ms. Pelayo…" Erick began.

"Elizabeth," she corrected.

"Elizabeth, I'm thinking I might be able to help unravel the mystery as it were. I work for a firm called Covert Intelligence. We are private investigators."

"Why does that name ring a bell," her eyes drifted backward and she sucked in her cheeks. Suddenly, she bolted to the back of the store and began examining a bookshelf. Finding the one she was looking for she approached Erick flapping it back and forth over her head.

"This!" she exclaimed triumphantly.

"Ah yes," Erick said looking at the cover. "Debra Figueroa."

"Poor Debra! This is one good book. I'm so happy you guys found her mother. How did you know she was in Texas?"

"Through our detective network," Erick said reluctantly.

Debra Figueroa was a forty something deaf lady who appeared in a local TV station looking for her biological mother. That was another case where Fernandez felt compelled to do his civic duty for free, and located Debra's missing relatives. The TV people followed the whole thing from start to end, and one of the reporters wrote a book about it. It had been Fernandez's most high profile case since Tirso Guerra's disappearing plane.

"Yes! And after the family was reunited I saw you on the news. Only it wasn't you, it looked like you," she drifted off confused.

"Yes, that would have been my boss, Fernando Fernandez," Erick explained.

She started laughing, ironically.

"Of course. I'm sorry Mr. Suarez, but there's no way I can afford to pay for something like that. You might want to go to the station. I'm sure they have the resources," she admitted sadly.

Family owned the building, Erick concluded.

"Oh don't worry about that. We're going to take care of it. I was just wondering if I could see where he lived, go through his personal effects, that kind of thing."

Erick was already removing his business card from his wallet before Pelayo had time to ask. She accepted it and fingered the embossed CI logo in the corner.

"Do you think you'll find anyone?" she asked still looking down.

"We'll certainly try. The firm has done a ton of this kind of work before. My boss has an extensive network of people he can count on all over the world. If Joaquin has relatives that are alive, it's a good bet we'll find them."

"Why does he want to do this?" she looked up at him warily.

"He doesn't like the idea of the old man dying alone and his family not knowing. That and it's good publicity, I'm not gonna lie to you, Elizabeth," Erick laughed.

She smiled and turned to walk toward the back of the shop, motioning for him to follow.

"Well, at least you're honest," she said over her shoulder. "I'm not going to lie to you either, he didn't have much. He lived like a monk. I already cleaned out his apartment. Aside from his clothes everything else fit into one box. It's up here."

Erick left the shop with a box containing some of Joaquin's mail and documents, his social security card, an expired passport, and photos. He put it on the passenger seat and made a beeline for the office in Carolina.

The offices of Ten Caribbean News were located about ten miles south of San Juan in the high-end area of Montehiedra. Fernandez pulled his brand new Chrysler 300S into the parking garage under the high rise, taking two parking spaces so no one could scratch it. Muscular, sleek and jet black, the powerful sedan was everything his tan Sienna daddy van wasn't. The monster engine purred menacingly and echoed off the walls of the enclosed area and smartly dressed business people milling about the adjacent courtyard getting their afternoon coffee fix turned to look. Fernandez relished in the new and unfamiliar feeling of coolness. The car had even prompted him to update his look as well. Sporting a tailored suit and designer shades, Fernandez was finally allowing himself to get a little Burn Notice.

He was here to meet Nelly Santana, Program Coordinator for Ten Caribbean. As he found a seat in the waiting room he gazed around at the station's talent plastered all over the walls. Ten Caribbean was mainly a weather station that also featured travel programming of interest to tourists and natives alike. Their big star and face of the company was an overweight and jolly weatherman transplanted from the icy wastes of Minnesota by the name of Cal Shelby.

Clad in an ever-present Tommy Bahama shirt, Shelby was

unusual as he was a prop weatherman. He carried a white, plush cockatoo puppet named Mr. Schnickens who he would use to offer commentary and terrible one-liners during his weather and travel reports. Shelby was, however, an inexpert ventriloquist with absolutely no training in the discipline. So every time Mr. Schnickens wanted to talk, the weatherman would have to hoist the avian up to obscure his own moving lips.

Shelby's "aw shucks" attitude and jovial presentation more or less insulated him from public criticism. Ten Caribbean tended not to complain much either, mainly because their next most popular on-air personality was a man in a frog suit named Captain Coqui.

As Fernandez waited, he felt as if he was shrinking into the sofa as Shelby's giant gin blossomed face bore down upon him. Mr. Schnickens had his own poster on the opposite wall.

"Mr. Fernandez?"

He stood up to find a woman of about 29 going on 50.

"I'm Nelly Santana." She extended her hand and smiled weakly.

Disheveled and distracted, everything about Santana looked as if supreme effort had been made just to preserve the appearance of normal. Her eyes scanned back and forth, meeting his for only a split second during the introduction. Her clothes were of the quality and character of the upper management office worker, but ill fitting and thrown on her body carelessly. Fernandez was reasonably sure he could categorize her quickly, she was the kind of person that spent most of her time struggling with a very loud internal dialogue.

People like this went about their duties and commitments in the real world in a mechanical fashion. Things got done because they had to get done. Her urgent and oh so important dilemmas invisible to the rest of us. Fernandez always marveled when people like Santana managed to do well, even excel in their jobs. They had a natural handicap, always paying half attention.

"Would you come this way please?"

She ushered Fernandez down a long hallway. Considering the station's tropical theme he was expecting to hear Bob Marley or Jimmy Cliff from the cubicles. Instead, his ears were met with the soft murmur of Australian hipsters Tame Impala. The only reason he knew the band was because of Erick.

Since he began, Erick had been making a conscious effort to expand Fernandez's musical horizons beyond Ricky Martin and Don Omar. When it came to rock, he started playing the Eagles and Steely Dan in the office and car. Inoffensive, middle of the road type stuff he was sure Fernandez would like. Then he'd moved to the 80's bands he approved of, like the Cars and the Police, taking care to stay away from anything too punk, or post-punk. He'd then glossed over hair metal and grunge, diving straight into Radiohead's first three albums. Before he could object, Fernandez was now familiar with, and enjoying, the Black Keys, Arcade Fire, and the Hold Steady.

A great lover of all songs, Erick's roots ran deep. He tried to get Fernandez into old blues and jazz recordings, but Fernandez couldn't deal with the poor sound quality. One of Erick's biggest triumphs though, was getting his boss to listen to Bachata. Fernandez had always disdained the ubiquitous, tinkling Dominican genre. His last experiences in the DR only served to reinforce this. But Erick unearthed some recordings from the 60's, before the musicians made the terrible decision to insert the jarring, over-effected electric guitar into nearly every song. Without that distraction, Fernandez could hear the haunting beauty of the music.

As he followed Santana he passed the cubicle that was the source of the music. Inside sat a young man with an enormous beard and those earrings that stretch out your ears like a Maasai tribeswoman. He looked up as Fernandez passed. Fernandez smiled as he mouthed the words to the song. Disgusted, the employee looked away. Fernandez thought for a moment the kid would be forced to delete all his Tame Impala songs if someone as unhip as himself knew the words.

"Right this way, Mr. Fernandez," Santana said distractedly, ushering him into a large corner office. The view was remarkably clear and he could see all the way to the high rises in Hato Rey. Santana collapsed in her chair so hard he thought for a second the back of her head would smack into the window. Upon recoil, the chair creaked so painfully he found himself feeling sorry for it. He took the seat in front of her.

"So. My assistant said you were interested in helping us find the old man's relatives?" she said while massaging her closed eyes. She spoke to him like he was being forced upon her.

"That's right, yes," Fernandez couldn't shake the feeling that he was being treated like the CEO's fuck-up nephew, and Santana had been ordered to find him a job. He wasn't expecting a parade, but he did think they'd be a little appreciative of his services, considering the mountain of useless bullshittery they were no doubt accumulating via 1-800-CAR-ALOT.

Looking to the side of her desk he saw a framed M.A. from the Columbia School of Journalism. It looked like it had been taken down and hidden as the screw still remained in the wall right above it.

"Getting a new frame for that?" he joked.

"I'm not a doctor Mr. Fernandez. It's a silly thing to put on your wall in this business," she explained.

"I don't know about that. Columbia? That's a pretty big deal in my book," he smiled trying to break through whatever she was building between them.

She looked for a second as if she would soften, but then remembered something. Her face turned stern, internally cursing herself for almost being tricked.

"So what do you propose to do Mr. Fernandez?" she said dryly.

"Ms. Santana, would you like me to come back another time?"

"No. Why? Are you busy?" It came out as almost an accusation.

"You seem not to want me here," he explained.

"Is that what your shrewd powers of deduction are telling you?"

"I don't have to be a private investigator to see that. I don't mean to toot my own horn but I'm pretty good. I'm sure I can help you on this…"

"Yeah yeah, I saw you in the papers. We're so lucky you called," she cut him off.

"You know what? I'm just going to fuck off."

He got up, irritated, thinking it was the last time he'd do any favors for anybody. Turning around he walked straight into the Tame Impala guy and spilled the stack of folders he was carrying all over the hallway..

"Dude, what the fuck?" he whined. "Take it easy man."

"Sorry," Fernandez said helping him pick everything up.

"Mr. Fernandez wait, come back. Alan will pick those up," Nelly Santana pleaded from behind him. She grabbed him softly by the arm and stood him up.

"Please come back in and sit down. I apologize. You've caught me in the middle of a nervous breakdown. It's not your fault," she led him back inside, patting him on the back sympathetically.

"Why? Did your correspondent get lost on the way to the St. Lucia Jazz and Arts Fest?" he taunted.

"I deserved that," she said sitting down once again. "I'm experiencing some pretty heavy disillusion right now and you just happen to be here. This job is taking a lot out of me."

Some people just naturally had bad boundaries. Santana didn't strike Fernandez as one of them. She was sharing personal information with a stranger because she really was nearing the end of her rope. Fernandez wondered what on earth could be the problem, though. True, all jobs contained a certain degree of stress and pressure, but to all outward appearances Ten Caribbean's work environment was as lightweight and frothy as its programming.

"I watch the channel. I would think this would be a pretty fun job," Fernandez offered.

"Have you seen our web presence?" she asked.

Fernandez shook his head.

"I worked in New York for three years after I graduated, for NY1. It's the local station, like this," she explained.

"Yeah I've seen it, the last time I was staying in Manhattan."

"I'm Puerto Rican," she continued. "I was born here and

I always planned on coming back. The station offered me a pretty sweet deal. To tell you the truth Mr. Fernandez, I was close to burning out up there. It was just like a conveyor belt of depressing stories that just got progressively more horrifying. It was a no brainer, coming back to family, and the salary was generous by island standards."

"This wasn't what you expected?" he asked.

"It's what I expected as a job, but not what I expected the job to be, if you catch my meaning."

"I don't," he confessed.

"You'd know if you checked out the website. It's sort of phase one in a plan to concentrate on actual news. I was hired for that purpose given my experience in New York, to move the station in a more legitimate direction, I guess."

"Away from Mr. Shingles the Cockatoo," Fernandez added.

"Mr. Schnickens," she corrected. "And honestly given what we've been covering I'd take that stupid fucking bird any day of the week. I knew full well why they were hiring me, but I didn't expect things to be this bad."

"Everyplace has it's share of problems. You're not going to escape, Ms. Santana," he tried not to sound like he was talking down to her.

"You know, I spend the day watching local news from all over the country on youtube. Do you know what was the lead story for WNEX Pleasantville, North Dakota last week?"

"Not off hand."

"An unknown F-150 illegally dumped a load of yard trash in a Walmart parking lot and set it on fire. That was the lead story for the whole week."

"Point taken," Fernandez conceded.

"Just in the last six months I've covered two instances of child rape and murder, where the prime suspect in both cases was a parent. We did a story last year about a man who hired a prostitute and was taken at gunpoint to an ATM by her and her pimp. After they got his money they lit him on fire, as one does. There's closed circuit video of the whole thing. They were laughing, belly laughing and making fun of him as he was burning up and begging to be shot. I'm not sure who to feel bad for in that one."

Fernandez began to understand her attitude toward him. In retrospect he'd come in rather casual and cocky while she was screaming in her own private hell of injustice. In his sharp suit and sunglasses he probably looked like part of the problem. He resisted the urge to tell her he was intimately familiar with the cases and let her continue. She'd obviously been keeping it in and needed the release.

"And the coup de grace, last month there was a home invasion where the parents were beaten to death in front of their children. The fucking animals took the two boys away, kidnapped them. When they couldn't think of what to do, they executed the younger boy in front of his older brother. Then they shot him. Somehow he survived and is in police custody. He said his baby brother was apologizing to him when the gun was to his head, saying he was sorry if he was a bad brother."

She was starting to cry.

"Six years old. What the fuck does a six year old have to apologize for? Such nice little boys," she was barely audible, her voice came out as a gurgle between sobs. "You know about that one I'm sure."

"Of course," he answered. The whole nation did.

"Do you know why they did it?" she asked.

"Because the parents were their landlord and they didn't have the rent," he said, though not wanting to.

She looked at him like a magician finishing a trick, throwing her arms to her sides and taking a bow.

"I'm sorry Mr. Fernandez. I've become a bit jaded. When you walked in here to talk about this crap...I mean don't get me wrong it's important I just find it difficult to preserve the air of professionalism with all this shit that's going down. Also forgive me if I don't trust your motives. As far as I can see nobody does anything for anybody here. It's all about what you can do for me. But I suppose you're right, that's going on everywhere."

"I understand perfectly. Finding the old man's relatives would be great publicity for my firm. I have all kinds of good ideas to make me look like a hero. If we find them, we could fly them here. You and I could meet them at the airport with the Governor. Ten Caribbean would have the scoop of course. Then I'll have Covert Intelligence t-shirts printed, small sizes though because their Asian."

"Cut it out," she started to laugh through her tears.

"We could throw a ticker tape parade for them through the streets of Old San Juan all the way to their father's grave site. And the finishing touch? A brand new headstone with the engraving 'Here lies Beijing Joaquin. Father, Inspiration, Beer Enthusiast. This Burial Brought To You By Ten Caribbean And Covert Intelligence,'" he finished.

Nelly Santana had put her head down on her desk and was shaking violently with laughter. He allowed himself a brief moment of satisfaction. She was a tough one. After about 30 seconds she lifted her head up. Her tears had stuck some of her hair to her face.

"Look," he began. "There's going to be self interest in anything we do. Business is business. But I assure you I do care about this. I had a long talk with my wife." Fernandez was surprised at himself, and unsure why he'd brought up Nicole.

"Everyone deserves closure in this world. If it was my father..." he wasn't sure where he was going with this anymore.

"Go on."

"If it was my father," Fernandez continued unsure of why he was pausing and finding it difficult to collect his thoughts. "I mean, it's a basic human need isn't it? I suppose I'd feel like I was betraying him if I didn't find out what happened."

"Well, we know what happened, it's not like Joaquin was murdered or anything. We just want to find his family," she proceeded slowly.

"Yes of course," Fernandez hastily replied, only subconsciously aware he might be confusing two different things. He quickly recovered.

"That's what I meant. I know it's a fluff piece but think about it, the old man was clearly beloved by the community. If we get it done, I mean, how much do people need this right now! Especially because of the guy getting set on fire, and those assholes killing that family. You're thinking it would mean diverting attention from the real problems, but it's not like we're covering a hot dog eating contest. We are trying to bring closure to a family. We can have a happy ending for once."

She looked at him hard, respect was beginning to kindle. He used the opportunity to continue his offensive.

"Look at it this way. Instead of just passively reciting a list of horrendous occurrences, it would show how journalism can have a real impact on the country. It would motivate people to care, to get involved."

Fernandez now totally felt he was at a job interview, throwing out buzzwords. Santana was clearly too clever to be won over by sweet talking her profession, or appealing to her passion and ethics. Her bemused expression notwithstanding, he could tell that he'd driven the point home. He'd come in expecting to get his ass kissed and he'd somehow ended up having to convince Nelly Santana that his motives were pure. All for a job that was probably going to cost a lot for which CI would not be paid. He briefly wondered if this is what it was like to work in the non-profit sector.

"We don't even know," he said. "He might have been some kind of asshole and the family wanted nothing to do with him."

"I can still see a headline there," she said without sarcasm.

"Yeah. 'Beijing Joaquin Was World Class Prick, Says Family.'"

"Alright. We'll put the fact you're taking the case for free as the lead story on the website. We'll also mention you and your firm, what was it called again? Covert Options?"

"Covert Intelligence," he snapped with a little too much force. Santana ignored it.

"We're continuing to run that spot on the channel. I'll have them add an update you have taken the case. We could put it in text over the coffin and flowers thing."

"Fantastic," Fernandez groaned.

"If you turn anything up I guess we'll take it from there. Just out of curiosity, do you know where you're going to start?"

"My assistant has already gathered Joaquin's personal effects. I'm going to need to get access to all the documents regarding his death."

"Well, this is your lucky day. I'm the station's liaison to the Department of Forensics. Let me talk to the supervisor and I'll get back to you. She can be a little particular," Santana explained.

"There's just one more thing," Fernandez said hurriedly.

"That is?"

"I want to get interviewed by the parrot."

"Get out of my office," she got up smiling and took him by the arm.

"Thank you Mr. Fernandez. Please be in touch."

He'd realized it was the first time she'd looked him in the eye for more than a split second.

Fernandez made his way back to the entrance on the verge of panting, feeling like he'd just gone a couple rounds with Mayweather. As he approached the glass doors he became aware of a loud, but pint-sized commotion in the elevator bay. A small group of schoolchildren who were on a field trip to see the television station were positively losing their collective shit.

Cal Shelby had arrived.

The corpulent weatherman in the Hawaiian shirt was wearing his sunglasses, indoors, and looking rather the worse for wear. Still he was all smiles as he waded through his adoring fans, signing autographs and patting them on the heads.

"Hey kids! This is Cal Shelby with Ten Caribbean coming to you live from Caribbean Plaza in Montehiedra! Don't forget to join us next week in St. Maarten the friendly island for the 87th annual Corn and Nut Expo at the Princess Juliana Convention Center. We hope to see you all there," Shelby broadcast in full voice as the children beamed.

What a pro, Fernandez thought.

"Hey kids, what should you never do?" he asked.

"Drugs!" the children shouted in unison. Then a different chant began.

"Where's Mr. Schnickens? We want Mr. Schnickens!" Shelby had whipped the excitable tots, zooming from free Pepsi, into a frenzy. There was clearly going to be trouble if he didn't produce the parrot, and soon.

Fernandez began to open the door to the elevator bay when he was pushed aside by someone from behind. Tame Impala guy had come to the rescue bearing the Cockatoo puppet. The kids went apeshit.

Fernandez slipped around the throng and pushed the elevator button. He couldn't be sure but when Shelby put Mr. Schnickens on his hand, Fernandez thought he saw a bottle of Pepto Bismol inside.

"No, no, Pan Ji Ke. Pan. Ji. Ke. Can you understand me? Hello? She fucking hung up again," Fernandez turned to Simon and Erick, exasperated.

One of the things they unearthed among the Asian guy's stuff was a photo showed Pan Ji Ke examining prawns in a sidewalk fish market as the attendant laughed in the background. He had the friendly and satisfied expression of someone who had just told a funny joke. It was winter. He was bundled up to the neck and dirty snowdrift was visible on the side of the street behind him.

The phone number on the store awning in the background

had a 212 area code. As in New York.

Fernandez had called three times to no avail. The woman on the other end seemed to speak some rudimentary English, but he really couldn't make heads or tails of what she was saying. On the second call he'd asked her if she had children, betting the younger generation would be easier to speak with. The excitable woman apparently took some kind of offense to this and was sufficiently pissed off by the third try.

"Simon, shouldn't you speak Chinese or something?" Fernandez asked.

"What do you mean?"

"With all the Buddha crap," he explained.

"You know, I'm just going to pretend not to take offense to that, and think about it as an occupational hazard. I'm going to lunch."

He got up and left the office in a huff. A minute later Fernandez could see out the window that Simon was in the driver's seat of his car sitting in a lotus position. No doubt trying to meditate away the hostility he was feeling toward his boss. Fernandez was vaguely aware of the effect his mood was having on the staff as of late.

Beijing Joaquin had pricked something deep and obsessive that was only aggravated by his conversation with Nelly Santana. He was short and irritable, and he was taking his wife's cold shoulder out on the staff. It manifested itself as a kind of teenage sassiness that he knew was incredibly unbecoming. Only he couldn't stop himself. He made a mental note to be nicer to Simon and Erick.

Nicole had taken his "died alone" remark as an admonishment, even though he never intended it to be. As a result, they'd been in a perpetual state of unpleasantness and disagreement ever since. Every time he'd tried to explain she'd leave the room.

Her father now shared prime real estate with Joaquin in his brain. The more he tried to push him out, the more ferociously he stuck around. The mental image that kept popping up was of a tanned grey haired man standing outside the Rio Piedras marketplace. This was a photo from 1983 that Nicole kept in her wallet.

Fernandez had actually never met his father-in-law.

He began dating Nicole after he died, when he was still working in the computer business. As a green P.I. he'd been very keen on helping her family, and they had been somewhat receptive to this. But slowly, Nicole developed a resistance to the notion of investigating her father's murder. She had, in her mind, come to terms with it and wanted to leave the whole thing at peace. It became certain to Fernandez that, were he to push the subject any further, there would be problems in their relationship. Either he had to be prepared to swallow something that was irrational, or he'd lose her forever.

So it lie dormant and unspoken at the base of their marriage. The compromise. One of the things they shared. It somehow perversely gave their union's strength. How many marriages were like this?

It was simply one of those things. There was nothing he could do, no angle he could work. Over the years, he'd stood up to cops and judges, gone toe to toe with cold blooded murderers, coerced confessions out of shivering pedophiles, yet he still feared his own wife's reaction when it came to the subject of her father. Not that Nicole was domineering or a bully in any way, it was just that his whole domestic life and persona hinged upon keeping his hands off the dormant and unspoken.

Over the years he'd heard things, he'd made connections, he knew where to start. Garcia.

But it was simply one of those things. His obsession to conclude things was every bit as strong as her denial. Deep down, did they both always know the blow up was coming? Were they so gullible as to just stay in the moment for as long as the ride lasted? Or did she genuinely have faith in him? This would be the biggest problem of them all. What she considered so right was to him, to his core, so overwhelmingly wrong.

And now an offhand comment about a dead Asian man had wreaked havoc in his house. He'd worked on cases much more similar to the Furniture Man than this one. What was it about Beijing Joaquin? Why now? Did it have to do with his anniversary, both in the business and to Nicole? Silly. But not so silly to someone with obsessive compulsive disorder.

"I'm going to call Dan Johnson in New York. He owes me a favor. Scan his social security card and the picture," he handed Erick the passport.

"Boss, check this out," Erick called from the makeshift evidence table. All of Joaquin's possessions had been carefully laid out, and Erick was going through them all.

"Whatcha got?" Fernandez approached, relieved to be pulled out of his train of thought.

"There's also this, nothing else really. Just this and the photo."

Erick handed Fernandez a document granting power of attorney over Joaquin's belongings to a law firm in Singapore.

"So I guess it's Singapore Joaquin now," Erick joked. "I don't suppose you have any contacts there."

"As a matter of fact..."

Fernandez's talk with Major Ho Chang was promising. He'd met the ex army man at the same Irish conference where he suffered the ignominy of being labeled Detective Daiquiri. Ho served in the Singapore Armed Forces for nine years before retiring and opening up his own investigation firm, gloriously titled Wing Command Security Consulting. Fernandez, suffering from a bit of moniker envy, became enamored with the Special Forces-trained Singaporean.

As the conference seemed to be dominated entirely by ass-kicking, fraud busting Jay Lauderdale-type Americans, and the dour, hard drinking, job weary Irish mocking them quietly behind their backs, Fernandez and Ho struck up an unusual friendship born of the feeling of being thoroughly ignored and out of place. Major Ho revealed to Fernandez that keeping pace with globalization was Wing Command's biggest priority. Indeed, in half the conferences Fernandez had attended since Dublin, Ho had been there.

He had even extended an open invitation for Ho to come to Puerto Rico and check out Covert Intelligence's operation. Fernandez wanted to learn all he could from the Major, especially considering his special forces experience.

When Fernandez related all the details of the Beijing Joaquin case he was only too happy to help, especially because the guy appeared to be a fellow countryman. Fernandez left to do his afternoon errands feeling hopeful.

"I'm looking for the sorry old bastard support group. Is this the right place?" Fernandez asked opening the door to Julio Gonzalez's Ocean Park office.

Deeply involved with something else before Fernandez's arrival, Gonzalez searched valiantly for the mother of all comebacks, but couldn't manage it.

"Fuck you," he sputtered, acutely aware of his inelegance. He glanced at Garcia in apology. Both men expected more from the old vulgarian.

"Lovely," Fernandez teased. "You could have gone with 'I know you are but what am I.'"

Garcia laughed.

"I stand by my last statement. Do you need those notarized?" Gonzalez indicated the folder in Fernandez's hand. "Put it on the desk," he snapped and turned his attention back to whatever he was doing.

"How are you, Antonio? I saw your car outside," Fernandez said taking the big man by the hand.

"I've been better, Fernando. They want me back on the force. I'm getting a lot of pressure here. That's why I came to talk to Julio, wanted his advice on the subject," Garcia explained.

"They want you back on the force? At your age? Are they starting a new geriatric crime unit?" Fernandez joked. Now it was Garcia's turn.

"Fuck you. See how clever I am too, Julio?"

Antonio Garcia was a 30-year veteran of the San Juan police department. He'd got the job through his old man and worked his way up from the mail-room to Homicide Chief Inspector. Five years ago, he'd packed it all in and started his own firm just like Major Ho. Fernandez frequently collaborated with Garcia. His endless list of contacts and collaborators from his time on the force was an invaluable resource.

Six foot five and built like a gorilla, Garcia barely fit in
Gonzalez's office chair. His stature had its good points and
bad. He certainly was intimidating, but intimidating could be a
positive drawback in some of the more clandestine and subtle
aspects of the investigation business. He enlisted Fernandez on
occasions he deemed himself too visible or too much cop to fly
under the radar. In return, he helped Fernandez out whenever
he asked. It was a mutual back scratching arrangement.

"I was actually going to call you, Fernando," Garcia said. He
painfully extracted himself from the chair and opted to lean
against the wall instead.

"What's up?"

"They're really laying it on thick. Appealing to my patriotism
and civic duty…"

"And dangling a lot of money in his face," Gonzalez sneered
without looking up.

"They're saying the nation is in a particular crisis right now,"
Garcia continued ignoring him. "I have to agree with them.
Things are worse than they've ever been. The drug activity
is out of control. They want me back. I've even received a
call from the Governor. I'm beginning to think I don't have a
choice."

"It was the report." Fernandez said.

"What report?" Gonzalez asked.

"The Department of Justice came out with this report last
year," Fernandez explained. "It basically said the police force
was rotten to the fucking core. Corruption…:"

"Systemic corruption they called it," Garcia added.

"And drug trafficking, civil rights abuses. It was pretty bad.

The American Civil Liberties Union is on their case, pressuring for a federal monitor to come down and kick some police ass. Don't you pay attention to the news, Julio?"

The old man shrugged.

"That wasn't the worst of it," Garcia picked up. "They found instances of officers getting shitloads of money to be bodyguards for drug shipments. It's sick."

"I heard the feds were coming down," Fernandez added.

"Are you kidding?" Garcia shot back. "They don't give a fuck about us, we're just a headache that pops up every now and then."

"Here we go," Gonzalez sighed.

"We're out of sight and out of mind, a historical curiosity along with Guam and the USVI, a remnant of the USA's late foray into imperialism. I don't know how bad it's gotta get for these people to wake up. We need to be independent, Fernando. Until then, we'll be forever relegated to tit-sucking mediocrity."

"Sounds like you're more mad at us than the States," Fernandez offered.

"Maybe I am," the big man went to the window and surveyed the stretch of beach. A couple of teenagers were strolling alongside some vacant houses covered in graffiti. He shook his head. "I don't like the US but I don't expect anything from it either. How do you vilify someone who doesn't seem aware that you even exist? We're the only ones who can help ourselves."

Fernandez felt he had been having this discussion with Garcia for years. The old cop was a fervent supporter of the Independence Party. Every so often the government would hold a referendum on the status of the island. Three choices were usually given: statehood, independence, or leave things as they are. Leave things as they are routinely got the overwhelming vote to the eternal consternation of men like Antonio Garcia. In a twisted way, even statehood was preferable to him, because at least it would show the population was interested enough to make some kind of fucking call.

"I'd be on the first plane out," Gonzalez said.

"Yeah, that's because you're a racist, Julio," Garcia observed spinning around at the window.

"You guys want to hear about what I'm working on right now?" Fernandez quickly butt in trying to cut off the argument before it had a chance to start. He then explained all the details about Beijing Joaquin and Ten Caribbean.

"That's that asshole with the bird puppet?" Garcia asked when he was finished.

"Yeah."

"Certainly a good move from a Public Relations perspective, Fernandez," Gonzalez offered. "I applaud you."

"Likewise," Garcia added. "Even if you don't find him."

"I fully intend to find him. I have Johnson and Chang working on it. We'll turn something up if something's there to turn up."

"And then?" Garcia asked.

"If he's got relatives that are willing, the station will fly them here to see his final resting place as an end to the story."

"Ugh how schmaltzy," Gonzalez gasped and Fernandez laughed.

"So what is it you wanted to talk to me about, Tony?"

He left Gonzalez's with a lot on his mind. Garcia had a week to make a decision about re-joining the police force Cold Case Squad. If he did, he'd have to freeze his P.I. license and close his investigation business. He asked Fernandez if he'd be ok with accepting a ton of still-open cases. Considering everything else on his plate, Fernandez couldn't imagine how the hell he could do it, Erick or no Erick. He told Garcia he'd have to think about it.

Although unnoticed by Garcia and Gonzalez, Fernandez had spent the encounter in a perplexed state of alarm. He couldn't believe in light of current events that he just happened to run into Antonio Garcia. It took a Herculean effort in restraint not to give into obsession and bring it up to Garcia. He now walked to his car in a peculiar confusion, unaware if he had succeeded or failed. Garcia had been one of the detectives on the Furniture Man case.

"So far Johnson's come up empty. No one knows him at the store in the photo, and there's another family at the address on the passport. Dan even brought along an interpreter. Zilch. Chang on the other hand, when I talked to him, he said something about how the case sounded familiar, which I couldn't believe. So that sounds promising, right?" Fernandez asked Erick.

"Uh..."

Erick was in no condition to pay attention. He watched the traffic before them with his face clenched in anticipated pain and his knuckles white on the oh shit bar. Fernandez was booming down Baldorioty Avenue in his new toy, weaving through traffic and running straight up people's asses.

"Erick, what are you doing?"

Erick realized he'd been slamming his right foot into the floor every time Fernandez cut somebody off. He tried to calm himself, secretly cursing Fernandez's new high-powered vehicle and missing the days of the bland minivan. No doubt, driving in the minivan had been stressful as well, as Fernandez was that kind of driver, but the minivan only possessed so much power. With the arrival of the new Chrysler, the full fury of Fernandez's potential had been released. Every time Fernandez had even a few car lengths of clear road he'd jam the accelerator so hard Erick felt like he was aboard an Antares rocket just as it was clearing the tower. He wondered if he'd pass out from the g-forces.

"Do you want me to slow down?"

"Yes," Erick squeaked.

"Ok, just say so man, we got time. We don't have to meet Nelly until 11:30am," he mercifully eased off the gas and fell in line with the rest of the traffic.

"So you were saying Major Ho knew about it?" Erick asked breathing a little more easy.

"Not that he knew about it per se, he just sounded intrigued, like I'd jogged a memory," Fernandez explained. "There's millions of people in Singapore, his knowing anything about this would basically be a miracle."

"You've told me he's performed them in the past," Erick observed.

"I know. The man is borderline uncanny. What are we listening to, by the way?"

"It's called Tidal Islands. I thought you might like it."

Before Erick had left Parakeets he'd picked up the album specifically to play for Fernandez while driving, thinking the relaxing rhythms would lull him into a state of tranquility. It hadn't worked. Barreling down Highway 26, narrowly averting death with each overtaking accompanied by the dulcet tinkling of pan flutes was an experience Erick was not keen to ever repeat.

"I do," Fernandez smiled enthusiastically. "You see, this is the kind of stuff you should be playing for me!"

He roared off the exit and Erick once again did a full-body clench.

After spending half an hour finding a parking space in Santurce during the afternoon lunch rush, Fernandez and Erick were met by Nelly Santana outside the Department of Forensics in the huge Government Center Plaza. The woman Fernandez's approached seemed wholly different than the stressed out wreck he'd encountered the week before. She wore tight designer Seven jeans and a black Ramones t-shirt. The whole breezy ensemble was topped off by a New York Mets baseball cap. A gust came up off the Atlantic and blew her uncovered hair all over her face. When it hit Fernandez he could smell the ocean.

"Where is the concert?" Fernandez joked.

"Wherever I am," she said kissing him on the cheek. Fernandez introduced his assistant.

"I see you got a Queens motif going on here," Erick observed.

"Music fan?" Nelly asked.

"Big time, they invented punk."

"I'm not getting into that futile and endless debate," she smiled shaking Erick's hand. "Follow me."

She led the two of them across the wide, windswept plaza to a cluster of government high rises, weaving in and out of the obligatory large scale modern art installations. Everywhere Fernandez looked there were people waiting for something: health insurance, passports, business licenses. Some looked supremely pissed off, but most didn't. Joking, chilling, drinking coffee, accepting and jolly in the face of something they could never hope to change.

Fernandez watched a particularly angry gentleman yell at a security guard while stomping his feet and waving some documents up and down. From what he could hear, the man was told to go three different places and waited in line for an hour in each. All three places were wrong. The fact that the guard refused, or was unable, to mirror any kind of reaction to his escalating anger only served to infuriate the man all the more.

A couple of clerks strolled casually up to the guard, obviously returning from lunch. They gave him a sandwich and coffee, and the three exchanged pleasant laughs and smiles. The complaining man looked about ready to explode.

The relaxed people were right, Fernandez thought. Even though the ineptitude was inexcusable what the fuck were you actually going to do? The relaxed people were right.

"You look a little more relaxed," he said to Santana as they walked.

"I decided to start smoking pot," she explained.

"That's great!" Fernandez exclaimed, picking up the sarcasm.

"Just kidding, they test us," she giggled. Her playfulness was infectious. He found himself wondering if she'd had some kind of religious experience in the last week. He looked over at Erick, googly-eyed and grinning like an idiot. He must be in love.

"Now, I have to warn you guys. The woman I'm taking you to meet is rather...particular. She takes her job deadly serious, but she also is one of those people whose sense of importance is disproportionate," Santana said as she opened the glass door to the lobby. She signed them in at the security desk and the three had to then pass through a metal detector.

"As Supervisor of Forensics?" Fernandez asked as he removed his belongings from the bin. He had to leave his gun with the guard.

"She's more. Press liaison, right hand to the Director," Santana continued. "Get ready, I'm just telling you that you're probably going to have to kiss her ass."

"Your referral isn't good enough?" Fernandez asked.

"Good enough to get you in there. The rest is on you. Between the two of us I think she's got something against men. She wants to make them crawl."

"I crawl for no one," Fernandez boomed dramatically.

"Me too," Erick had finally found his voice.

"It's up to you then," she opened a door, shut it again and drew them close. "In spite of her outward appearance she's very susceptible to flattery, and flirting. Go figure."

The three entered the Department of Forensics. Fernandez had to momentarily catch his breath when the sole figure in the room looked up from her desk.

"Hi Estrella! These are the guys I was talking to you about. Fernando Fernandez, this is Estrella Leon."

"Hmmm," Leon regarded them both, frowning.

The first thought that came to Fernandez was that if he had

to kiss her ass it was going to take a while as Leon was a woman of significant size. The second thought was that he'd never in his life seen someone quite so red. Her dress was red, lipstick blood red, nails and shoes were redder, all framing the beauty of a taino-looking woman with long, straight, thick black hair. He peered intently at her face, expecting to see crimson eyes staring back at him. Instead he found they were solid black and accusatory, burrowing directly into his soul, telling him he was a very bad boy indeed. Erick must have picked up on the same vibe as he stood looking at Leon with his jaw open.

"Whoa," he said, then hurriedly cut the interjection off with a fake cough.

"Please excuse yourself young man. I can't afford to get sick," she stated plainly and with endless authority.

"I just had a tickle in my throat," Erick explained.

Estrella didn't look amused.

"Mr. Fernandez is a private investigator. Do you remember the case we were talking about the other week? The one with the deaf woman looking for her mother…, anyway Fernando was the one who solved that. It was in the newspapers and TV, do you remember?" Nelly sped up as she talked and ended the sentence in a full out sprint, breathing heavily and relieved to be finished.

"How nice," was Leon's reply.

"Well, anyway," Nelly continued seeing Fernandez was not yet intent on speaking. "He needs…"

Leon cocked an eyebrow and gave Nelly a 'you should know better' look.

"Excuse me. He would like to request the file on…"

"Can he speak?" she said calmly. "If he needs a file he needs to follow procedure."

"Of course," Nelly laughed nervously. "You can, can't you?" She was looking at Fernandez like if looking for a life saver.

Fernandez smiled at Leon in silence. The room's two other occupants stared at each other, shuffling their feet while the lady in red sat cool as a cucumber at her desk, the epicenter of bureaucratic importance. She was intrigued but still secure with Fernandez. Realizing her sphere of intimidation was encountering a different kind of sphere, she'd determined to keep cool until she'd discerned its nature. In the end it wouldn't matter, though. She'd torn apart far more egotistical and important men than Fernandez.

"If you're trying to be mysterious, know that it's incredibly boring" she directed at Fernandez.

He sighed heavily and sat on the corner of her desk. He picked up a picture frame and started studying it. Leon didn't move. Behind her Nelly looked as if someone had just farted in the Vatican.

"Help yourself," she said in a voice that suggested not a trace of bother.

As he examined the photo, Fernandez was building up a mental profile. Leon was one of those people who used discomfort as fuel for her ego. The more Nelly and Erick searched desperately for something to say or do to fill the silence, the more intimidating and expecting she became. Paradoxically the more she increased the anxiety in the room the less likely anyone was to say anything. When someone finally found their voice, whatever they said would inevitably come out as nervous nonsense or a half-assed and pathetic attempt at humor.

About twenty full seconds had passed in silence. Fernandez looked at Nelly, she returned his gaze with a desperate 'go ahead' kind of expression. He then looked at Erick. His assistant stood empty eyed and mouth open like a mental patient who'd just been administered his medication and was watching a test pattern on television.

In truth, Erick was being momentarily transported back in time to elementary school. In fourth grade, he and three friends had gotten the idiotic idea to make a game of throwing rocks at each other. Erick managed to score a direct hit to the forehead of a boy named Melvin. The wound gushed blood and Melvin, understandably, went screaming and crying to the teacher.

As the school nurse sewed the poor boy up and gave him ice cream in the infirmary, Erick and the two other boys were next door in Principal Sanchez's office. The imposing man sat behind his desk waiting in silence for one of them to confess in the exact same way Estrella Leon was waiting now. At the peak of the moment, when his nerves had achieved critical mass, the mother of all moronic statements managed to escape from his mouth.

"I guess we're between a rock and a hard place Mr. Sanchez."

Saying the wrong thing in moments of supreme nervousness had been an issue ever since. Fernandez had been working with Erick on this, so he wasn't surprised to hear his faithful assistant say:

"I heard people are dying to get in here." It wasn't so much a sentence as a car crash. The nine words hit and stacked upon each other, coming out more like four.

Fernandez winced. He'd got the gist of the ancient joke and hoped it was unintelligible to the rest of the room.

"Ha! That's such a good one! Right Estrella?" Santana nervously laughed too loud. In trying to help Erick turn the release valve she'd only increased the pressure.

Leon, who had still not taken her eyes from the man sitting on her desk, slowly and deliberately turned her neck to the right to look at Nelly.

"I couldn't understand," she said with a patronizing smile. "If it's so funny let him share it with all of us. Please say it again young man."

Erick's head buzzed and he felt dizzy.

"Nothing. It was just a bad joke," Erick started.

"Maybe I'm the kind of person that likes bad jokes. It's rather rude of you to make that decision for me, coming into my office. Do you usually employ rude people, Mr. Fernandez?"

Up until now Fernandez was content to let Erick make his own mistakes. Mrs. Leon was indeed a particular woman, just as Nelly had warned, but enough was enough. She was holding court from a thoroughly meager position of power and it was only her personality that was intimidating.

As she calmly manipulated the situation, she was making one thing clear: your life, your history, all the things you do or don't do to make you are irrelevant once you walk through my door. My rules, learn them well or I will calmly lecture and humiliate you into compliance. She was a judge in a courtroom drama and Fernandez was about ready to turn off the TV.

"I only employ rude people Mrs. Leon."

In a way, she and everyone like her were their friends' and coworkers' fault. We create the monster by never challenging it. We never challenge it because we don't want to upset it. We create the bubble in which the monster lives. It a tense and electrified bubble that will shock when touched. To the monster inside it is normal life.

Fernandez knew that to get results, one simply had to do what everyone else was too afraid to do, burst the bubble.

"Mrs. Leon, I'm a very busy man and I don't have time to sit here all day. Please get me the file on Pan Ji Ke. I believe he was known locally as Beijing Joaquin. Produce the proper forms and my assistant will fill them out. Then we'll be on our way."

"Excuse me." she half shouted. It wasn't a question it was a command. "You can't just come in here…"

"You're a government official," he cut her off. "I'm requesting a government document. This is your function. What else is there to discuss? Just do your job and get the file please. We'll wait."

Momentarily silenced by the monumental lack of respect, Estrella Leon remembered who she was and quickly rallied.

"I know you're particularly good and finding out important things like who left a deaf baby behind, but in case you didn't realize it, you are not the police Mr. Fernandez. I don't have to give you a damn thing. The only reason I've agreed to see you is because of Nelly. Speaking of which, why did you bring this asshole in here?" Leon turned her wrath toward Nelly Santana.

"Estrella, I'm really sorry," Nelly began.

"Fine I'll get it myself," Fernandez jumped off the desk and proceeded to the door behind Leon's desk.

"Oh hell no!" The big woman was up in an instant. Displaying surprising agility she used her knee to push her rolling chair in Fernandez's way on her way to barricade the door. On the way she pushed Nelly Santana out of the way with a big arm. The young woman doubled over on top of a low bookcase taking a stack of magazines right in the stomach. Her Mets hat fell off on impact.

"Ooof!"

"Nelly!"

Erick sprang into action.

"Let me help!"

On his way over to Santana, Erick got his feet jumbled in the throw rug and ended up stepping on her toes.

"Oh jeez, I'm sorry Nelly."

"It's ok. I'm ok. Are you stepping on my hat also?" she said through her hair propping herself up.

"I think so, let me get it."

Erick retrieved her flattened hat from the floor. Nelly accepted and looked at it pathetically.

"I'll totally get you a new one," Erick offered but realized he no longer had her attention.

Nelly was looking at the standoff now occurring at the door to the file room. Erick stood up, intrigued. Fernandez and Leon were eye to eye in front of each other. He'd expected to see gritted teeth and blazing eyes, but during the course of his encounter with Nelly Santana and the bookcase the vibe in the room had significantly changed. Leon was looking positively smitten and Fernandez was gazing into her eyes in earnest.

"What the fuck?" Erick half whispered in shock.

Neither party acknowledged him, mesmerized by the scene that was playing out before them.

"I'm sorry," Fernandez breathed into Leon's face. "I don't like being nervous, it's bad for business."

"Whose business?" she said, her voice cracking.

"My business," he affirmed solidly, locking her gaze through the tops of his eyes. If it was even possible he drew closer. Estrella Leon had to catch her breath.

"And what business is that?" she taunted, leaving her mouth to hang open on the last syllable.

"This city is my business, it's streets are in my veins. Every two bit punk and back alley miscreant are my business. Every dink that busts out of the joint, every outhouse, henhouse and whorehouse within fifteen miles. I don't need no stinking badge, Mrs. Leon, cause King Kong ain't got shit on me."

Erick was momentarily perplexed by all the movie lines Fernandez was mixing up. He thought for a second Leon would laugh, but no dice. She was swallowing it hook, line and sinker. The two of them stood nose to nose like in a telenovela. Erick marveled as his boss was manipulating the situation masterfully.

Nelly Santana, on the other hand, had a look on her face like she'd just walked in on her parents having sex.

"It's hard on a man," Fernandez closed his eyes and made a pained face. "To see the things I've seen in this job. I only wish I could unsee them, but that's not going to happen. Once you see something, it's seed. Forever."

She nodded. Fernandez used the opportunity to shoot a quick glance at Erick that said stay where you are and don't smile at my grammatical error.

"So tell me then," Leon whispered. "How could I make a man like you nervous Mr. Fernandez?"

"You remind me of someone," he explained.

"Who?"

"A woman I was terribly in love with, ever since I was a boy. It's silly, I know."

He changed his expression to one of wistful sadness. There was no distance to look off into, so he stared painfully at a terrible painting of a clown riding a unicycle on the office wall.

"No, on the contrary, it's not silly at all," she said playing with her hair. "Tell me," she said looking at him in sympathy. "Who was she?"

As Fernandez, Erick and Nelly Santana walked out the building Fernandez handed Erick the file on Beijing Joaquin. Erick promptly stowed it in his leather briefcase and the two exchanged devious smiles. They walked across the hot and windswept plaza toward Avenida de Diego. Nelly was shaking her head back and forth still trying to process what the hell she had just seen.

"That was a hell of a gamble boss, saying she looked like Charo," Erick offered.

"I know," Fernandez replied. "It could have gone either way. I mean, I had to keep it realistic. I couldn't have said Scarlett Johansson. She would have seen right through that."

"I was thinking Sophia Loren would have been good."

"Yeah that would have worked too," Fernandez concurred.

"Maria Conchita Alonso?"

"Who's that?"

"Remember Running Man?" Erick asked.

"Oh yeah! I don't like her." Fernandez disagreed enthusiastically. "Remember when I said I'd kill you last," he droned in a terrible Schwarzenegger. "I lied."

"No that was Commando," Erick countered.

Still reeling from the events inside, Nelly Santana watched the exchange in disbelief.

"Remember when he threw the circular saw blade at that dude and sliced off half of his head?" Fernandez reminisced.

The two started acting out the scene, laughing.

"Wait, wait, wait!" Nelly yelled having finally had enough. "What the fuck just happened in there?"

"You told me she was susceptible to flattery," Fernandez explained innocently.

"Yeah, but what was all that? You looked about ready to make out with her. First you come to my office and knock people down in the hallway. Then you have me thinking you're some kind of asshole opportunist, but you end up winning me over. I introduce you to Estrella and you cause this huge scene, I end up being pushed into a bookcase with this guy trying to help me and before I know it you're teasing her and have one of the world's most difficult women eating out of your hand. This is not the way you're supposed to do things!"

Fernandez narrowed his eyes and reverted to his Dirty Harry voice.

"It's the way I do things, punk."

Two months had passed since the incident in Forensics and Covert Intelligence had so far turned up nothing on Beijing Joaquin. Fernandez and Erick had expended considerable effort and time following every lead however small and researching every aspect of the old man's life. Through Datasledge Fernandez had turned up possible relatives in Chicago and San Francisco. He'd tried to contact anybody on Facebook he thought could be related. He'd spent weeks culling pages and pages of prior addresses and dead phone numbers only to come up empty handed.

Erick's job, however, was even more mind numbingly complicated. He researched Asian naming conventions to find out what parts of Pan Ji ke's name relatives or children would share, if any. Then he took to social media. Even narrowing the search to the US and Singapore there were literally thousands of possible permutations of Joaquin's given name, and that was assuming he was even from Singapore. Then there were the privacy settings to contend with. Erick realized there was really no way he was coming off as not a stalker. Although he'd told Fernandez it was futile several times, his boss pushed him to continue.

To Fernandez it was looking more and more like his best option was going to be Major Ho Chang. Ho had explained to him early on that when working on missing persons cases in Singapore, the families often bought classified ads in a certain newspaper asking the public for any information concerning the whereabouts of their loved one. The Major had a contact at the paper that had access to its database of ad payments, but had turned up nothing yet. He was also doing his own newspaper search, but the problem was going through paper after paper, year after year, was almost as time consuming an endeavor as Erick's Internet odyssey.

Ho had initially put two employees on the task but had to call them back to the office as he'd scored a high profile government corruption case that would require all Wing Command's resources. He'd apologized to Fernandez and assured him he'd pick up the trail as soon as he could spare someone.

There was good news however. Things on the home front

had improved. Time had dulled the tension and Nicole was talking to him again, which in turn had a beneficial effect on the entire work environment. Simon was smiling again, and even Erick seemed somewhat contented in his irritation. As he watched the two of them busy themselves, involved, naturally distracted, he realized his staff genuinely enjoyed working for him. He had good employees. They'd taken his pissiness as out of character.

The Furniture Man was still bubbling under the surface of his mind but far less menacingly than before. Fernandez figured it was due to the all-consuming and procedurally rote task of tracking down Joaquin's relatives. Burying his head in busy work afforded him the convenience of not fucking up his domestic situation. He'd made a subconscious, but sadly temporary, truce with his automatic convictions.

Then one afternoon, he got a visit from Antonio Garcia.

"They waited a little longer than I expected but they're demanding to know by Friday," the big man said, shuffling uncomfortably in Simon's chair.

"What are you going to do?" Fernandez asked.

"I'm going...Jesus what is that? Everything at this desk smells like jasmine incense."

"Sorry about that, Tony. We're going through a happy and permissive phase here," Fernandez explained.

"I'm going to take the job. You know me. I'm not stupid enough to fall for all that jingoistic shit, but at the end of the day I do care way more than they think. These government officials are appealing to my patriotism just because they want to look good for big brother. I care about Puerto Rico. If that sounds naive and uncool I don't care."

"You know I don't think that, man."

"It's funny, no matter what I've done in my career, I'm still just some hick from the countryside to them. These youngsters really think they are manipulating me, laughing after I leave the room."

Garcia started examining the spiritual knick knacks on Simon's desk. In Fernandez's experience it was best to let the old cop roll until he was finished. If he'd tried to join the conversation or interrupt, Garcia would have redirected whatever he said to flow back into his line of reasoning anyway. One simply had to wait until he finished.

As Garcia ranted, Fernandez became unpleasantly aware he barely paying attention and with an inner dilemma of his own. It was gnawing at the cuff of his jeans like a yappy little dog. The harder he kicked it away the more ferociously it came back. Nicole was gone, the kids were out of school and she'd taken them to Luquillo for the day.

"But it matters to me, dammit!" Garcia declared. Fernandez realized he'd missed the last minute of his monologue. "So what do you think?"

"What?"

"Have you got the time?" Garcia said.

"I'm sorry Tony, I was thinking of something else for a second."

"Can you take the cases?" he asked.

"How many are we talking?"

"Say 25 that are still open."

"Damn that's a lot, Tony. I'm totally snowed under here in case you didn't notice."

"I'm not going to take this position with all these hanging out there. Look Fernando, about half of them you really don't have to do much, they're basically in the can, just wrapping up and paperwork. I'd consider it a personal favor. You'd be helping your country, indirectly, but you'd be helping your country nonetheless, and you'd be making money."

"You're planning to swoop in there like Elliot Ness?" Fernandez joked.

"Yes," Garcia stated plainly.

Something had to be done about the state of affairs, that was plain. Fernandez knew there was no better man for the job than the one who sat in his office at that very moment. Despite Beijing Joaquin and the enormous workload from Dirk Saban and Interference International, he found himself considering Garcia's proposition. It wasn't out of national pride though. He'd got hung up on "a personal favor".

Obsession is uncontrollable. The thought comes back again and again, unasked for, unwanted and dreaded. One's only choice was to ignore it, to adopt an attitude of indifference. But that course of action goes against every natural instinct, and deep down one knew the feared thought would one day find its way to the surface and have to be reckoned with.

In this way Fernandez lived in a mental environment that would send most men directly to the psychiatrist. There were medications to silence the primal scream of obsession, medications that worked well apparently. But in this world there was a certain flavor of person who'd see an inability to deal with his own mind as unacceptable, and medication as cheating. The professionals would identify this kind of thinking as just another manifestation of said obsession. Perhaps they were right. In the end, all one had to deal with was one's mind until death and no further, and what another person would see as a disorder Fernandez saw as occupational advantage.

"Tony, you worked on my father-in-law's case, didn't you?"

The words were out of his mouth and into Garcia's brain. There was no going back. Maybe he could play it cool with Nicole, keep it a secret. Why not?

"Yeah, I was there, but it was Raul Hernandez who was heading up the whole thing. He's the guy you want to talk to. He retired about five years ago. Why?"

"Just curious."

A devious grin appeared on Garcia's face.

"I can put you in touch with him," he taunted.

"If I take your cases," Fernandez guessed.

Garcia leaned back in Simon's chair and folded his arms. The appeals to national pride and doing the right thing had gone. Now it was good old fashioned tit for tat.

"I was going to take them anyway, Tony."

"So you do care about your island," he boomed triumphantly.

"No, I just like you a lot," Fernandez said with a trace of sarcasm.

Simon entered and Garcia got up to let him work. Frowning, he rearranged all the items Garcia had been messing with and put them in their proper place.

"You know, I do remember one thing about the case," Garcia revealed. "It wasn't handled well, it took a lot of family involvement to get Hernandez off his ass. I think it was actually the family that found the body after the cops did a crappy search and gave up, one of his kids. Can you believe that shit? I guess some things never change."

"I never heard that," Fernandez said the shock washing over him. Connections were being made immediately, attitudes were being explained. He sat transfixed on the mystery in his own house. How many things had she not told him? Picking up the girls from school, going to dinner, watching TV on a Sunday night. All the while things were there, inside. Living that way, utterly inexplicable to him. This was just one piece of information. What else did she have the capacity to disregard?

If he hadn't scratched the surface, it was entirely possible things would have been unsaid permanently. He struggled hard to sympathize and not take offense. He didn't know what it was like.

"Something else," Garcia looked at the ceiling and clenched his face, trying to remember.

"Yes?" Fernandez said tersely, wondering if he would be able to handle it.

"When the family stopped pressing the detectives stopped too. It's so ironic that we're having this conversation right now, considering this whole thing with the new job. I mean, what could be more indicative of the systemic problems we're facing than this? And this was years ago Fernando. You know it's kind of psyching me up to tell you the truth, no offense."

"None taken."

"Anyway, I remember there was a lot of unsorted evidence. They dropped the ball because they didn't give a shit. I bet you it's sitting there in Forensics to this day."

"In Forensics." Fernandez deadpanned.

"Yeah, good luck getting it, though," Garcia laughed. "The

woman down there is a fucking nutcase. Your best bet is to go through Hernandez. I got his contact info at home, I'll send it today. Thanks a lot for this, Fernando. I knew I could count on you. Let me know when you're free to meet so we can go through all this stuff. We'll do dinner at Metropol, my treat of course."

Fernandez saw Garcia to the door and walked him outside to his car. Even though Garcia drove a large SUV it still seemed to Fernandez it took a mammoth effort for the big man to squeeze inside. Garcia shut the door but lowered the window.

"Hey, how's it going with the old Chinese man thing? I saw an update on that Ten Caribbean channel."

"He's from Singapore, not China. We're kind of stuck in neutral right now, it's been a lot harder than I thought it would be initially," Fernandez explained.

"Well, you better hurry up before Interpol gets the drop on you."

"Yeah sure," Fernandez laughed. He looked down at Garcia and his face hadn't changed.

"No, I'm serious Fernando. You didn't know?"

"What are you talking about, Tony?"

"It was online. I think I saw it on the BBC Latin America site, a little public interest story just like with Ten Caribbean. We don't usually make international news. A friend of mine emailed it to me. Shit man I should have sent it to you..."

The words weren't even out of his mouth before Fernandez had turned on his heel and ran to his office screaming for his assistant.

The next hour brought a flurry of activity to the Covert Intelligence office. The BBC news story Garcia had referenced was a week old. It was basically the same story Ten Caribbean aired two months ago, only adding in a last paragraph that Interpol was planning to conduct its own investigation.

Fernandez immediately called Nelly Santana. After pulling her from a meeting she confirmed that she had contacted Interpol.

"Lugo from Forensics told me she called them, Fernandez," she explained. "I couldn't let that pass. Upper management would just can me and assign this to somebody else."

"And what would happen if Interpol found something?" Fernandez asked, knowing the answer.

"They'd run with it, of course. They don't give a shit about you."

He hung up the phone and felt the rising possibility of panic. Two months of work could potentially be going straight down the toilet. Interpol spanned 190 countries (including Singapore), employed 800 people, and had an annual operating budget close to 100 million bucks.

He heard a loud smack and turned to see Simon and Erick struggling to make the coffee machine work. The two smiled at him feebly.

Interpol would take full credit for everything without giving Covert Intelligence a thought. Fernandez was immediately on the horn with Major Ho Chang. After he explained the situation, Ho regrettably said that Wing Command was still neck deep in the corruption investigation and he had no staff to spare.

"Can you hire someone?" Fernandez asked.

"Excuse me?"

"Can you hire a temp? Hire five temps! Invoice me, Ho, I'll pay for it, I promise. We've been busting our asses over here and they're going to steal my baby!"

Ho agreed, no doubt picking up on the desperation in his friend's voice. He told Fernandez there was a firm he sometimes made use of when Wing Command was overstretched and he'd hire as many people as they had available to search the newspaper database.

"If there is something there, we'll find it. Don't worry Fernando."

Fernandez hung up the second call breathing considerably more easy than when he hung up the first. He pulled up Datasledge on his computer and sighed heavily as he looked at the empty fields on the search screen. He'd already followed the best leads. Continuing to sort through the records for Pan Ji Ke at this point would be like throwing darts blindfolded. He had to admit the social media thing had also gone nowhere. Beijing Joaquin was effectively in Major Ho's basket. He found the loss of control profoundly disconcerting.

Perhaps that's why against a lifetime of better judgment he decided to do what he did next.

In a previous life working in IT, Fernandez had gotten quite adept at using design programs. Many of his contracts were advertising firms in San Juan and Hato Rey. He often spent his downtime picking up tips and tricks from the graphic artists.

In a fit of inspiration, he screen grabbed a shot of the front page of the newspaper El Nuevo Dia and opened it up in photoshop. He pulled up Estrella Leon's Facebook profile and selected an appropriate photo of her (there were more than enough to choose from). He siloed Estrella, and tweaked the levels.

The result didn't look entirely natural but it didn't have to. He then replaced the headline with "After 15 Years, Furniture Man Case Finally Solved With Help From Forensics". It would be the ultimate appeal to the red lady's ego.

Fernandez printed his masterpiece and left the office without a word. On his way to the Department of Forensics he remembered something Nelly Santana had once said about Leon and stopped by a liquor store.

By the time he arrived at Estrella Leon's office he'd accumulated a case of Don Julio Reposado, and the fake newspaper headline in a cheap dollar store frame.

Estrella Leon wasn't in.

He placed the fake news article squarely in the middle of her desk and arranged the gift around it. He then left the stupidest note he could think of:

> Beautiful Estrella - Charo,
> I was crushed to find you not here.
> I need another favor from the impressive lady in red.
> I left these gifts, a pathetic attempt to have you remember me.
> When can I see you again?
> -Fernando

Feeling like an idiot Fernandez left Forensics, jumped into his Chrysler 300S, and pointed it west. Before he knew it, he was halfway to Arecibo on Rte. 22 and going like a bat out of hell.

The Interpol thing had rattled him, and everything he had

since then had been done in a kind of willing amnesia. Like when you get drunk and you do something you know you're not supposed to do, fully aware the entire time you will regret it the next day. Fernandez wasn't drunk, but he couldn't shake the unpleasant feeling that he was being that stupid.

Night was falling and the craggy peaks of Vega Baja gave way to the flat plain of Barceloneta. His head abuzz, he tried to concentrate on the landscape and not dwell on the possible repercussions of his actions. Pressing forward dangerously fast, he had to weave back and forth between cars as the passing lane was largely ignored.

The freeway made a broad turn to the north at Arecibo and Fernandez could see the distant ocean rise up before him, seeming much higher than the land. As a child the illusion frightened him, a gargantuan and unstoppable wall of water coming to envelop the entire island, and then the entire world. When he descended to Highway 2, things had returned to their proper proportions.

The surface road was riddled with stoplights and he was no longer able to drown his thoughts in speed. Things had calmed down. Why had he done it? Did he really think he could keep it a secret?

"What the fuck is wrong with me?" he said aloud as he pulled into a service station to fill up.

The last rays of the dying sun lit the ocean as he entered the wide and picturesque coast outside Quebradillas. He slowed to take in the view and was once again brought back to his youth. Always on this part of the trip his father would point out the disused railroad tunnel at the base of the mountain next to the sea. He'd then launch into the history of the Puerto Rican railroad, and how the highway system had destroyed it. As a child, Fernandez never understood why his father talked like this was a bad thing. Ten hours from San Juan to Ponce? Surely one and a half hours by car was preferable.

As he shot through the dark rain forest road that heralded the approach to Isabela he made note of the giant Taino head landmark at the turn off to Highway 113. Usually he would take this route, but Fernandez had no idea where he was going on this night. He was being pulled somewhere else, mindlessly.

He finally turned right on 4494 and began his approach to the center of Isabela. Weaving through the angular and tiny streets, he passed the town plaza and made his way down the steep slope that led to Playa Jobos just out of town. About a mile down the road to the right he saw his destination. It was Casa Delgado.

He hadn't thought much of Henry Delgado or his family in the last four years. Now their sumptuous golf resort lay sprawled out before him.

"Sir? Sir? Can I help you sir?"

He was parked at the security gate staring straight ahead. He didn't know how long the guard had been talking.

"Yes. I'm just here to go to the restaurant."

The guard opened the gate which led to a winding, pine tree lined avenue. The unostentatious and neat semi-detached units radiated upper class peace and quiet. He swung a right and meandered past a single, well-maintained tennis court and a basic, rectangular pool. Somehow, the no frills facilities gave the impression of wealth all the more. He thought of the enormous and multi-level resort pools back in San Juan and Fajardo, built to seem rich. This was where the rich people actually were.

The Penumbra restaurant lay near the ocean's edge in a

corner of the property obviously reserved for full-time residents. Fernandez could tell this as the units were considerably more lived in, their porches and patios littered with beach gear and personal effects. He wondered what it would be like to live in Casa Delgado. Even if he was rich enough to do nothing and simply exist day after day. It was a dream come true to most, but he had to wonder if he'd be happy. Playing golf, playing tennis, scuba diving, eating at the Penumbra restaurant three meals a day, wasting away in a sleepy old hole.

It was Friday night and the restaurant was packed. He'd forgotten.

"Sir, to provide you with our accustomed level of service you're going to have to wait an hour and a half for a seat," the hostess chirped.

"Can't I just sit at the bar?"

Fernandez squeezed in at the end of the bar uncomfortably close to the waiter's station. A group of large Americans who looked prematurely middle age by drink and leisure swayed around him like a herd of drunken bison. As they bragged loudly about other hotel bars they've visited in far flung places all over the world, Fernandez tried to imagine the desperate and movable party. Gstaad, Saint Tropez, Lake Como, The Maldives, all the same bar, all the same golf course, the only difference the quality of hangover depending on the local cuisine. Why did they even bother? Because they could.

He phoned Nicole and explained he was working and would be eating out. She was in a good mood and her happy voice made him feel another onslaught of wretchedness.

Draft beer wasn't very widespread in Puerto Rico, where the natives preferred ten ounce cans to ensure the experience remained freezing from top to bottom. Penumbra had an

American style row of taps. He chose a silly looking microbrew that he'd never heard of before.

"Fernando Fernandez?"

He whirled around to see a stunned looking pregnant woman approach him from around the bar. She was dressed in black like the staff and her hands were full of receipts. As she drew near Fernandez read her name tag: Sylvia Delgado, Manager.

"You didn't recognize me?"

"I'm sorry, Sylvia."

They embraced, taking care of the third party.

"I'm not surprised," she laughed rubbing her belly.

The last time Fernandez had seen her was at her brother Henry's funeral. He'd marveled at her composure then, but knew Henry had given her plenty of opportunities to grow hard. As she stood smiling at him he realized it had all started here, in the resort their parents had made. This is where Sylvia and her wayward brother had grown up. Why was she here again?

"What are you, ah…" Fernandez searched.

"What am I doing here?"

"Yeah."

"Come over here out of the noise. You can bring your beer."

She motioned to the bartender to put Fernandez's beer in a plastic cup. Taking him by the arm she led him to the side of the restaurant where there was a miniature, lagoon-like swimming pool. A couple children were night-swimming as their parents relaxed at the bar.

"Now this is a good idea," he said pointing at the pool.

"Everybody's happy."

They sat down on some deck chairs.

"You might find this perverse," Sylvia began. "But right after Henry's funeral I realized how much I missed this place. I got in touch with Radisson, they had a vacancy for manager, end of story."

"I would think that after owning the place it..."

"It would be a step down?" she guessed. "Well, I'm more of a consultant really. They were losing some of my parents' original vision and I'm helping them get it back. Don't let the outfit fool you, they're paying me a load."

"Well, I'm happy you're happy then," Fernandez grinned.

"Fernando, I never got around to it but I wanted to thank you. I know it's easy to just pick up the phone, but you keep pushing something off until it doesn't matter anymore. If it wasn't for you I wouldn't have seen my brother before he died."

"He was in bad shape," Fernandez breathed.

"But he smiled at me. He saw me and he smiled at me. In the end he didn't die alone."

Nicole's father had.

"Do you know what determinism is?" she asked.

"No."

"I don't really have a grip on it myself. But when he was dying and we were smiling at each other I knew that there was no other way our lives could have played out. It was going to happen, as fucked up and tragic as his life was there was this beauty, this permanence and relief in his exit from it."

"Sounds like you're saying you can't escape fate," Fernandez offered, remembering some of his religious studies.

"I know, but it's not, he still had free will…ugh."

She searched the blazing night sky for an explanation but found none. When her eyes fixed on the full moon her expression softened out. The young hostess came running up in a panic.

"Syl, Syl, one of the big gringos is barfing all over section four!"

"Calm down, I'll be right there," she said with infinite patience.

"You're going to make a great mom," Fernandez said. She kissed him on the cheek.

"I gotta go take care of this. I'll find you when it calms down. Again, thanks for everything."

"Anytime Sylvia. I'm glad I could be of assistance."

She turned away and hobbled toward the restaurant to take care of the current disaster. When she reached the bar she turned around.

"And they caught the bad ones too! It was your report that did it. I don't think I could live with myself if those assholes were still on the street."

She disappeared into the restaurant. Fernandez watched a rush of busboy activity as she gave orders above the din of clinking glassware and Friday night conversation. One of the Yankee Doodles he'd seen earlier at the bar was being escorted limply off the premises by his friends.

"I shaid what i shaid! And that bith knew what I shaid!" Fernandez could hear him slur in the night.

"Yes I understand, Dale. Let's just get you home, big guy," a more sensible friend encouraged.

"I don't think I could live with myself if those assholes were still on the street," Fernandez said aloud to himself not without irony.

Just as he was about to get up his phone rang. It was Major Ho Chang.

"Fernandez!" The Army man's voice crackled in the poor reception, but the signal was there.

"What?"

"We got it!" We found the family! His daughter placed an ad in the Singapore News fifteen years ago, trying to declare him legally dead."

Terminal B Arrivals at Luis Muñoz Marín Airport was positively heaving. In addition to the normal mass of people getting in from New York, Orlando, and Miami, this Saturday morning found the airport crawling with press. Every local newspaper had sent a reporter, and every local TV station had sent a crew. Telemundo had even come from Miami to cover the affair.

Their vans and equipment choked the already narrow area and limited traffic to just one lane. The taxi drivers were screaming at the police, the police were screaming at the press, and the press were screaming back at the police as they'd been forced to remain behind a large barricade that had been constructed outside the terminal entrance. Only one station had been granted access to go inside the baggage claim area to film the arrival of Beijing Joaquin's two daughters, and it was Ten Caribbean News.

Nelly Santana was testing the mic at a small podium set up

for the exclusive press conference. Columnists from the San Juan Star, Primera Hora, El Vocero and El Nuevo Dia were seated in front, the only other press invited.

She had ditched the punk theme for the occasion and looked radiant in her slim business skirt and white sport jacket. Fernandez couldn't believe her transformation. When he'd first met her the same kind of clothes looked a bunched up mess, now the young lady looked sharp as a tack. Smiling, happy, and on point, attitude really did make all the difference in the world. The weight of the island's woes had lifted off her shoulders a bit, and Fernandez was pleased he had something to do with it. She was far too young to have already been broken down the way she had been.

Erick stood behind her, staring at her rear with a wistful and faraway look in his eye.

"For God's sake, get it together man," Fernandez whispered to his assistant.

"Sorry boss," Erick said taking out his phone, pretending to be interested in something.

"You know, you really can't blame him," Julio Gonzalez said elbowing Fernandez painfully in the ribs.

"Remind me again why I invited you to this?" Fernandez asked.

"Security," Gonzalez replied motioning to the barrier outside.

Two agents from Interpol were arguing with officers from the SJPD. Fernandez and Santana had made sure they were not in the list of people airport security would let inside. Since the SJPD were there to offer support to the airport, there was nothing they could do. They were not to be admitted. Covert

Intelligence had put in all the work, and Covert Intelligence was going to get the glory this day.

"Where do they get off?" Gonzalez asked.

"It's the nature of the big boys to gobble everything up," Fernandez explained. "It's policy. Besides, apparently they were close. Maybe it's some new agent that wants his face on the news."

"Man, they look pissed off," Gonzalez observed.

From this distance Fernandez couldn't hear the exchange, but saw the shocked, 'don't you know who I am' look on the Interpol guy's face and thought it was priceless.

Airport security was used to this, since they spent a lot of their lives listening to people who bitch about service, bitch about the facilities, bitch about everything under the sun. After a while it becomes white noise, a desensitized feature of everyday life. The more angry and self important someone got, the more maddeningly static the response remained. Celebrity, politician, artist, CEO...sorry, not impressed.

That's why the agents at the barrier almost looked bored. It was par for the course. Fernandez knew, though, that there was a point. If Secret Agent Man pushed past it, the response would be quick and unpleasant. To outward appearances it could seem that the security people were fucking around, but they most certainly were not fucking around.

The two agents gave up in frustration and retreated to the curb for a private and exasperated powwow. Fernandez watched in satisfaction. There was no other way in.

He didn't feel badly for them, not one little bit. He, with the assistance of his colleagues Ho Chang and Dan Johnson, had closed this. He remembered the call he got shortly after

Chang's. It was Nancy Ji Ke, the daughter of the deceased. She wanted to explain the ad thing.

When she graduated high school there was no money for college. She tried to find her father through the newspaper ads, and since she got no response, tried to declare him dead to be able to access some funds. The courts told her to place ads in Singapore and New York as well. As a little girl, she'd been told he'd gone to the Big Apple to find work.

The ads were fifteen years old now, and her name didn't appear in the newspapers databases any longer, which was why it had been so hard for Chang to find her. A reporter from the newspaper had found the payment receipt for the ads, and it led them to the family's lawyer. That was how Chang was able to finally get her information.

Fernandez got to think about the turmoil this father's disappearance had put on his kids, and his family. Now he turned his attention to his wife who sat silently in a pod of chairs across from the baggage claim, close to where the Secretary of Estate was answering questions from the press. After Estrella Leon's phone message and Fernandez's subsequent admission, she'd returned to a tense and tight-lipped silence. They hadn't spoken since he told her he was trying to get the evidence on her father's case.

To Fernandez, though, the quality of her silence appeared to be different than it had been in the past considering this subject. She was thinking. Where before there was nothing but a knee jerk reaction of anger, unquestioned in its validity, there was now conflict. Interest had reared its long-dead head and was in competition with the anger. He could tell that her irritation at herself was sharing stage with her irritation at him. He'd decided the best course of action was to shut up and see how it all played out.

"That's great Cal. As usual, you've come up with a really good angle, but I'm thinking maybe on this occasion we leave Mr. Schnickens out."

Fernandez turned to see Nelly Santana in conversation with the venerable weatherman. Cal Shelby had been chosen by Ten Caribbean to do the live report. For the occasion he'd picked a slightly more subdued and earth-toned Hawaiian shirt with white linen pants. He'd actually offered to wear a suit but Ten Caribbean felt they still wanted to preserve the integrity of the character and the station's number one star. Fernandez assumed their move toward hard news was going to be done incrementally.

"Ok, so you're thinking it a little more of a serious piece?" Shelby was engaged and spoke sharply.

"Exactly! You got it a hundred and ten percent, Cal." Nelly responded a bit too enthusiastically, like she was dealing with a child in grade school.

"Good, good," Shelby rubbed his hands together in anticipation.

"Fernandez, Erick, can you guys come over here? I want to walk through this. The plane has just landed but it's going to take them a while to get through customs."

Fernandez and his assistant joined Nelly at the podium. Nicole remained sitting by the baggage belt, staring at her feet.

"Fernando, this is Cal Shelby, he's going to be doing the live report."

"Cal," Fernandez grasped his hand and the weatherman gave him a firm Midwestern shake.

"Cal, this is Fernando Fernandez, the investigator that took the case pro bono," Nelly explained.

"Wonderful thing you've done sir," Cal said. "Should be more people like you around."

Fernandez was momentarily thrown off guard by Shelby's five figure smile and earnestness. His praise was no doubt genuine.

"Well, thank you. I'm a big fan," he lied. "I actually saw you at the office the day I took the case. I wanted to introduce myself but you were being mauled by a bunch of children at the elevator."

"Sheesh I remember that morning," he sighed painfully and Fernandez laughed. "I was out at this whiskey bar in Santurce the night before with a bunch of friends from Ocean Park. I like to think I've reached an age where I know how to pace myself, but man!"

"You still made those kids' day though," Fernandez said.

"Hey," Shelby shook his head. "I'm the luckiest weatherman on earth and I got the best gig in the world down here. I get to hop from island to island, cover restaurants and hotels. I owe it to those kids. My dad used to say just because you're hungover doesn't give you the right to act like an asshole."

"Amen," Fernandez replied.

"Anyway, I'm incidental for the most part. All the kids want to see is Mr. Schnickens."

"Who's Mr. Shitins?" Erick asked.

"Ok," Nelly interrupted. "Their names are Nancy and Penny Ji Ke. They'll emerge from those doors and Cal is going to interview them over there."

She pointed to a white backdrop dotted with logos of Ten Caribbean and el Nuevo Dia.

"What, are they going to a film premiere?" Fernandez joked.

"I know. I know," Nelly waved him off. "Don't think I didn't fight it, let's just move on and pretend it's not there. Then we'll have the press conference. Fernando, you'll join me at the podium."

"They speak English, right?" Shelby asked.

"Yes," Fernandez responded. "I spoke to them both on the phone in Singapore."

"Here they are," Nelly said excitedly. "Cal you're on, work your magic my friend. Fernando, you're with me."

"You got it boss," Shelby chirped diligently and ran to the backdrop.

"Do you want me to go sit with your wife?" Julio Gonzalez asked innocently appearing behind Fernandez.

"Absolutely not."

The old man skulked off, offended as the two Singaporean women walked out of customs accompanied by a TSA escort. Fernandez was momentarily taken aback. He observed two sharply dressed and thoroughly modern middle-aged women make their way toward Cal Shelby.

"What were you expecting?" Nelly whispered to him, obviously picking up on his bewilderment.

"Not sure...I," he stammered.

"A couple of Geishas in kimonos?" she teased.

"No, of course not," he asserted but wondered himself, what had he been expecting this whole time?

Cal Shelby was on point, delivering a somber and parrot-free interview to thousands of homes across the Caribbean. He'd made the transformation from jolly, island hopping travel reporter, to respectful and hard-hitting journalist effortlessly. Shelby's performance forced Fernandez to wonder about his past. It was apparent the weatherman had a ton of real experience up his sleeve from back in the States. The cockatoo routine notwithstanding.

Nancy Ji Ke did all of the talking. Penny, older and seemingly shy, stood in the background always on the verge of weeping. Lost in his own thoughts Fernandez missed the majority of the interview.

"We are very grateful," Nancy said. "Of course we are very sad as well to have discovered our father is dead, but after all these years our minds can finally be at peace. It's quite a relief."

"I'm sure it is," Shelby interjected. "It must have been heartbreaking, all this time, not knowing what happened to your father."

"Yes," Nancy fought back tears as she put her arm around her crying sister. "Now we have closure. Now he can rest in peace."

Nicole was watching the interview intently. Fernandez couldn't be sure from this distance, but it looked like his wife was crying as well. On the other side of the window behind her he suddenly noticed a commotion. Antonio Garcia was behind the police barricade and frantically trying to get his attention. When he realized Fernandez had seen him, Garcia started waving his arms up and down, beckoning him forward. As he made for Garcia, Nelly Santana grabbed him by the arm and moved him in the opposite direction.

"They're coming now," she said between clenched teeth.

"Well, we're going to meet the people who made it happen right now," Shelby announced. "Ten Caribbean Program Coordinator Nelly Santana, and from Covert Intelligence Private Investigator Fernando Fernandez."

The cameras swung to the podium and Fernandez blinked in the glare. Nelly Santana read a short speech and took a few questions. Fernandez put on his sunglasses and hung in the background. In his black tailored suit he looked like secret service. Everyone was just waiting to get on with it and bring the two sisters to Old San Juan, the reason they were there in the first place.

"Well, that's about it," Nelly concluded. "And now I give you the man who found Nancy and Penny Ji Ke, Fernando Fernandez, P.I."

Fernandez cleared his throat and sent off a salvo of feedback. He moved away from the mic and in a moment of trepidation realized this was the first time he'd ever done anything like this.

"Thank you," he began. "First of all I would like to recognize and thank two people without whom we wouldn't be standing here today. Detective Dan Johnson in New York and Major Ho Chang in Singapore helped me immensely in bringing this case to a conclusion. You know…"

He paused for a second, looked at Nelly Santana next to him and to his wife. Nicole was far away but he was certain she was paying attention. Fernandez decided to ditch the rest of his prepared statement and wing it.

"You know my friends," he continued. "It's very easy to get wrapped up in what is wrong with this world. And it's necessary to a certain degree. After all, we need to in order to make things better. I'll admit right now, when I first saw Ten Caribbean's coverage of this initiative I thought: 'great another public interest story'. Then I realized I'd fallen victim to this thinking too. I don't think you can blame me, though, considering my line of work."

A light chuckle ran through the audience.

"My point is that we have to keep trying, and we must never give up. If anything the case of Beijing Joaquin proves that we can make positive changes in this world, one thing at a time. We must be relentlessly optimistic in the face of darkness and never despair. Because if we don't do this, who will?"

Nelly was smiling at him from ear to ear.

"Thank you," he concluded to applause. She grabbed him in a huge bear hug.

"Nice one, Winston Churchill," she whispered into his ear.

"Thank you all for coming," she said turning to the mic. "And thanks to Covert Intelligence for making this day happen."

On the way to the car Fernandez tried to spot Garcia to find out what was so important but he'd apparently vanished. The drive to the Department of Forensics was silent. Erick sat in the front with Fernandez while Nicole sat with Gonzalez in the back. After several abortive attempts at conversation even the old lawyer picked up on the tension and shut his mouth.

The trip to the morgue was a mercifully brief affair. The sisters had to identify their father by photos as his body was in such a state of decomposition they were not allowed to view it. The looks on their faces when they'd received the news was heart wrenching. Fernandez was sure, there and then, that the memory of the moment would be tattooed on his brain till his dying day. They'd come so far.

After signing forms consenting for their father to be cremated, the group once again piled into their vehicles and headed for Old San Juan and the neighborhood the old man had called home for so long.

Fernandez followed the minivan that Ten Caribbean had rented to carry the Ji Ke sisters up the narrow streets of the old town. Turning left on Calle del Cristo they descended sharply. The minivan paused briefly in front of Parakeets. Nelly Santana was no doubt pointing out that this is where their father had lived and worked.

The caravan continued on and parked in a small area near the Governor's mansion that the police had cordoned off for the occasion. The group alighted and Nelly Santana led the sisters back up Calle del Cristo followed by a lone Ten Caribbean camera and the Covert Intelligence contingent.

Nelly introduced the Ji Ke sisters to Eliza Pelayo, who was standing outside of Parakeets. Fernandez remained outside and watched Joaquin's old friend show his daughters around the store. At one point he could see the sisters giggling and figured Pelayo had recounted some amusing and inoffensive anecdote about their father. She then led the ladies up the narrow back staircase to their father's apartment. The cameraman followed.

About halfway up the stairs Penny looked ready to swoon. Pelayo was already up inside the room and Nancy, walking in front, didn't have the strength or the right angle on the tiny stairway to help her sister. As the cameraman was clearly not putting his camera down, Fernandez rushed forward through the store and caught Penny just as she pitched backward.

"Sorry I spoiled the shot," he said sarcastically over his shoulder. The cameraman remained silent.

"It's ok," he heard his own voice saying to the limp woman

in his arms. It was a lie. It wasn't ok.

You say the things you're supposed to say. You embody the hollow and empty platitude. The Ji Ke sisters were about to see their father's things, now unused. This was often harder than viewing the body in Fernandez's experience. It was when finality first peeked around the corner and made it's incredible and unalterable presence known. It was sweet and it was sad, it was wistful and angry. But most of all, it was where we all were headed. Subconsciously, this was the pin that pricked everyone in this situation whether they'd admit it or not, whether they even knew it or not.

One day, they'll be going through your stuff. And unless you're a monk or struggled with severe depression you weren't used to this idea. It arrived unwanted, unasked for, a spoiler you were always somewhat aware of in the distraction that was life itself. The lights went on. The movie's over. The worry, the joy, the anxiety, the pain, the constant doing. None of it was real. Time to go.

Those who had the most to lose materially, those invested neck deep in this mortal coil met the notion with rage. Most normal and sensitive souls met it with confusion and sadness. As he looked at Penny Ji Ke's watery eyes, Fernandez was sure this would be the sisters' reaction.

"It's ok," he repeated. This was not the place to be clever, or realistic, or profound. It's precisely the place to be dull, predictable and boring, because that's what someone who is grieving needs most.

Fernandez brought Penny to a standing position and walked her the rest of the way up the stairs. His wife and Nelly Santana followed close behind the cameraman, in a dream.

Eliza Pelayo stood in front of the closet. Joaquin's clothes were still neatly hung. Nancy approached first and retrieved a beaten old Fedora from a cubbyhole. Penny came up behind her and the two women caressed the material.

"I'm sorry," Fernandez said.

They began weeping freely, pressing their heads to the hat, subconsciously trying to somehow touch their father. It was Nancy who found her voice first, choked by sobs.

"Daddy! Daddy! Why did you leave us?"

Fernandez heard a muffled cry from behind and turned to see his wife's face, a mask of tears and agony, looking herself about to fall backward down the stairs. He rushed over and took her in his arms.

"I'm sorry," he said again, this time apologizing for that which he could not control. She looked at him and perhaps for the first time felt pity and understood. Expecting him to stop was like expecting his eyes not to be brown.

"Fernando," she began in a conciliatory voice he'd never heard before.

"Let's not talk about it," he quickly cut her off. "Do you want to get out of here?"

She nodded and the two made their way back down the staircase, leaving the Ji Ke sisters keening furiously in their father's room. When he reached the bottom he was happy to hear Nelly Santana give the order to the cameraman to stop filming. Enough was enough.

Fernandez led his wife back up the street to the plaza outside the Cathedral of San Juan Bautista. They took a seat on a park bench and he handed her a tissue. There was so much he wanted to say but he didn't know how to start. At that moment he would have sold his entire practice and taken a job in I.T.

again, he would have switched to something sensible like a bank
manager and never mention her father's name again for the rest
of his life. He sensed they were on the verge of some kind of
understanding. After all these years. It was a kinetic and unsta-
ble nucleus that needed protection. And, paradoxically, in the
eve of this reconciliation he was possessed with the incredible
urge to throw it all away, to do anything to make his wife happy
and peaceful.

"Nicole," he began softly.

"Fernando, there you are! I thought I'd find you here!"
Antonio Garcia came bounding up to him smiling from ear to
ear. He was with someone dressed as a priest.

"Tony, now is not a…"

"I missed you at the airport," Garcia was laser intent on his
purpose and not listening. "This is Raul Hernandez, the guy I
was talking about. He was the lead detective on your father-in-
law's case."

"Stop!" Nicole cried. Garcia and Hernandez reeled in
surprise. She got up and bolted full speed up Calle del Cristo.
Fernandez followed her. Yoga and the gym had given her a considerable advantage on the steeply sloping street. She cleared
the top and disappeared from view while Fernandez was still
stuck halfway down, panting uncontrollably.

He pushed himself double hard, all the while amazed by
Garcia's bad timing. Why then? Why right fucking then?

He reached the top of the street and entered Plaza San Jose
a rumpled and sweating mess. He removed his sport jacket
and untucked his shirt for more freedom of motion. Scanning
the area he finally spotted Nicole. She'd made good distance.
Beyond the plaza and the totem monument he saw her working

her way down the grassy hill that led to the huge lawn spread before El Morro. Before her were only the castle walls, a cliff, and the ocean. She had nowhere else to go.

Fernandez chugged down the hill. When he reached the lawn Nicole was nowhere to be found. Impossible, unless she jumped into the water there was only one place she could be.

He carefully made his way through the narrow slot that gave access to the garita. The sentry box was built in times of old to house a lookout. There was only space enough to accommodate two or three soldiers. Inside it was pitch black, even in the afternoon sun. The guard tower was lit only by a narrow slit of a window, providing maximum protection for the men inside.

"Honey?" he called into the darkness. She was sitting against the wall, her head buried in her arms. The entire place reeked of urine.

"Nicole? I promise I'll let it go. I'm sorry but…"

"I never told you I found him Fernando," the voice seemed to him remarkably small.

"Your father?"

"Yes. That son of a bitch back there, Hernandez, he didn't do a damn thing. They said they couldn't find him so we went looking for him. He didn't take long to find, the lazy bastards."

Fernandez was unaccustomed to the language. After years of trying to set an example she was finally letting loose. He decided to let her continue and not interrupt until she was done.

"He was beaten. They never did anything! It's like beating your head against a wall Fernando. The only way it doesn't hurt is to stop. My father was a good man. He didn't deserve it! And those assholes didn't give a shit!"

He understood now. Nicole had absolutely zero faith that the police could ever do anything about her father. She'd built an impenetrable wall and stopped beating her head against it. The truth was far too painful. You knew there was foul play, you knew things were not what they seemed, but the cops treated you the same way a doctor treats a hypochondriac. Put a note in the file, this one's crazy.

"I'm not them," Fernandez said.

"I know, that's why this has been so hard. I gave up so I could have a life, don't you see?"

To live with an outrageous injustice was only possible if you became utterly convinced it never happened. Everything he was, loved, important, the warm circle of a family, a universe unto itself, was ripped apart by some piece of shit who didn't care.

Fernandez extended his hand. She took it and stood up.

"C'mon, it smells like piss in here," he said leading her out into the fresh ocean air. The two of them sat down on the ledge of the battlement. The breeze blew her hair all around her face. She'd stopped crying.

"Consider the case closed," he said finally. She turned to him, he was astonished to see her smiling.

"You still don't get it, do you?"

For the first time in a long time Fernandez had nothing. He searched his wife's face but found her expression completely foreign.

"Enlighten me," he said after a long moment.

"I want you to do it," she pulled him close. "I want you to go ahead. You managed to reunite those ladies with their father.

I think you made me believe again."

"What a terrible thing to do to someone. I apologize."

The two embraced. The island breeze left her hair, curled around the tombstones of Santa Maria Magdalena, flowed over the lighthouse and out to the open sea.

Epilogue
2015

She didn't do it. Esmeralda Caro didn't kill her alleged step-daughter. The case that had absolutely monopolized national news and Fernando Fernandez since September 2013 was finally over. He'd been the woman's most fervent voice of defense when the entire system was calling for her head.

Grainy footage from a hospital parking lot security showed Esmeralda arriving in her car, with the girl's father in the passenger seat, frantically trying to resuscitate the little kid at the same time she was driving. The father was just there, doing nothing. Four-year-old Gilamarie Blanco was pronounced dead on arrival, and the cause of death was severe trauma to the body, especially the liver which had been completely dislodged by a blow. In an amazing and bewildering turn of events, the district attorney accused Esmeralda of the deadly beating, even though the father had complaints for child abuse against him already filed within the Department of Family Affairs.

The police investigation was open and shut. A combination of the district attorney's moves of granting immunity to the father, and twisting the meaning of the actions seen in the security footage, had helped in getting Esmeralda accused, but it was the little girl's brother's testimony that got her locked up for good. The boy, only 7, testified he witnessed Esmeralda beating the girl hard, on her chest and her back. This all but sealed Esmeralda Caro's fate. Never mind Fernandez uncovered those were obvious CPR attempts. The boy had obviously rehearsed his answers with the district attorney, and learned his lines in earnest.

In coming to her defense, Fernandez had become hated by the members of the district attorney's office and the police department involved in the case. According to them, it was tight, it was satisfying, it was good news, the police had per-formed well and the person who'd committed the awful murder by beating was going to get what she deserved for a change. Why was this asshole Fernandez rocking the boat?

Because having 100 criminals out on the streets is better than putting an innocent person in jail. He'd seen things in the video everyone else hadn't, including the police. He tirelessly conducted his own investigation, which didn't find the killer, but irrefutably exonerated Caro and pointed to the father. He had analyzed the expert reports from the district attorneys office. He analyzed the crime scene. He developed a time line, which gave Esmeralda a less than two minute window of opportunity to perform the beating, which Fernandez concluded was almost impossible. He interviewed more than 30 witnesses. He did background checks for all of the witnesses, looking for any one with a propensity to lie. He helped the lawyers in choosing the jury, along with Erick and another lady P.I. hired just for this case.

One of the witnesses, a nurse working on the girl the night she died, testified there was a distinct sandal mark at the spot of the fatal blow, like the girl was kicked. The only one wearing sandals the night of the events was the father.

Yet Esmeralda Caro was sentenced and sent to jail in February, 2014, five months after the murder.

The public asked for justice. The vast majority of the people who had followed the case through the media didn't buy the district attorney's nonsense. They rallied asking for Esmeralda's release, for the father to be investigated, for due diligence from the justice department in order to come to terms with the horrid crime.

An innocent woman's life hung in the balance, but it had paid off. The lawyers were able to appeal, and on February 2015, a full year after she was incarcerated, the Appeals Court ordered a new trial, and for Esmeralda to be released from prison.

Fernando Fernandez was right. He had helped in this case pro-bono, thinking it was important for the general public to understand just how valuable the P.I.'s work is in a criminal investigation. The investigator does the running around, the dirty work, the hard prying, the culling of details for the attorneys to build their case. And in this case, it seemed to have paid off at the end. The only problem was that the urgency of Esmeralda Caro's case had drawn him away from the Furniture Man for a considerable amount of time.

It was time to put Esmeralda behind him, place his father-in-law's case in the forefront, honor Nicole's trust in him, and finally let Furniture Man rest in peace.

His name was Alejandro Martinez, a respected business man and father of three. He lived in the town of Rio Piedras, in the middle of the metropolitan area. Originally from Vega Alta, he had moved to Philadelphia in the 60's, in an attempt to better his opportunities. There, he had found the love of his life, and married Laura Rodriguez, starting his family and his first retail business.

Nicole had actually been born in Philly. By the time she was three they moved back to Puerto Rico, where Alejandro started a couple of businesses which ended in the purchase of his furniture store. It had been a very successful endeavor for a long time, allowing him to raise his kids not with extravagance, but with all their needs taken care of without worries. Alejandro and Laura ran a tight household, where discipline was dished out regularly but lovingly. All three kids grew up as responsible, critical thinkers, and very independent.

At the time of her father's death, Nicole was 28 years old.

In his mind Fernandez kept calling Alejandro "The Furniture Man". Somehow this made it possible for him to detach himself from the misery of what his wife and her family had experienced, and keep a professional, if passionate, determination to close the case.

In the long months since he had last touched the case, his reluctant liaison of sorts in Forensics, Estrella Leon, had resigned unable to handle the pressures of her position, and without time to help Fernandez at all. Fernandez assigned Erick the task of procuring the evidence, which he was trying to do with the help of Antonio Garcia and his vast connections. Garcia told him, though, just how difficult this task could prove to be.

"Son, you know where the evidence for this cold case is?" Garcia was chewing on stale gum while talking to Erick. He was trying to cut back on his smoking. Gum chewing had not helped as of yet, but he had hope.

Erick saw the jittery hands, and the unsteady eyes. Nicotine was a bad one to conquer. "I have no idea, but I would expect a file room of some sort."

"Some sort is right! It's a room, but there are no files there. It's a jumble of boxes containing evidence, all in a complete mess. No catalog, no database, no nothing. You go in there and start digging. It's like a freaking grandma's attic on hormones."

Erick was dismayed, but determined. "We'll take Simon to keep us calm. Let's get in there! When can we do this?"

"Hold your horses, kiddo. First we have to gain access to the place. I am inside the police force and I don't have it. We'll have to take this one hurdle at a time," Garcia said to a tired Erick, who was trying hard to remain faithful.

With the evidence still out of his reach, Fernandez began a

long dialogue with the cop turned priest Father Raul Hernandez and was able to piece together a time line.

In July, 1993, the Furniture Man went out on a sales call in Trujillo Alto and never returned home. When Nicole's family reported him missing the police did a very crappy job of trying to locate him. Three days after this the family searched the area themselves and found his car down in a ravine, in the area known as the Road of the Dead (known for body dumping and nefarious executions). When they reported this, Detective Hernandez conducted a half-assed search of the area, found nothing, and confiscated the car.

Undeterred, the family kept going. In the late afternoon Nicole found her father, beaten and bloodied in a dry river bed. She sat with him alone in silence, until the rest of her family found her.

Raul Hernandez, who should have been ashamed but wasn't, finally opened an investigation. Maybe it was fate, maybe it was luck, but evidence was literally handed to him. An alert neighbor had seen a slow moving suspicious car in the neighborhood the week before the Furniture Man disappeared and actually managed to write down the license tag number. When it was traced it was found to be on a different car in another town. Hernandez's investigation also turned up receipts from one of the Furniture Man's stolen credit cards after his death. Those had been signed by someone impersonating him.

The owner of the second car promptly got a lawyer. He was then brought in for a handwriting analysis but the results were inconclusive. After a month, Hernandez lost interest and dropped the case. Fernandez openly wondered if the cop was already distracted by thoughts of a higher calling at the time. The family was furious.

Now that he had Nicole's cooperation and access to her father's files from Hernandez' point of view (who was not fazed or embarrassed in the least by his obvious incompetence at the time of the events), Fernando was able to put together an intimate picture of the father-in-law he never knew.

Though not on the scale of a Tirso Guerra, Nicole's father owned a successful franchise of furniture and appliance stores. Similarly to Guerra though, the Furniture Man was drowning in debt and at the time of his murder was financing his family and businesses primarily by borrowing from loan sharks.

Sifting through journals and random notes, Fernandez was able to verify that the Furniture Man was visited by henchmen at his office the Friday before he died. They threatened to start taking his stock and personal possessions as collateral. Nicole's father stopped them by guaranteeing he'd have the money Monday.

When they returned, he showed them a bankruptcy letter. He'd filed for bankruptcy right after they'd left on Friday. It was obvious he had everything planned and ready. Fernandez was sure the Furniture Man had been killed by the loan sharks, either themselves or with a hit man.

Then in December of 2014, Fernandez managed to uncover a newspaper article about the case from two days after the alleged murder.

"Hey, Erick, take a look at this," Fernandez was elated. This was the first new thing they had unearthed about the case in a long, long time.

"It looks awful, boss."

"What do you mean? It's precious! It's the scene!"

"I mean the quality of the picture sucks! Where did you

get it?" Erick came from the age of technology, where a bad, heavily dark and grainy picture was like a personal affront. After all, anybody could take a perfectly good pic from their smartphone nowadays.

"I had to go to the city archives to get the microfilms of the newspapers back then. This is what they've got. Bad photocopies of bad pictures. But this is gold! It shows the car and this other one has the body!"

Erick took the impossibly dark copy and looked at it carefully. "If you say so. All I see is a mess of black with a crime tape and the name of the photographer."

Erick was still trying to make sense of the image when Fernandez took it from him in a rush, leaving Erick staring at his boss, empty-handed.

"Hey! I was looking at that!

Fernandez was getting a magnifying glass and looking through it at the newspaper copy. Simon entered the office after a satisfying short meditation brake. He felt refreshed and renewed.

"Wow, you actually have one of those? I thought it was a prop for Sherlock Holmes movies," he couldn't help the comment when he saw his boss hunched over a paper with a magnifying glass.

"Sherlock my ass. He couldn't do shit without his faithful Watson."

Erick cleared his throat. Fernandez looked at him in disbelief.

"Erick, you don't want to be Watson. He was a total wuss. And, you don't want Fernandez to call you "my dear anything", do you?" Simon was clearly enjoying himself.

Fernandez shoved the paper he was inspecting into Simon's hands, who unsuspectingly stared at the picture, frowning.

"What's this?"

"That's the newspaper picture of Nicole's father's car as it was found three days after his death, and his mangled, bloodied body" said Fernandez perversely, knowing how Simon hated gore. "I need you to tell me the name of the photographer."

"Maybe you should wear your reading glasses."

"Maybe you should make yourself useful before I feel like kicking somebody's butt out of here today."

"Permanently?"

"Nah, just for the fun of it. But without pay."

Simon dutifully grabbed the paper and scanned it, to enlarge it once it was on the big monitor on his desk. He felt the freshness and contentment from his meditating session wash away as he looked at the dreadful scene on the screen. Even with the bad quality of the picture, you could make out the outlines of the Furniture Man's car. It was in a very dense forest-like area, on its side on a sharp embankment.

All three felt silent as they stared at the monitor and looked at the graphic evidence of a violent, untimely death.

Then there was the photo of the body from a distance. Fernandez got a bit misty himself when he saw that one of the figures next to the deceased was his wife, a young lady that he'd yet to meet.

The photographer's name was Danny Franco and lived in New York now. Getting his number had been easy, and when he called him Franco remembered the article and revealed to Fernandez he'd taken "at least a hundred pictures" that day.

They were, however, somewhere in storage as he'd moved to a small apartment and his boxes didn't all fit. He told Fernandez he would go there as soon as possible.

Fernandez redoubled his efforts to get the evidence still in San Juan. By his conversations with both Garcia and Hernandez, he knew there was a bag containing some sort of heavy, metal-clanging object that could very well be the murder weapon. There was also a glove, taken from the trunk of the deceased's car. And there had to be pictures. Forensic was supposed to have at least the pictures and the glove. But the mysterious heavy object should be in the police evidence warehouse.

Using his contacts, and a little help from Garcia, Fernandez was granted permission to search the police unsorted evidence warehouse for the evidence, with an escort. However, the red tape he needed to navigate in order to finally get inside the warehouse's door was ridiculous.

Danny Franco called him at the beginning of February 2015. He was ready to go searching for the photos in his out-of-the-city warehouse just as a massive blizzard paralyzed the city of New York. It had taken New Yorkers by surprise, and the roads were impassable. On top of that, his building had sustained extensive damage from the heavy snowfall and he was forced to seek refuge at a friend's house. There was no way he was going to get to the suburbs any time soon.

Finally, Fernandez made it to the police unsolved-cases evidence warehouse in March. It had taken considerable clout, a number of contacts, and some favors to gain access, but he was ready, accompanied by a small set, rookie-looking cop kid who couldn't have been more than 20. When he pushed open the door to the warehouse, he stood for a second mouth agape, in shock.

Stack after stack of plain brown boxes stretching into infinity. The storage space was so tall and cavernous birds had nested on the upper shelves and scaffolding. It was the scene from the end of Raiders of the Lost Ark, and Fernandez was rooted to the spot in horror.

He looked at his valiant escort, and the poor kid looked as if he were going to faint.

"Ha!" came a voice from behind him. "I know that look."

An old janitor appeared from behind a stack of nameless files.

"I know it can be rather daunting, but believe me, there is a system," he explained.

If there was, Fernandez felt he could spend the rest of his life learning it.

"Can you tell me what the system is?" Fernandez was trying very hard not to feel utterly defeated.

"I would if I could. I just clean around here. However, I can tell the stacks are positioned in a sort of organized way, by size, and by weight." The old man was slowly making his way towards the door, mopping after himself. "Now, there have been those who can't deal with it, and I've seen them here day after day only to go away empty handed. But you seem to be an intelligent man. No doubt you'll figure it out in no time!"

"Right...I," Fernandez stared hard at the labyrinth before him. No words.

"Good luck, buddy!"

The janitor chuckled and mopped the area just before the door, closing it after his exit with a loud bang.

ABOUT THE AUTHOR

"When your work becomes your passion, success is imminent."

-Fernando Fernandez, P.I.

Fernando Fernandez is a licensed private investigator with a proven 10-year track record of solving cases across the Caribbean and United States. From his home base in Puerto Rico, Fernandez is well known for creatively and efficiently handling complex criminal and domestic investigations and has developed a worldwide reputation for his reliability, ingenuity, honesty, and impeccable attention to detail.

Working independently, as well as with local and international government authorities, law enforcement personnel, and attorneys, Fernando Fernandez has cracked some of the most difficult cases and brought justice and closure to all parties involved. From large scale criminal and corporate investigations like tracking down fugitives from justice and exposing multi-million dollar insurance scams, to personal, single client-based investigations like finding missing persons or conducting background checks, no case is beyond the scope or capabilities of this veteran P.I..

Passion and dedication, experience and intuition, credentials and education, Fernando Fernandez brings all the weapons of the most successful private investigators to bear in his work. His previous 10-years' experience as a computer specialist gives him a unique edge and enables him to stay at the forefront of cybernetic investigations and all the latest detection technologies. Fernandez' varied workload includes areas like lie detection, undercover surveillance, interrogations, fraud investigation, missing persons, fugitive search, and of course computer forensics and cyber-crimes, among others. In addition, he also boasts some of the most prestigious and sought after certifications in the field of private investigation: certified counter-terrorism specialist, certified fingerprint specialist, certified email tracing investigator, certified criminal defense investigator, forensic photography specialist and board accredited investigator. He is a member of 8 international P.I. organizations and is constantly circling the globe, meeting with the best and brightest in his field to share knowledge and stay in the vanguard of innovation.

Fernando Fernandez has been featured in all major Puerto Rican publications, TV and Radio broadcasts, as well as international media venues like P.I. Declassified, Voice of America, and others. He's a published author and contributor for trade publications like P.I. Magazine and International Intelligence Network's newsletter.

Fernando Fernandez graduated Summa Cum Laude from the Caribbean Forensic and Technical College in 2004 and achieved one of the highest grades of the year on his Private Investigator Exam. In 2013 & 2014, his colleagues at the World Association of Detectives honored Fernando by nominating him Investigator of the Year. Paradise Undercover is his first novel.

STRAWBOY
TIDAL ISLANDS

'Iona' the oficial song of Paradise Undercover by Strawboy
From the album Tidal Islands
Out now on Spotify/iTunes/Bandcamp
https://www.facebook.com/strawboymusic

Made in the USA
Columbia, SC
26 May 2017